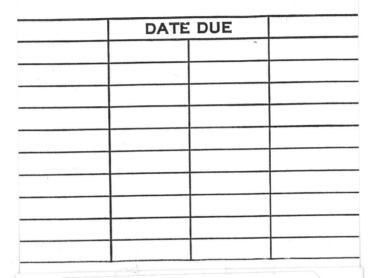

DATE DUE			

'*Clitoris.* 1615. Phys. A homologue of the male penis, present in the females of many of the higher vertebrata.'

The Oxford English Dictionary

'The marvellous is always beautiful, anything marvellous is beautiful, in fact only the marvellous is beautiful.'

André Breton
The First Manifesto of Surrealism

Adèle

Adèle

Adèle

Mary Flanagan

W. W. NORTON & COMPANY
New York   London

First American edition 1997

For information about permission to reproduce selections from this book,
write to Permissions, W. W. Norton & Company, Inc., 500 Fifth Avenue,
New York, NY 10110.

Manufacturing by The Courier Companies, Inc.

Library of Congress Cataloging-in-Publication Data

Flanagan, Mary.
Adèle / Mary Flanagan. — 1st American ed.
p. cm.
ISBN 0-393-04547-1
I.   Title.

PS3556.L32A65   1997   97–6775
813'.54—dc21   CIP

W. W. Norton & Company, Inc., 500 Fifth Avenue, New York, N.Y. 10110
http://www.wwnorton.com

W. W. Norton & Company Ltd., 10 Coptic Street, London WC1A 1PU

1 2 3 4 5 6 7 8 9 0

FLA

With thanks to Liz Calder,
Mary Tomlinson, and Nigel
Greenhill. And to the Authors'
Foundation for their generous grant.

CHAPTER ONE

At first Celia Pippet thought she had opened the wrong drawer. According to her instructions L504 contained only one antiquity. But here were two. Clearly she'd made a mistake, and no wonder. These specs were terrible, too big and blurring her vision. She adjusted them, but they slid down the bridge of her nose.

She closed the drawer with what sounded to her like a crash that echoed through the wood-panelled room. Then she hurried behind the oak cabinet and backed herself into a corner. Checking to see if anyone was watching, she took Martin's diagram from her handbag. Her feet in high-heels were pinched and sore. Celia always wore flat shoes.

Mole stood in the doorway glaring at her. She could feel him wanting her out, out, out. He regarded her as some sort of ghoul and was suspicious of her motives, as if he guessed he was about to be double-crossed. Celia felt entitled to ignore him. He'd collected his reward, hadn't he, and in advance. She'd never believed herself capable of such ruthlessness, assumed she didn't have the equipment, and perhaps she didn't. She willed him to go and he went.

'I'm an honest person,' she wanted to remind him. 'I neither steal nor deceive. Normally.'

It was now eleven-thirty and the museum lunchtime began at twelve. She must hurry if she was to slip out unnoticed, as planned, amidst the confusion of employees and visitors. Again she read the directions. She'd been right, after all. Then why did L504 contain two items? She might have imagined the second, what with these awful glasses and a bad case of nerves. Yet she'd felt something, she was certain. It had slipped under her fingers and rolled to the back of the drawer.

Exasperated, she again adjusted the glasses and scratched her hot head that was itching badly. Really, she must get on. Time was running out. And no more misplaced scruples. They were merely a product of cultural conditioning. Besides, this was not a theft. It was a public service.

A member of staff entered, and Celia detached herself from the wall, unsure whether to smile or even to acknowledge his presence. She hoped he noticed her laminated visitor's pass, her respectable green suit and black courts. She tried to project legitimacy as he shuffled towards the cabinet on the opposite side of the room and opened several drawers, registering their contents in a notebook. Then he left. He hadn't seen her. Cautiously she returned to L504, sensing herself observed by concealed electronic devices. A chill breeze tickled the back of her neck, like wind through an underground tunnel.

'This is for you, Adèle,' she whispered, and did not feel in the least melodramatic. She was only frightened, a noble fear. She opened the drawer. The object lay in its clear plastic box, anonymous, horrible, perfect. It had been stretched and flattened to the thickness of a fingernail and shaped into an oval 9 cm long and 6 cm wide. Its centre was russet gold and its exterior frills a faded rose, smooth and glowing as the inside of a sea shell.

Celia took the smart black Canon from her bag and

put the viewfinder to her eye, controlling her fingers with difficulty. Why had she never been taught any prayers, a single incantation, a mantra, a spell, however silly, to calm her nerves and stoke her courage? She pushed the button and there was a whirr like the revving of a motorcycle. She froze. They'd get her now. But no one looked; no one came. She took another shot and another. She shut the drawer, carefully this time, and photographed the catalogue number framed in brass. Mole had repositioned himself by the door. She nodded but did not smile. She took three steps backwards and photographed the entire cabinet, turned 180 degrees to shoot the one behind her, made a quarter-turn and took a view of the room, then back to L504 for another view of the room.

Mole pointed to his watch, panic in the small weak eyes that were the source of his nickname. She didn't know his real name. She'd met him only this afternoon, as arranged, at the Information Desk. He'd been waiting for her, pasty and hunched from a life spent ministering to precious dead things. Sullenly he had verified her as a bona fide journalist researching a piece for the Sunday arts pages on the disruption caused by the much-postponed move of the British Library to its new residence in St Pancras.

She sent Mole a minatory look and waved him away. Again he pointed to his watch. 'Please,' she mouthed, holding up an index finger to indicate one more minute. When he was gone she returned to her business with the drawer. Until now she'd worried she might not find what she was after, that the stories had been rumour and fantasy, that the contents of the Cone letters were a figment of Tamara Sass's vivid imagination. But here it was, proof of the grotesque event, the unpunished crime. She removed the box, wrapped it in a green silk scarf and put it in her organizer bag along with the camera.

She tried to close the drawer, but it stuck. She heard voices behind her. The drawer wouldn't budge. Sweat began to bead her upper lip and her peripheral vision blurred. She wondered if her arm could reach to the end of L504 and imagined it was a secret passage to whose dimensions she might suddenly shrink and be sucked down into the depths of the cabinet where she would find herself in Wonderland or Hell.

Something rolled beneath her fingers, almost thrust itself into her hand. She pulled it out and hastily inspected it. The tubular object in her palm was about 16 cm long and a dark brown flecked with red and gold. Though firm to the touch, it gave slightly under pressure in a way that was repellent but very interesting. Celia pushed it into her handbag and shut the drawer just as the voices reached the room.

I *am* a thief, she thought. What would Patrick have said? But Patrick would understand. He would see how this was an act of liberation.

Three men entered. Low voices speaking an unfamiliar language – Mongolian, Malagasy. Celia waited by the cabinet, paralysed. What would they do if they found her? She pressed the handbag to her stomach and held it there, a black leather baby. As the men came nearer, she tiptoed round to the back of the cabinet and out of view. (Really, this was absurd. She had her visitor's pass.) Her breathing was quick and shallow, and she feared she was about to hyperventilate. Any minute now they'd be sure to accost her.

But here came Mole to inform them that they were in the wrong room, and they were obligingly following him to the exit. Now they were gone and so was Mole.

4

Adèle

Celia was experiencing tunnel vision, her eyes fixed only on what was in front of her. She moved, robot-like, through other rooms with oak panelling and identical wooden cabinets that contained yet more antiquities, numberless, beautiful and weird. But none as strange as what she carried in her bag. Once Patrick had said, 'Whatever you do is good, darling. Whatever you want is fine.' Could that still be true? Celia supposed she must believe him. She had to, having committed what would otherwise be called a crime.

She was walking too fast; she couldn't help it. She imagined employees turning as she passed, felt their eyes on her retreating back. She must look so obvious – a marked woman, radiating guilt. She reached the exit and handed her pass back to the uniformed guard who nodded her through. The glass door opened and closed behind her. Nothing happened. But, she reminded herself, this part of the building's security system had not been modernized, so the antiquities carried no electronic tags.

She crossed the large entrance hall where pillars cast giant shadows and tourists earnestly consulted floor plans. It no longer mattered if her heels clicked. They wouldn't be heard among hundreds of murmuring voices. Yet all the while she expected alarm bells to ring or to be met by guards who would seize her arms and advise her to come along quietly. Now she was parallel with the Manuscript Room, now with the Bookshop. She pushed through the revolving doors and stepped out into the sunshine. A sharp breeze stung her face and made her clutch at her head in a telltale way. She sensed shadows behind her, heard someone hurrying to catch her up. Leave me alone, leave me alone. I've done nothing wrong. It's you, you're the criminals . . .

Celia descended the wide stone steps, disregarding Mole who waited on the last one, looking as if he'd like a word with her. He made a move to follow, but she marched resolutely past him towards the gates. Could it really be Celia Pippet adopting this bold attitude? She hoped he would not pursue her, saying things she did not wish to hear. He would find out soon enough what she'd accomplished. Then rat on her, no doubt.

Celia was through the gates and out, but was still unable to breathe normally, stop the lurching in her stomach or allow her hunched shoulders to relax. At the pedestrian crossing she hesitated, certain she could hear deliberate footsteps among all the other footsteps. She crossed, the sun hurting her eyes as it always did. By the Museum pub she removed the glasses and glanced behind to gauge the distance of the security men sure to be trailing her. There was no one except Mole who stood behind the bars of the mighty iron fence, as if imprisoned within its perimeter. She wished it could be so and walked on, slicing him from her mind and discarding him.

It was time to discard. On Bloomsbury Way she passed St George's Church and turned into an alley she'd investigated the day before. In the semi-darkness she removed the pins that had secured the black wig, the cheap hot wig itself and the courts which had maimed her feet and dropped them, along with the spectacles, in a half-filled skip. She fluffed out her short blonde hair and slipped into the flat shoes she'd kept in the bag. She looked both ways before quitting the alley, then ran to catch a 38 bus to Victoria.

Even the conductor seemed menacing, but as she paid her fare she reminded herself that he, like everyone else on the bus, was entirely ignorant of what she'd done. She looked like an ordinary person, maybe a little sweeter than ordinary. So they assumed she was ordinary and not the avenging bandit heroine she'd just become.

CHAPTER TWO

There was no horizon, only an opaque merger of sea and sky. The Channel was choppy with real waves, not the usual blip blip of shoreline ripples. The equinoctial tides had begun. Down on the beach Celia could smell the fish and chips from Come Fry Away, where in their teens she and Martin would purchase their weekend treat if they had the money. On warm evenings they'd walk to the Martello Tower where she now waited in a sharp drizzle, and devour their food on the shale, their backs against the fortress walls. Silly, she thought, to meet here. Sentimental, melodramatic. And very uncomfortable. *His* idea.

But Martin's parents still lived close by, and he and Celia had wanted an anonymous place to rendezvous and continue their journey together. Hard to be more anonymous than Seaford. And the Newhaven ferry was only a short drive away. Even in the mist she could make out the silhouette of the town. Sometimes you could see Brighton beyond, but not today. This was how she remembered the place – wet, chilly and grey with its little streets off the seafront struggling to approximate old-world charm, boasting half a dozen antique shops where most of the objects displayed had travelled steadily down-market to this, their final resting place, their last chance before the scrap merchant's or the recycling bin. On the outskirts, solid brick dwellings obscured the Downs. Behind her an isolated row of Victorian houses, vacant for decades, had been recently renovated and sold. There was now the odd window box with its courageous daffs and a tipped-over tricycle on the pavement. The hotel, the only large one in town, was closed for what appeared to be leisurely repairs. Next door, the pub, full of tourists in high summer, looked barely patronized.

Celia paced the beach, fighting to hold her brolly aloft. She was keeping an eye, even in this deserted place, on the travel bag she'd taken from Left Luggage, swapping it with her organizer bag before boarding the train. The locker key and the antiquities she kept safe in her shoulder bag. A man in a green mac was striding towards her. Not Martin, he'd never wear a mac. And she'd have recognized him instantly by his walk and the set of his shoulders. She squinted to make out the stranger, still anticipating Mole or his superiors or MI5. Every passenger in the railway carriage had been briefly suspect.

A retriever caught up with the man and dropped a ball at his feet, and together they went off towards the Seven Sisters. Going home. How lovely. Returning. Celia hugged the bag. She was shivering with cold and anxiety. Where was Martin? Dealing with the domestic backlash, probably.

Martin had a baby as well as a wife. It was peculiar to watch someone who'd been your best platonic friend for so many years slide suddenly into conventional emotions. Martin Cleary a dad. She wasn't jealous of his new arrangements. (She'd analysed her feelings at length, not only alone, but with Martin and with Nasreen, her deputy editor.) She was merely bored by them. She saw him with Frances as little as possible, insisting that most of their meetings remain à deux.

Celia had been reluctant to inform his wife of their travel plans, and when Martin had insisted that, sooner or later, he'd be forced to tell her, Celia invented a lie she hoped he could live with, at least for the next ten days. But live with it he couldn't, so in the end she capitulated and settled for his promise that he would swear Frances to secrecy. Later, if all went according to plan, everyone would know the terrible story it had become her obligation to tell, and it wouldn't matter if Frances gossiped as usual with her large and garrulous family.

Celia tried to be understanding and not mind about the way Frances had trained Martin to be a dependable father and husband. She herself preferred the more anarchistic version and had misgivings about his new leaf. She tried not to resent Frances, she really did. She didn't blame women who still chose to be domestic. Why should everyone want or even need a career? The fact that she and her women friends had carved out some professional niche, however unconventional or insecure, did not give them the right to be contemptuous of those who went the maternal route. Or so she liked saying. And there was no denying Frances was pretty (the kind that peaked at eighteen then ran to happy fat after the first child) with her white skin and white teeth and full white breasts and hair so blonde it was almost white. No wonder Martin . . .

Even at a distance she recognized him at once. He waved to her and she waved back, feigning a confidence she wished she felt. She picked up her travel bag and went to meet him. His walk and his square-set demeanour were the same as when she'd first noticed him during a dull lunch hour on her second day at South Ham School seventeen years ago. After that they'd spent every break leaning against the brick wall conversing about movies they hadn't seen and politics they didn't understand. Femate and Hemate he'd called them. They still were. Celia smiled to herself, guessing his thoughts. He'd be imagining the beach as an English version of some scene in a Fellini film, he and she the approaching figures on an empty strand, linked but alienated.

They came face to face but didn't touch. In seventeen years they'd hardly kissed, only hugged each other if they hadn't met for a long time or if one of them was depressed.

'Hi.' He smiled at her. 'How's the public enemy?' He had no umbrella and his black hair was separating into damp tendrils. His jacket hung open over old jeans, he had no proper footgear and she could see the dark bristles he'd missed during a hasty shave. Frankly, he looked a slob. A not unappealing slob.

'Where's the camcorder?' Celia asked.

'In Dad's car. Ready to go. You won't believe this, but everything's ready to go.' He glanced at her bag. 'So, you did a successful runner?'

'Please, Martin, don't tease. It wasn't easy.'

'I'll bet. Any problems with the Mole person?'

'Just very bad vibes. Wait until he finds out . . .'

'He won't be forgiving me in this incarnation. Things I do for you, sweetheart.'

'I do appreciate them,' she assured him. 'But he *has* been paid − and in advance. It's not as though he didn't get something for his trouble,' she rationalized, still uneasy about her trickery. 'You found a baby-sitter then?'

'Frannie's sister found one. Thanks for the cheque,' he added.

Frances had refused to be left alone with baby Tom unless they supplied her with back-up. She probably didn't much like the idea of Celia and her husband running off to Paris together either. Not because of jealousy. How could she be jealous of Celia? Frances just needed Martin, present and accounted for, to do her bidding. But Celia realized she wasn't being fair. Frances only wanted what most women of her acquaintance claimed they wanted: an equal partnership. Except Frances fought for it, demanded it, won it. She'd done what the others hadn't managed. Of course she'd had a head start with Martin. He was a good man, if an impecunious one. And it wasn't his fault that Thatcher had wrecked the British film industry, or that the last job he'd had was eighteen months ago making a documentary on family planning in Jordan.

He took her bag and they walked on, the wind at their backs.

'I have to sign on Monday week. I told you that, didn't I?'

'You told me.'

'That means leaving no later than next Sunday morning. Otherwise there won't be time to do even a rough edit.'

'I'm aware of that.' He was making her nervous. A hundred things could go wrong during the coming week. 'Please don't fret. The lecture, the film and my piece for *Dia* all have to be ready by Sunday morning, so we must be back in Paris by Friday night.'

'I'm still worried about the rough edit.'

'Martin, please. It's all organized.'

'OK, I'm sorry.' He shook out his wet head like a dog. 'So how does it feel to be a felon? Miss Muffet, who'd have thought . . . By the way, do I get to see the contraband?'

'Not here. Too wet.'

'Whatever you say, ma'am.' He took her arm and they went on through the rain. She made token gestures with the brolly, but she was too short to keep it above his head, and so it protected neither of them.

'Give it here, titch.' He held the brolly for her. He never minded getting wet.

'We'd better hurry. It's getting dark.' She checked the watch that Patrick had bought for her on her twenty-eighth birthday. She'd been surprised and very touched, though a trifle uncomfortable when he'd slipped it on to her wrist. Lavish jewellery wasn't her style.

'Ferry doesn't leave until six. Have you eaten?' He studied the pale face with its large eyes and gamine fringe.

'Not much of an appetite.' She smiled. 'But thanks for asking.'

Martin squeezed her arm. He was just so nice sometimes. So lovely to be with. Better than a lover with all the conflicting demands and infantile behaviour and lack of privacy. Yet he could not still her anxieties. Not now. Celia was well-acquainted with anxious states. They dogged her daily. They seemed the currency of all enterprise, no matter how carefully planned. (She had always been an excellent planner, even as a child.) Since the launch of *Dia* they had plagued her incessantly, despite the journal's modest success: first prize last year for New Ventures in Women's Publishing, shortlisted for the Small Press Award. She hoped that somehow Patrick knew. She'd started *Dia* with money he'd given her. Of course most of that had been spent long ago, and she worried constantly that the Arts Council would withdraw its small grant. She'd nurtured the journal cautiously, forcing it to conform to rules and procedures, a kind of benign Five Year Plan. No jumping of developmental phases. The journal took an academic slant, exploring, promoting and often discovering women's writing past and present. It offered essays, reviews, an interview written by herself and poetry, plus some graphics she was aware needed improving. Her own special interest focused on art and culture between 1920 and 1945, which was how she'd come across Adèle Louisante and later Tamara Sass.

They reached the car-park and discovered that Martin had forgotten to lock the boot. However, the camcorder was still there, alongside the shabby rucksack, borrowed from a nephew, that was his only luggage. Personal appearance meant little to Martin. He looked out at the world with his kindly, critical eyes, one of which turned decidedly downwards with an effect that was at first disturbing but later endearing. Beside him in the front seat, Celia watched a drop of water slide down his nose to fall between his thighs on to the regularly hoovered seat-covers. He didn't notice.

Mr Cleary had lent Martin the car with reluctance, convinced his youngest son was a magnet for catastrophe, but finding it difficult to refuse him any request despite the inevitable effects on his and Mrs Cleary's nerves.

'Go on with you,' he'd concede in mock disgust. 'Have fun with your Miss Pippet.'

To him she would always be Miss Pippet, and she wished this were not the case. It reminded her of a part of herself she didn't much like. From the day she'd met him, she suspected Tom Cleary regarded her as a snotty little middle-class sourpuss. No good to joke with, though occasionally fun to tease. She remembered the glint in his blue eyes when, with a face perfectly straight and a tone all innocence, he'd casually put to her his embarrassing questions and watch her ensuing discomfort. Family and friends were used to his mischief and able to give as good as they got.

Their only intention was to keep the insults flying. They sharpened their wits at every opportunity. But though she longed to do so she'd never been able to join in the banter. She lacked the right tone, the right attitude and, above all, the right background.

The Pippets were experts at deflecting any threat of confrontation. Safe in their padded world of middle-class speech patterns and social formulae, they hid their disapproving and judgemental natures while handling each other with kid gloves. Celia resented it – and her inheritance of it – fiercely. She sometimes felt like a trained animal. But how to un-train herself? Besides, to be honest, she preferred organization and arrangements. She was good at them. At four she was marshalling her dolls and soft toys in domestic hierarchies; at seven teaching them geography and correcting their spelling as their orderly ranks swelled in her neat primrose-and-white bedroom.

Celia excelled at school. Naturally her classmates mocked and shunned her and she was seldom invited to parties or chosen for games. It was all so painful. But what could you do with an insatiable little brain that snatched up every scrap of information and mentally filed it for future use? How to suppress or at least disguise your intellectual curiosity? How to tolerate or even enjoy people and behaviour that were alien to you? How to please naughty, attractive, good-humoured folk such as Tom Cleary whom you secretly liked? How to be messy and silly – how to have fun?

And then, to further annoy her, there was her appearance. At five foot three, and a size eight, she looked pretty in a vulnerable way, so that strangers assumed she wouldn't say boo to a goose, and were surprised or shocked when she displayed her strength of will.

Meeting Martin had helped. He created an atmosphere and a space where she could come out and show herself in a better light. Yes, she'd improved, though she could not understand how it had happened. She wasn't so sure about the effects of her five years with Patrick. He'd certainly indulged her, so that she felt both protected and free. And he was madly generous, giving her the money for *Dia* and all. Perhaps he'd only detained her in the role of Daddy's Girl, ignoring certain features of her character, because, from his point of view, she was so absurdly young. Whatever the motives or the results, she missed him badly.

The windows of the car were steamy now, so she felt safe enough to display her treasures. She showed Martin the clear plastic box but refused to open it. Somehow she wasn't ready to touch its contents. He stared at the thing, his brow creased.

'How the hell did you manage this?'

'Someone had to. The woman as usual – doing all the dirty work.' They finished the sentence in unison and laughed.

'Listen.' Celia placed a hand on his arm. 'There was something else. Something Mole never told you about.' Celia opened her bag and drew out her second discovery. 'This was in the drawer along with Adèle's – ' She held up the speckled brown object for him to see. 'What do you suppose it is?'

Martin grinned. 'Well, I know what it looks like.'

She half smiled.

He examined it closely, his eyes wide in mock excitement. 'Maybe a sort of ritual object. And maybe very old. Hey, you may have stolen a real antiquity. With a clever fence we could even – '

'Honestly, Martin.' She snatched back her treasure and replaced it in the bag.

16

They were silent as they waited for the engine to kick over. They felt out of place in the immaculate interior.

'This'll soon be more homely,' said Martin, glancing around.

The engine coughed, gagged, spat then roared unconvincingly before settling down to a comfy purr. They turned into the Newhaven Road. It would be a longer journey via Dieppe but less obvious than the Dover–Calais route. They tried to be crafty while knowing they could never be crafty enough.

'Feels a bit like the beginning of *Kiss Me Deadly*,' said Martin.

'Does, sort of.' The reference chilled her, reminding her that she was now a genuine thief. 'I only hope I don't end up like Cloris Leachman. Ralph Meeker wasn't much help, was he?'

'He did his best, as I recall. And got regularly thumped for his pains.'

They drove on, Celia glancing nervously at every car that passed them.

'So.' Martin hit the steering wheel with the palms of his hands. 'Tell me about this Tamara person.'

'I've only spoken to her on the telephone.'

'Yeah, but you write to each other. And you know people who know her.'

'True.'

'I mean how famous is she? Famous within a select coterie or world-wide like Paglia, only I haven't noticed, or famous for fifteen minutes?'

He was chewing gum. She wished he wouldn't.

'I suppose she's fairly famous. Quite famous, actually. Among feminist academics and people who read a lot.' She looked at Martin who didn't read all that much, except for *Sight and Sound* and *Cahiers du*

Cinéma. 'This book on prostitution should enhance her reputation.'

'You've read it.'

'I published an extract,' she emphasized.

'OK, so I don't read every word of your magazine. I'm not pretending I do. But I'm here, aren't I? I'm doing what you want and escorting you on this lunatic enterprise.'

'Of course you are. And I'm very grateful. I just assumed you understood it had an important purpose – at least I consider it important.'

'I do understand. You want to present your dramatic discovery to all the delegates at the Female Futures Conference. Tell the story of this beautiful, exploited child courtesan, strike a blow for justice for your sex. Isn't that right?'

'Martin, are you being facetious?'

'Me?'

They were approaching the front at Newhaven. Through the mist and rain the docks were just visible.

'Hell, I believe in what you're doing. I mean it's really good.'

He turned into the waiting area. Celia produced their tickets as Martin steered Tom Cleary's car into the correct lane.

'See? We're early.' He switched off the engine and faced Celia, his arm resting across the back of the seat. 'But isn't one of your criminals a woman as well?'

'They're not *my* criminals. And it must be obvious to you after eleven years with a certain PM that women can be oppressors. Or collaborate with male oppressors. Sometimes they have very few options.'

'What was her name? That nurse, baby-sitter – what was she anyway?'

18

Her own words surprised her. 'Blanche Jessel was an evil woman.' She stared at the huge ferries lined up at the dock. Blurred by the weather, they made her think of white sea cows resting on their river banks, harmless and doomed. She corrected herself. 'I mean her behaviour was evil. We don't know what she was really like. Perhaps it was all her brother's influence and she was forced to act against her will. That person in yellow is waving us on,' she warned Martin. 'There seems to be rather a lot of over-manning here.'

'Celia, that is the least of our problems.'

'Sorry. It's my stupid fretting. You mustn't let me do it.'

'I won't.' He started the engine.

'Martin?'

'Yes.'

'Thank you for escorting me on this lunatic enterprise.'

'De rien.' He smiled at her. 'Is that correct?'

On an uncharacteristic impulse, she seized his hand and pressed it. Then she quickly let it go.

CHAPTER THREE

A human tongue is so sensitive, so engorged with
memory, that it can analyse the components of the most
sophisticated cuisine, isolate flavours, test their strength,
trace their origins, inform the brain of their proportions,
pass judgement on the success of their combinations. It
can do the same with a human body.

This afternoon I am remembering the taste of your
skin. I have remembered it thousands of times. Yet on
each occasion the pleasure of the evocation is shocking
and fresh – the mushroom volutes of your ears, the salt
of your neck, the swamp of your underarms, the garlicky
fur between your legs, the mineral traces on your palms
and feet. And behind all these tastes, conjoining and
confusing them, the taste that was really a smell, the
smell of excrement, your root smell which we had
continually to drench with perfume. But that is an
olfactory recollection which must be kept for the
appropriate hour.

The surface of your tongue was rough as a cat's and
full of prickles to ignite every sense. It wrestled with
my own like a sea creature, too slippery to manage
coition. I would explore the furrows of your mouth's
roof and the thick camellias of your inner cheeks, caress
your middle tooth (which he removed against my will),
then invade your throat, straining for your larynx.

The taste of you changed according to the time of
day. I used to think it was best in the early mornings,
just before I left you at five-thirty to hurry to my room,

frightened he would see me, catch me. Before I went I would lick you everywhere, your sleeping body moist like a baby's. You tasted of baby then (or rather the way I imagine a baby tastes, since I have known so few – only inhaled the tops of two or three downy heads as I planted soft kisses there, feigning love). Then there was the thundery ozone taste that signalled arousal. I savour it again, along with the anticipation that accompanied it. I would run my tongue along the pattern of fine dark hair that formed a galactic swirl between your shoulder blades, then trace the line of your spinal column to dive into the notch where your buttocks divided, your deepest crevasse, the source of yourself. It was your smoothest, dearest place, and my tongue longed to linger there, to curl up and dream. But your ridged interior would draw it on, further and deeper.

I travelled you with my tongue. It was a journey that had no end, returning to the beginning only to set off again on new adventures. In my mind I travel you still, even here in this prison, the roads and hills of your body a fertile landscape in which I am completely at home. (And they think I'm immobile, that because I neither read nor write any more or listen to the wireless, I don't and never will venture beyond the confines of this room.)

The texture of your skin felt cool and metallic, as if made of crushed crystals that alternately trapped and freed the light. It glistened and shimmered, reminding me of the ground jewels Jonas said were used in the windows of Chartres and that fling magic bands of colour across the mazed floor. But that is another story, a visual memory which must be kept for the appropriate hour.

You loved to please me. It made you happy to

please, like a child whose first word is yes. Of course, I was not the only one you pleased. There were others under whose tongues you also spread and stretched yourself; who left their trails of slime, like slugs, across your body.

After these encounters I would bath you. Gently I would wash away the excretions of the night and pleasure you again if you asked me. I tended you in every way. You were my vocation, my life's work. I tend you still. I watch over you when all the others have abandoned you. I'm only sorry I can't visit the churchyard any more. A boy now looks after the grave. I pay him well to plant, and water the flowers which I can see sometimes, yellow flags waving on the grass. When you were buried under that grass I felt my life was over. Nothing could prepare me for the pain of your physical absence. I even longed for the terrible times when you were merely a freak, when we fled and lived the life of freaks. I am not disgusted by these episodes. Our life together was beautiful, even, I often think – probably because I'm old and will die soon – holy.

The memories and sensations are beginning to fade. I can't sustain them as I once did. Even your image is fading, and I am back in the room where I'm told I live. My eyelids are heavy, and it's difficult to keep my head erect. Forgive me, my dear, I can't go on. As I said, I am old, and the old must sleep.

CHAPTER FOUR

America's leading female authority on prostitution opened the door to a tiny flat in the Place Jeanne d'Arc. Its interior was self-consciously spare and made clever use of space as Parisian flats must. Tamara Sass appeared much too large and spontaneous for the place, prone to sudden explanatory gestures that could topple a green glass shelf or spill a bottle of claret on to the pale carpet.

'It's so cramped,' she complained, as though accustomed to living arrangements the size of the Pantheon. 'Thank God I'm only renting and don't have to stay here. At least the view's good.' She opened a full-length window on to a minute balcony. Two floors below was a square enclosed by plane trees. 'Nice, huh?' She smiled and adjusted the two lacquer chopsticks that pierced her chaotic bouffant. 'There's a great market here on Sunday mornings. Saucisson sec right from the campagne. Twenty different kinds of goat's cheese.' Her smile was atomic, her teeth large and white. She looked as if she liked her saucisson sec.

'Could I have a drink?' asked Martin. She hadn't offered.

'Sure. There's a bottle of Badois in the ice box and some apple juice – unless you'd prefer the hard stuff.'

'I would, actually. But not right this minute.' He hesitated, smiled uncertainly, then wandered off in search of the kitchen to which he had not been directed.

23

Tamara watched him go. 'Cute,' she said. 'Will he be any use?'

'I trust him completely,' Celia answered.

'In other words he's all we've got.' Tamara leaned back on the dove-grey divan and opened a packet of Gitanes. 'Boyfriend?'

'Old friend.'

'I see.' Tamara lit up. 'Hey, it's freezing in here. Are you freezing?' She looked around for her missing baronial fireplace. At five foot ten, she was a lovely big girl, a fine healthy woman in the bloom of middle age and probably with a spectacular immune system. She switched a small electric heater on to high. 'I had to buy this myself,' she said, disgusted. 'So you've got it.' Her greedy eyes fastened on Celia.

'In here.' Celia patted the bag she'd refused to part with since noon the previous day.

'Well, come on.' Tamara sat up, excited, and made a 'Gimme' gesture with her hands. 'Let's see it.'

'Right.' Celia removed the green silk scarf and its contents and held it out to Tamara. She hadn't yet opened the transparent box, hadn't touched the item for which she'd risked jail and disgrace. She'd wanted to be the first to do so and was reluctant to hand it over. But Tamara was now her partner and collaborator, and without her she would never have come this far.

Tamara opened the box and stared at its contents. Her eyes met Celia's with undisguised respect. 'God,' she breathed, 'were you brave.'

Celia felt hot. She was blushing. How awful.

'Weren't you scared?'

'Very. I think I still am.' She turned away from Tamara's smoke.

Tamara took out the artefact and held it up to the

24

light. Martin entered and squatted beside the glass table and the three of them stared at their prize. It was stiff like parchment and translucent as fine china.

'How can you be so sure it's Adèle's?' Martin asked.

'The BM says it is.' Tamara offered him a cigarette, but he shook his head. 'So pure, the two of you,' she teased.

'You trust the BM, do you?'

Celia watched him play devil's advocate.

'Certainly not.' Tamara wasn't offended. 'I have other verifications.'

'Discovered by you.'

'Yeah, if you want to know. Hasn't she told you?' She settled herself with an air of messy grandeur, adjusting cushions, skirt, mohair cardigan, cut velvet scarf, crossing feet in high-heeled ankle boots. 'I'd been working on this prostitution project for a couple of years. One afternoon in the Houston Library I came across a photograph in a book about Paris between the World Wars. It was taken by Yves Gervais – ever heard of him? – of some night ladies, expensive pros by the looks of them. I was struck by this one face, beautiful but not quite human, do you know? I got interested and started tracking the picture down.'

'How?' Martin asked.

'Let's say I followed my instincts. There were hints and little references here and there from which I drew a rather large conclusion.' She chuckled.

Celia listened to this clearly excellent but disquieting person while studying her face from a safe distance. It was smooth and moon-round, framed by hennaed curls that fell past her shoulders. A generous mouth, with just a hint of a pout, had been enhanced by brown-red lipstick, expertly applied. The fleshiness of the cheeks and jaw contrasted with sharp green eyes, so that the overall expression was both sceptical and sympathetic.

'I found a couple of mentions of Adèle in contemporary journals, but they were only a tease, didn't cohere. Then came the Breakthrough. Like discovering buried treasure, I swear. I was researching a paper I was meant to give at Cornell and checking some minor reference in the memoirs of Professor Oscar Cone, once a highly regarded anthropologist, now discredited by his politics, although there's a sinister resurgence of interest in the professor's so-called theories.' She shuddered. 'Anyway, in the midst of five hundred pages of gunge were these extracts from his correspondence with one Dr Jonas Sylvester. Apparently they'd been friends since university, had some interests in common, went to Germany together for a year. Well, I was beside myself, you can imagine. Nearly had kittens.' She burst out laughing. 'You guys want a drink now? I personally could use one after seeing this amazing object.'

Celia drank her Sancerre slowly, as usual. In general she preferred her consciousness unaltered.

'So Sylvester lived with this mysterious girl Adèle and his weird sister in a big spooky house.' Martin wanted the Tamara version.

'Yeah, in the Tenth. There were very few one-family buildings of that type and I don't know how he acquired it. Obviously he was desperate for complete privacy. Anyway, he was there, I think, until about 1940. Adèle had disappeared by then, and he writes to Cone saying she's gone and he's living alone, trying to get to Germany. By 1942 he's back in England. I'm not sure whether he came home because of the fall of Paris or whether he was drafted or whether he left France because nobody liked him. 1940 was a bad

year for Franco– British relations. There was a wave of anglophobia after England attacked the French fleet.'
'But why do you think he did this to her?' Martin pointed to the box.
Tamara shrugged. 'Lost control of his meal ticket and couldn't manipulate her any more. Thought he'd made a Lulu and discovered he'd created Frankenstein's monster. Went the way of all Svengalis. My guess of the moment is that it was an act of vengeance, either for himself or for a threatened male sex – about whose safety he was most concerned.'
'A very sick boy.'
'You said it.' Tamara swallowed audibly.
'And was she really so fabulous?'
'Oh yes. Very special. Gervais mentions her in the introduction to one of his photographic essays. Says she was scandalously beautiful. And there are a couple of references to her in memoirs of the period – old roués chalking up their conquests, artists talking about their models and girlfriends and whores, that kind of thing. None of them had managed to purchase her favours, but they all say she was this mysterious alluring creature, barely out of adolescence. No one knew where she came from. Maybe Spain or North Africa. She was very dark, and dark skin was a big number in thirties Paris. Josephine Baker and the Bal Nègre, you know. But let me finish. The letters turned out to be a dead end. Nothing else came up, and I began to worry that I was going off at a tangent, getting caught up in fancy speculation and not progressing with the sex workers' book. Then one day this letter arrived from Celia telling me in guarded terms about an item tucked away in the British Museum and asking was I interested. Was I, hell.'
'Really it was Martin's discovery.'

'I know this guy who's worked in the museum since university,' he explained. 'As kids we were great mates. Then his parents moved from Seaford to Luton when we were about twelve. We sort of kept in touch until we got too sophisticated to bother about the past. Then a couple of years ago I ran into him again in London. Time had not improved him. He was a dour bloke, and I wondered what I ever saw in him. Impressed by his rat-like cunning, probably. Anyway, we met a couple of times for a drink. One night we got talking in a pub, and Mole, as he is known to his acquaintances, since he has no friends, got drunk and started telling me all this apocryphal BM lore – resident ghosts and people being dead at their desks for weeks before anyone noticed and the shenanigans that used to go on in the cataloguers' residences. I was gripped. I asked him about the secret stuff, antiquities stashed away and just forgotten. Or maybe too upsetting and dangerous to see.'

'Like John Dee's obsidian mirror.'

'Like that. Normally Mole's a reticent grump, but by this time he was pretty newted and acting out of character. That's when he spilled the beans about L504. And I thought this is something my friend Celia might find interesting.'

'But how did you persuade Mole to get her in, for Christ's sake?'

'Bribed him, didn't we?'

'With what?'

'Nintendo games.'

'Huh. And was Mole aware of your larcenous intentions?'

'To my shame, no.' Martin bowed his head. He was now on his third glass. 'He thought Celia was only taking photos.'

'Which I was.'

Celia watched him reconnoitre the room for another bottle. She took advantage of the break in their conversation to put a question of her own.

'I keep wondering how it got into the museum in the first place.'

'Cone. Only way that makes sense.'

'Why?'

'Well, initially I thought someone may have planted it there in secret.'

'But why?' Celia persisted.

'Temporary stashing, haste and confusion, like after a robbery. Then I figured maybe Sylvester gave it to Cone for safekeeping, Cone being the only person he trusted. The only one who knew about his crime. Afterwards Cone duly "donated" it to the museum.'

'Or slipped it into L504 himself. Also for safekeeping,' Martin offered then reconsidered. 'But what would be his motive?'

'Listen.' Tamara wriggled forward on the couch. 'You mentioned the residences for the cataloguers.'

'Yeah. Mole told me about them. Top museum scholars were given apartments free of charge from the eighteenth century until after World War II. One or two may still be tucked away in there pickled in Saint Emilion. Apparently they led the life of Riley. Maids upstairs, wine cellars en bas, jobs for the boys, jobs for life. Nothing to do but catalogue and carouse.'

'Well, my dears, Cone was awarded one of these residences, and there he lived for twenty years.'

'So when he died — when did he die?' asked Celia.

'1953.'

'A certain box got scooped up with his bequest.'

'You mean he left the BM all his loot.'

29

'Why not?' said Tamara. 'They'd been damned accommodating. Besides, I'm sure it was expected.'

'But what if it wasn't an accident?' Martin asked. 'What if it was a deal? The BM could have acquired it on purpose, maybe intending to transfer it to the Museum of Mankind. I've heard they have a collection of human remains.'

'That would be a nice irony,' said Tamara.

This was the moment. Celia reached for her bag. 'Speaking of men, I have something else to show you. I don't know how to interpret it. But I'm sure you'll have an idea.'

CHAPTER FIVE

In the beginning it was science. I'm sure it was. But science became obsession, which puzzled me because my brother was a cold rational man. (I too was cold until I cared for you.) He was polite and soft-spoken but withdrawn and socially reticent, especially with women. Odd, therefore, that he chose to practise gynaecology, announcing one day, without preliminaries, that it was to be his career. Stranger still that women actually came to consult him. Why choose a man like Jonas, I asked myself, until I discovered that choice was not a factor. All men who specialized in female maladies were more or less like Jonas. Behind encouraging smiles and impeccable manners was an ill-concealed hatred of our sex. Carrying his colleagues' antipathy much further, he rose in their esteem and was envied by all. While they applauded his medical skill, it was his clever and precise application of hatred they really admired. His friend Cone, for instance, seemed to venerate him, visiting us twice to marvel at the progress of the 'experiment'.

You were already installed in the house on Rue Beaurepaire when I arrived in Paris. It was 7 February 1934, and the city was recuperating from a hectic night. Men in crumpled blue uniforms were clearing the debris of the riots everyone was talking about. Wishing to test my French, I bought a copy of *Le Temps* whose headlines announced that the battle at the Palais Bourbon had ended with a failure of the attempted *coup d'état* and

31

that the Republic had been saved. Saved from what, I asked Jonas. But he answered only that it might have been better lost. I, however, was determined to regard the news as a good omen.

When I met you you were fourteen years old, and you had no name. For years I knew neither where you came from nor what you had been called there. These were Jonas's secrets, and you pretended not to remember. Perhaps you really didn't remember. You seemed at times to possess occult powers, while at others you were a beautiful imbecile, helpless in the world.

I hated our house in the 10th arrondissement, particularly during that first winter. Later, when I had come to love you, it didn't matter to me that it was unkempt or undecorated, save for three rooms. It was far too big for us, and I could not understand what expectations my brother had of it. It was draughty and, though the rooms were high-ceilinged with large windows, there was never enough light. A gloomy pall hung over the ugly expensive furniture Jonas had bought. Where the money was coming from I did not know. It was not my place to ask, and he would have resented any enquiries. I wondered what the housekeeper, Madame Monmousseau, thought of those bare dusty rooms. We discussed little aside from the shopping, the difficulties involved, during the strikes, of acquiring the most basic foodstuffs, and the few rooms to which she did attend. Whatever her reasons, she kept our secret.

I had never been to Paris. In fact, aside from a school trip to Brussels, I'd never left England in all my twenty-eight years. (Twenty-eight, though I looked older.) I was excited at the prospect of my new home, never imagining I would find myself in

the midst of universal conflict. Only two days after
the Palais Bourbon riots, the Place de la République
was in a state of siege, and from 7 p.m. to midnight
eastern Paris was the scene of violent battles between
police and people Madame Monmousseau assured me
were communists. Within forty-eight hours of the
restoration of order, one million strikers descended
on us. Communists again. I dared not leave the house.
I could not believe I had been summoned to take up
residence in such a chaotic city. Everyone was fighting
everyone and Paris seemed on the brink of collapse.

My brother's affection for the place, despite the
upheavals, surprised and puzzled me. He was so very
much the Englishman. He loved Paris, though he
would never admit to such an emotion, indeed to
any emotion.

He had given me the merest sketch of my duties and
no indication as to the singular nature of my charge.
An adolescent, I was told. But he had faith in me,
and − stupid woman − I was touched by his faith. I
felt encouraged. Perhaps, after all, I had a purpose and
would find it through caring for another. It would be
good for me, I believed, to be needed and depended
upon. I might overcome my shyness and negativity.
But this optimism would soon yield to my normal
torpor and feelings of inadequacy. What did I know
about children?

Though it seems incredible to me now, the combination of current events and the shock of meeting you
at last was nearly strong enough to send me straight back
to London. When I said as much to Jonas, he forbade
it. He said I would get used to you in time. He never
guessed the real source of my alarm, and no doubt I
myself was ignorant of it. Nothing in my experience
had prepared me for such a creature, let alone for an

intimate relation with it. Often I was gripped by real terror and would tremble as I climbed the narrow stairs, after a breakfast I'd hardly touched, to commence my duties for the day.

These began with your bath. Not that you were dirty. Dirt and grease slid from your umblemished skin which seemed to have special properties of resistance. It was your smell we could not get rid of. Jonas instructed me in the use of various oils – lavender, ylang-ylang, jasmine, geranium, sandalwood – alone or in combinations he would prescribe. (He'd developed an interest in herbal medicine which, until that time, he'd regarded with contempt. He'd also begun to experiment with plant essences, and his study was filled with dried flora and fungi as well as books, old and new, on the subject.) As he seldom opened the windows, the room was thick with their dust and decay. I did, as usual, what I was told to do, but none of the potions worked. Also as usual, I was suspected of being the cause of this failure.

You loved the hot water, the steaming scents, the whole ritual of bathing. You surrendered to my careful scrubbing like a happy child, though I cannot imagine ordinary children making the demands you did of me.

'Donne-moi ta main, Blanche,' you pleaded in the accent I struggled to comprehend. 'Mets la là.' And you'd gaze at me with your empty eyes.

'Non,' I would reply in my most severe tone. 'Non, Adèle.'

Twice a day for several months we tried to rid you of your smell. Eventually I became used to it, then tolerated it, grew fond of it, craved it. It reminded me of barns and cattle and spring mud. A comforting arousing smell, old as the earth. Why smother it? I asked. But Jonas insisted that he and 'others' found you malodorous. 'Born on a dung heap,' he'd grumble, 'born in shit.' More experiments ensued until at last he discovered the right fragrance, not of his own making but for sale at a select perfumery patronized by the very rich. The perfumier, it seemed, was interested in Jonas's work and promised to introduce him to some like-minded people. I was both relieved and sad that the baths were reduced to one a day. I confess I was finding it impossible to maintain a nurse's decorum. You both touched and horrified me, and the inability to control my own responses filled me with confusion and guilt. You see, until I knew you I was certain that I was incapable of response.

I found I could no longer arm myself against you. You were a charming snake, a blazing sun, a riotous field of flowers and grasses where I longed to fling myself down. I was frightened my personality, such as it was, would become submerged in yours. I felt you wanted to rob me of myself. Why did I cling so long to that self when its loss brought my only happiness? I suppose I believed I was not allowed to be happy. I resisted the very idea of happiness. Cold misery was what I was used to, and I feared change.

Even here I live in your smell. I suck it from the thin air of this room where I am interred. In a way, I love my tomb. Stone walls and locked doors exclude distraction. They encourage the self-hypnosis which your smell induces. Even the subliminal aroma of sulphur which permeates the building from beneath the earth cannot taint or dilute the perfume mixed with excrement. I breathe it as deeply as I am able. My lungs expand to their meagre capacity to inhale once more as much as they can of your mysterious essence.

My brother, despite his courtly façade, was a hard man. He exploited me as he exploited you, relying on what he regarded as my canine devotion and my useful female afflictions which, in his eyes, were the source of my fitness for the job. He believed me to be conscientious and honourable and claimed to admire these qualities while putting them to work for his own advantage. In fact he despised my compliance. But his attitude to me was not unique. I am even less agreeable to men than my brother is to women. He, at least, is used to their company; familiar, however perversely, with their bodies. My male society has been restricted to a father, a brother and a husband. How stunted and starved an existence this must seem to other women. But it was all I knew. Men both intimidated and bored me, and their reaction to me was clearly similar. I had nothing to offer, neither beauty nor charm nor intellect. I was incapable of joining in the rituals of flirtation that I witnessed all around me, especially in Paris.

Before coming to France I had made love three times in my life, and only to my husband. He too appeared to be a reserved man, though no one moved in such a chill atmosphere as myself. Yet he was grossly venal beneath his starched surface, starch which I applied and daily ironed. (He was vain and owned dozens of shirts.) Secretly sensual, he assumed I would ignite as he did once we had drawn the bedroom curtains. I did not.

We were not compatible. I shouldn't have married him, but I did not know what else to do. Why in heaven's name did he want me? To ingratiate himself with my brother? I was a prissy, old-fashioned woman, strapped into a moral code in which I could not believe but for which I had no replacement. The idea of living without any code whatsoever was inconceivable to me.

Adèle

Roger Jessel left me. I didn't blame him and I didn't miss him. I was only humiliated. He had confirmed what I had always believed and what all men had encouraged me to believe: that I was ugly and unlovable.

Jonas had purposely failed to inform me of the nature of my charge. He guessed, rightly, that if I had known the truth I would not have come. When my initial shock had subsided, I asked him what he intended to do with you. He replied, politely of course, that it was none of my concern. My job was to tend his creature like a rare and valuable animal he was attempting to breed in captivity. I was to be your keeper. That was all. It was then I realized that my brother's faith in me was based on the crude assumption that a woman as physically plain as myself was guaranteed to be trustworthy. Since I was also a nurse, he could not imagine that I would be interested in you other than as a patient.

In my work, I had seen many naked bodies, usually women's. I saw them when I was my brother's assistant. He would often ask me to be present during examinations. I would sit on a straight-backed chair, my hands folded in my lap, trying to ignore the distressing proceedings. To me what he did was obscene and terrible – probing the vulnerable recesses of these poor women with long gloved fingers and metal instruments as though assaulting them or inseminating them like cattle. Often they would cry out in pain, and I would wring my hands and bite my tongue to keep silent. Yet I could not help studying their bodies, most of which were creased and pocked and shadowed. They, of course, did not smell, but they were sullied nevertheless by time, maternity, inactivity or abuse. They looked unclean. In contrast, your body, which was so rank, was always pristine. You shone and flashed with cleanliness like a fish. But I was unable to admit that I found it more and more difficult to maintain my mask of benign restraint. The disinterested nurse I was required to be by Jonas – and myself – was unnerved by the wiles and poses of her patient. Where had you learnt such behaviour?

But it was not only your seductiveness that distressed me. It was your sweetness, your absence of artifice. It was your affection. I could sense your constantly looking for ways to please me, to tend me as I tended you. You guessed my needs and you wished to help me, to show me how I could be loved and satisfied; how you, at least, would never reject me, never say no. You didn't know the meaning of refusal. You could only say yes.

And so one autumn afternoon when water trickled over the walls and the bathroom was hazy with steam, I placed my hand where you had so often asked me to place it. I did what you wanted and while so engaged I heard something crack like the breaking of ice.

CHAPTER SIX

Tamara had been correct about the house on the Rue Beaurepaire. At least about its appearance: nineteenth-century French pomposity overlaid by fifties banal with more recent touches of fatuous po-mo. It looked a mess. But the refurbishments did not prevent Celia visualizing the doctor, the beautiful child and her nurse as they moved past its windows, whispered in the hallways, lit and extinguished lamps, welcomed their dubious visitors.

They should have left for the south that morning, but Tamara had proposed a tour they could not resist. Clearly she liked Celia and Martin and wanted them all to have time to get acquainted, discuss strategies, sort out agendas, prioritize, brainstorm. She also wanted to do a bit of feather-spreading, show them what she'd been up to with her research and give them a taste of thirties Paris, or what was left of it. This was essential, she insisted, the English had no idea, it had been a complex decade – and dark, very dark.

After the Sylvester house the tour consisted entirely of brothels.

'We'll start at the top,' she announced as they exited the Métro at Opéra. Crossing the Boulevard des Capucines, they turned into the Rue du Hanovre.

'This is it,' she said, bringing her party to a halt. 'This is where the photograph I showed you was taken.'

'What is it?' asked Martin.

'It was the Acropolis.' This *ne plus ultra* of Paris

brothels was now a nondescript urban façade. 'It was originally built to outdo the Chabanais, which was the grand *fin de siècle* establishment famously frequented by Edward VII. They spent hundreds of millions to make it into this paragon of French taste and style. The classiest whorehouse in Europe. All done in white marble, very elegant and spare with a glass dance floor lit from underneath. It catered only to the rich and famous who were served by these hetaerae darting around in diaphanous gowns. Quite a wow, I guess.'

'There's no street number. What makes you think this was the place?'

'The photograph. Remember all the girls are in ethnic gear, that is, some Madame's fantasy of it.' Adèle had been decked out in an Arab costume, the transparent veil across her nose and mouth making her eyes even more startling. 'And one was made up to look Chinese and another like an Eskimo. The whole place was a sexual theme park. My guess is Adèle worked the Desert Room. It was done up as a posh Arab tent. There was even an ingenious diorama of a desert sunset with dunes and a passing caravan.'

They turned back towards the Métro. 'You could screw in Turkey, Japan, Brazil. There was even a virgin's room and a bridal suite where liberated couples spent their wedding night. And a mirrored room where you could watch a thousand reflections of yourselves doing it. Plus a torture chamber built to look like a medieval dungeon. They had this machine that – '

'Don't tell me.' Celia covered her ears.

'What I can't figure out is what became of the Black Museum,' Tamara went on as they descended the stairs. 'It had a huge collection of erotic art. Not garden-variety porn, but real masters like Beardsley and Utamaro. Gives you an idea of the level of taste — and the level of expenditure.'

'They certainly catered to every little whim.'

'Yes, if you could afford your whim.'

'So where do we go from here?' Martin surveyed the platform as if he had no idea how he got there.

'The opposite end of the spectrum. Get on — quick!'

En route to Hôtel de Ville, Tamara hardly drew breath. She warmed increasingly to her subject; she knew her stuff, recounting stories of Degas at the Montyon and Lautrec sketching throughout the many hours he spent at the Moulins. At the Rue de Rivoli, she led them along what became increasingly like Oxford Street and then into the Marais. They turned into a tiny street interrupted by a square, not at all stylish, where a few students sipped coffee in the weak sunshine. The Rue Caron looked as though it had been stripped for a renovation which had never taken place. A plaque commemorated the site of an ancient convent dedicated to St Catherine.

'And what are we supposed to be seeing here?' Martin made a slow 360-degree turn in the middle of the square.

'Something horrible. Come on.' They followed their leader as she retraced their steps to a shabby three-storey structure. The clips in her hair kept slipping loose (no chopsticks today) so that she was constantly reinserting them, sweeping back fistfuls of the auburn strands as she did so. It was an unconscious action, performed a hundred times a day, as much a part of her persona as her laugh and her accent.

The establishment advertised itself by a small glassed-in sign, so dirty and cracked that the words

'Hôtel Modern' were barely legible. It struck Celia as the most depressing place in Paris.

'Creepy.' Martin peered through the dingy net curtains that concealed whatever lay behind the ground-floor window.

'This hasn't seen Windolene since 1955.'

The door stood open, the entrance to a black hole. Not even a flight of stairs was visible in the gloom.

'Is it still functioning?' Celia asked.

'Depends what you mean by function.'

'Have you been inside?'

'Once.'

'What was it like?'

'I confess I walked straight out again. Every little hair on my body was standing on end.'

'Was it somewhere – important?'

'It was a slaughterhouse.'

'You mean an abattoir?' Celia recoiled. Aside from the occasional fish from a non-endangered species, she was practically a vegetarian.

'Almost, but for people. There was this one, the Sun, and another on the Rue de Fourcy, but that whole side of the street is demolished now. And some on the Boulevard de La Villette. Let's grab a grand crème, shall we?'

Strange, thought Celia, to be so learned about human degradation. But perhaps Tamara didn't think of it that way.

'The Sun was a sexual assembly line.' Tamara stirred her coffee. 'The women would line up along one side of a long narrow corridor and the men, mainly North African, along the other. The two chains of bodies would move towards a desk where some Madame would sit like a fat spider. No parading around in a gauzy négligée or arranging charming little lewd

42

tableaux. You just stood stark naked or in an old skimpy dressing gown to hide any scars or bruises and took what came. Whoever was opposite you when you reached the desk, well, that was your trick, and you whisked him off to a filthy cubicle and turned him as fast as possible. Some of those girls screwed fifty or sixty men a day.'

Imagining the lurid scene, it occurred to Celia that there ought to be an equivalent of a blue plaque on these 'houses of illusion'. The citizens of Paris were ashamed of them, she supposed, or they'd completely forgotten. Were the lives of these poor women so worthless and insignificant as to be undeserving of some recognition? At least the girls at the Moulins and Montyon had been rendered immortal, if anonymous, by male artists. Victims of great disasters are honoured; surely this was also a human catastrophe. The slaughterhouses *were* a kind of slaughter. You didn't have to mow people down with machine guns to massacre them. When she could get a word in she said as much to Tamara who didn't seem as moved.

'In some ways it's worse now. Back then women risked pregnancy or a dose or a slug from their pimp. But now it's crack and AIDS babies and homelessness and attempted suicide. You name it.'

'Does anyone help them?'

'There is a place where they can go in the 18th, but funding's being cut, surprise, surprise.' She looked at her watch. 'Let's go to St Germain for a drink at La Palette. You guys will like that. On the way we can stop at Suzy, or rather at the shop where it used to be. This was an altogether different sort of operation. Some of the male clients would even bring their families along. It was very comfy, with stained-glass windows like a church. Course they're gone now. And the street's all prettified for the tourists.'

Celia and Martin were exhausted when at last they arrived at La Palette and battled their way through the smoky crush of patrons and staff to claim a table against the far wall. Celia wished never to see another brothel, however renowned, even if Adèle Louisante had been among its attractions.

'Coffee's overrated,' Tamara confided. 'But the atmosphere is good.'

Three coffees and two brandies preceded a litre of house red. Celia rationed her wine while Martin, clearly fascinated, grilled their new friend.

'Do you do boys as well?'

'Sure.' Tamara's second volume of her study of prostitution, *The Sexual Working Class*, dealt with Europe since 1900. This massive undertaking with no end in sight seemed likely to be her life's work.

'Do you interview people?'

She lit a cigarette and sent a plume of smoke rushing towards the adjoining table. 'I don't interview them so much as just meet them.'

'Are they very exotic?' Celia enquired politely.

'Rarely. These people are doing a job, trying to earn a living. Lots of them are under heavy pressure from corrupt cops and can't operate unless they pay out – either with cash or their person. A few are breathtakingly normal, considering what they risk.'

'Tamara, I'd like to hear your thoughts about the – other object.'

'I was afraid you were going to ask me that.' When presented with Celia's surprise discovery she had taken it to the window, donned the specs she wore on a chain around her neck, held it to the light, declined to turn in a verdict. 'I need to let this sink in.' Then she

44

guffawed. Her laugh was brash and infectious. 'Why don't we brainstorm it over some couscous. My treat,' she suggested, neatly skirting the issue.

'I'm not very hungry,' said Celia.

'Not even if we go to Les Fleurs de Marrakesh, which is in the neighbourhood where Adèle hid from Dr Sylvester?'

Celia's eyes brightened. Tamara caught their excitement.

'You have such beautiful eyes, doesn't she, Martin?'

'Outstanding.'

'Really luminous. Such an unusual colour.'

'They're only hazel.'

'They're not.' She studied them. 'They've got all this green in them and this orangey-gold. And those lashes!'

Celia gave her a quick self-conscious smile. Compliments made her uncomfortable, as did too much attention. She considered her eyes pretty enough but hardly extraordinary. Perhaps Tamara was praising them because she was a nice woman and could find nothing else to compliment.

'Want to go to that restaurant now?' the nice woman asked.

Once more they were following Tamara as though she had been imprinted on their baby brains. She led them along the steep narrow streets behind the Barbès. Every bakery was open, blazing with strings of electric lights and filled with fraternizing Arab men. All resources had been turned to the manufacture of a pink-orange pastry twisted into pretzel shapes, gleaming with fat and dripping with sugar syrup. Women with black hair straying from beneath kerchiefs and shawls were buying the sweets by the kilo.

'What are these?' asked Martin, licking his sticky fingers. Sweet-toothed Tamara had bought them one each.

'End of Ramadan.' She had already finished her treat and was purchasing another. 'Nasty, but I love them.' She blotted the corners of her mouth on the back of her glove.

They entered a small dark room which smelled like a spice market and was decorated with plastic flowers and winking fairy lights. A little man with a bald pate surrounded by a fringe of dark curls came forward to offer Tamara an extravagant greeting as she laughed her loud laugh. She introduced her friends to Driss the owner who spoke French with an accent Celia found easier to understand than the Parisian. Slower and without running the words together. He led them to the best table where he circled them, waving menus while making special recommendations to Tamara. The food was very cheap.

'He's a sweetheart.' She leaned towards them, speaking in a stage whisper. 'Runs the place with his wife and sons. I've told them I'm Jewish and they don't care at all. Marrakesh used to be a tolerant city with a large Jewish community. Now they're all in Tel Aviv. Quel dommage. Have the lamb tajine with pears and the carrot salad to start.'

After the meal, which was indeed delicious, but too lengthy for Celia's limited endurance, Tamara insisted on showing them what remained of the infamous Rue de la Goutte d'Or. She tottered down Rue de Sofia, hitting her normal stride once they'd reached the Boulevard Barbès. Celia and Martin hurried to keep up, trying to catch her commentary in the din of the overhead Métro. Under its arches an ancient Saturday market still thrived. Here had been the scene

46

of the great Pimp War. The big Arab chiefs had grown rich and fat in the neighbourhood and felt it was time to expand. They had moved in on Corsican territory, and a battle had ensued on the streets of the 9th and 18th arrondissements with gangster-style shootings and hundreds dead.

'The Arabs won,' she concluded.

'It'd make a great film.' Martin turned to survey the neighbourhood from the other side of the road. 'Can't you see it—the bosses in their Cadillacs, the trains roaring overhead as the shoot-out begins, bullets whizzing past, screaming veiled women, market stalls overturned, vegetables and ladies' knickers everywhere . . .'

They entered the Goutte d'Or to find themselves in what looked like a bombsite. The entire area was being demolished. Streetlamps cast spotlights on multiple layers of peeling wallpaper, ghostly outlines of mirrors, baths, chests of drawers. Smashed masonry rose in jagged peaks to the moon. Glassless windows afforded views of limitless devastation.

'They're building new flats,' said Tamara.

'But won't the community be destroyed?' Celia looked worried.

'It'll just re-make itself,' Tamara replied confidently. 'Did you know that Jonas Sylvester suspected Adèle of being North African?'

'Any particular reason?'

'Lunatics don't need a reason.'

'But Celia said she was born in this inaccessible village in the Pyrenees. Isn't that why we're going there?' Martin leaned past Celia to light Tamara's cigarette.

'I never said it was inaccessible,' Celia corrected him as they walked on towards the Boulevard Rochechouart. 'But I always thought she was from the Languedoc.'

'She almost certainly was. Sylvester had anxious fantasies, like maybe her mother had a fling with a passing soldier from the Maghreb and Adèle was the result. I got the impression his warped agenda might be wrecked if she weren't white European.'

'He was a racist?'

'Let's say his tone made me damned uncomfortable. Remember there was a lot of it about and not only in Germany. There were plenty of fascist sympathizers in France and many of them were doctors.'

Martin went out at 8 a.m. and returned to the flat to inform Celia and Tamara that the car would not start.

'It'll have to go to the garage.'

'Are you sure?'

'I'm sure. Only I don't have any money.' He glanced at Celia.

'Me neither,' Tamara put in quickly. 'Anyway, we've lost a whole day. I guess that was my fault, goofing around like we did, but we don't have time to check out garages. If it won't start, it won't start.' She picked up her lavender coat and red leather gloves. Her movements always set off the tinkling of bangles, the rustle of silk, a scented breeze. 'Come on, we'll grab a taxi to the Gare d'Austerlitz.'

'What for?' asked sleepy Celia who could sense structures crumbling.

'To catch a train to Toulouse.'

'Funny,' mused Martin. 'The old man never has trouble with the clutch.'

They waited with the bags while Tamara hailed a taxi. They'd had a late night and not much sleep, and Celia was worried she'd nod off in the car. She hated the idea of being seen unconscious while others remained awake

and judging, of being observed while defenceless, even
by Martin. Reflecting on these matters, she fell asleep.
After the passage of several decades, they'd arrived at the
Gare d'Austerlitz and Martin was shaking her gently.

'Wake up, babes. Train leaves in fifteen minutes.'

Blinking away the haze that surrounded her, she
watched him struggle out of the taxi. As he hitched
the camcorder over his shoulder she could see the tear
under the arm of his jacket, which was nowhere near
warm enough. Celia collected her mac and the small
travel bag she'd bought for £8 at a stall in Covent
Garden Market. It contained: one dark-green jumper,
three pairs of snowy-white cotton knickers decorated
at the waist with a modest band of lace and carefully
bleached once a fortnight, one white bra, a copy of
Jazz, a blue-and-white-striped flannel dressing gown
with matching pyjamas, two pairs of black woolly
socks and a pair of dangling Indian earrings which
looked quite attractive with her short hair and which
were her only jewellery apart from Patrick's watch.

Still in a daze and very cold, she followed Martin.
She was miserable when she hadn't slept properly,
she hated drinking too much and Tamara's Gitanes
were making her ill. She caught up with the other
two at the ticket booth where they were informed
that the train to Toulouse would be twenty minutes
late. No one would say why. Not, as Tamara pointed
out, that it mattered. Late was late. They could have
a grand crème in the meantime. God knew, she
personally could use one. Martin found a *Times* and
a *Guardian*. Neither newspaper mentioned anything
about a museum theft.

Celia's eyes felt dry and gritty. She, Martin and
Tamara had stayed at the restaurant until one, and
she'd drunk in order to keep awake, reasoning,

mistakenly, that the sugar content in the rosé would have an enlivening effect. Normally she went to bed at ten-thirty.

At the station café their table hadn't been cleaned, so they were obliged to drink their coffee amidst the remains of someone else's breakfast. Absently Celia cleared a patch on the steamy window with the tips of her fingers. Looking through her peephole she caught sight of a gangly man in a brown mac. The coat was unbuttoned so that its tails billowed slightly as he walked. He carried a briefcase and his stride was awkward and a bit unsteady, like that of someone unused to rapid movement. She recalled the rhyme: 'There was a crooked man and he walked a crooked mile.' Celia leaned closer to her aperture and studied him as he consulted the departure board then turned in the direction of the Toulouse platform. Hastily she cleared a larger circle on the glass then brought her hand to her mouth.

'Martin,' she said, touching his arm while keeping her eye on the receding mac until it disappeared among the other travellers.

Simultaneously Tamara checked her watch. 'Hey, time to go.'

'We haven't paid.'

'Ohhhhhh.' She fumbled with a purse then flung some coins on the table. 'Here!' Then she gathered up her three bags and marched out of the café, calling over her shoulder, 'Dépêchez-vous, troops!'

They raced to their platform, an exhausted Celia bringing up the rear while anxiously scanning the crowd for the person she was positive had been Mole.

CHAPTER SEVEN

'"We've come to this churchyard in Bez to administer long-overdue justice for a crime committed fifty years ago."'

'"Long-overdue" is redundant.'

Celia made a note on her script in blue pencil. Her writing was small and clear. '"A crime which to this day remains unpunished and unknown."'

'How about "unrecorded". More official.'

'Yes. Better. "UNRECORDED."'

'"Dr Jonas Sylvester was a highly regarded gynaecologist. He escaped retribution for a vicious and illegal operation upon a friendless and possibly retarded young girl who had for several years been his ward and chattel and to whom he became father, jailer and pimp."'

'How much time will this take?' Martin opened his eyes and looked out the window at the flat countryside that precedes Bordeaux.

'May I please finish? Where was I? "After surgical removal of Adèle Louisante's clitoris, Dr Sylvester preserved the organ by means of a mummification process of his own invention. The culprit – "'

'Oh please, darling. That's so Perils of Pauline.'

Celia considered it and changed the word to 'doctor'.

'" – acting on the principles of a debased science, transported the organ to London. During the fifties it came into the possession of the British Museum where, until last week, it has remained."'

'Celia.' Tamara looked at her hard through oval titanium-rimmed glasses. 'You know that if this comes off we might be asked to do more, maybe even a TV documentary.' She swallowed a triangle of Toblerone and offered some to the others who refused.

'It's what we've been planning, or rather hoping. That we'll get some money to do a longer and more technically sophisticated version of what we shoot over the next few days. Martin has a contact at Channel 4 who says he's interested. I've also approached an *Observer* journalist and the *Guardian* Women's Page isn't averse, so we may get some features.'

'Especially if Dr Sass is a smash at the conference.' Martin was awake again.

Celia looked at them both, checking their eyes. 'Am I being naive?'

'Just optimistic, but what's wrong with that? I'm sure lots of people will share our enthusiasm — or at least our curiosity. I know several women writers in America who'd pursue it. It's a good story and it has links with contemporary issues.'

Celia nodded, very serious.

'One thing keeps bothering me, though,' Tamara went on. 'What about the BM? I mean what if they nail us for theft or sue us for libel? They're not going to be charmed by the revelation that they've been stashing human remains.'

'We've considered this.' Celia hastened to reassure her. 'We don't think they'll be able to prosecute.'

'We're relying,' Martin explained, 'on standard radical logic. Since the museum's possession of the organ is itself illegal, they can't complain about the loss of something that wasn't theirs in the first place. It's called false provenance, I think. And the trustees won't be keen to get embroiled in litigation or any

52

sort of public squabble that could involve a lot of bad PR. Besides which – I mean if the worst came to the worst – Celia has no previous convictions.' He put an arm around her. 'She's a first-time offender with an otherwise spotless reputation.'

'And what about those with less spotless reputations who will be booked as accessories after the fact?'

'I really don't think it's a problem.' The corners of Celia's mouth drooped. 'But if you're worried, you can still leave.'

'Not on your life.' Tamara laughed. 'And don't take everything I say so seriously. I can see I'm going to have to watch myself with you.'

'Probably.' Celia smiled.

'OK, Larceny Lou, go on.'

Celia continued. '"Jonas Sylvester was able to escape retribution for his crime partly because of a talent for secrecy as well as the disappearance of his victim who never lodged a complaint. But especially because he was a successful practitioner within a powerful male establishment. An establishment that still exists."' She looked up. 'That's as far as I've gone.'

'Good. I particularly like the last point. I think we should develop it. The fact that the vast majority of gynaecologists are still men exercising almost complete control over women's bodies. But let me read you what I've written. You'll see we're moving in the same direction here.'

Celia studied Tamara with her twenty-twenty vision. Though she had often to remind herself that this person was a serious scholar, she was not surprised that Tamara received substantial grants for her projects, good publishers' advances, publicity for her work. Clearly she was an accomplished academic hustler.

Celia took advantage of a pause. 'Before you go on

I was also thinking about Victorian medicine and its methods of dealing with unruly women.'

'Excellent. Very relevant.'

'I've got something here . . .' Celia shuffled pages. 'A bit I wrote last . . . here we are. "Women called mad, that is, women who wouldn't obey their husbands or who simply wished to be independent, were often treated by clitoridectomy. Many gynaecologists, the most notorious of whom was a certain Dr Isaac Baker-Brown in London, routinely performed these operations, often without the women's knowledge or consent, after coming to an agreement with the father or husband. The treatment rendered the women docile and obedient. These 'unfeminine' women who had been depressed, self-destructive, even psychotic, were, or seemed to be, much happier. Therefore medical sophistry reasoned that such operations were for the women's own good. In fact, they had been robbed of their individuality by the removal of their independent source of pleasure." I think Sylvester was similarly motivated.'

'Please remember,' Martin mumbled, becoming drowsy, 'this is a short film.'

Tamara pounced. 'He's right. It should go in my Summit lecture. Link Adèle to the campaign to end female castration.' She punched some keys in her laptop. 'How about this? "Even now Harley Street doctors are performing these same illegal operations for fat fees. How many Arab, African or Indonesian girls are put to the knife against their will?" What if I go for that angle?'

'Excuse me.' Martin roused himself. 'I know I'm a male and generally insensitive, but I'm beginning to feel very upset. You seem to be forgetting the second organ which we've agreed is a penis – either very old and made of an unknown substance or mummified like the missing part of poor Adèle. Could you please tell me if you have any plans for it? I mean, can you somehow fit it into your Concept?'

'Frankly, I have no idea what to make of it,' Tamara replied. 'And I suggest we keep it on hold for a while longer.'

'I don't agree,' Celia snapped.

'You've got to admit' – Martin's elbows were spread wide on the table, one of them absorbing a puddle of coffee – 'it's muddying the waters.'

'At present, yes. But I'm sure it's going to tell us so much more.' Celia moved the elbow to dry ground. 'It's part of another story we never imagined existed. Obviously there's a lot we don't know, so wouldn't it be better to admit our ignorance? If we were to conceal it now and the truth, whatever it is, emerged later, our work might be completely discredited.'

'She'd make a terrible scholar.' Tamara addressed Martin. 'Got integrity. Wouldn't sacrifice awkward facts to the success of her theory. Never make any moolah that way.'

'Would you sacrifice the truth for success?' he asked her.

'Darling, do I look rich?'

'Sort of rich.'

Tamara smiled indulgently at Celia. 'You're quite right, pet. We ignore the penis at our peril. Just tell me what we should do with it and where we should start and I'll support you every step of the way.'

Celia opened her mouth to speak then abruptly closed it. She'd been counting on the others for inspiration.

Martin slid from his seat and stood up. 'Pardon me, but I need to sleep.' He made his unsteady way to an empty seat at the rear of the carriage. 'If you make any progress or you need any help, give me a shout.'

'Don't worry, we'll wake you at Toulouse,' called Celia who wished very much that she could speak to him alone.

CHAPTER EIGHT

A nurse in the veterans' hospital once asked if I had ever noticed how people with small neat ears were more capable and ambitious and organized than those whose ears were medium or large or malformed. I said no, I hadn't, expecting her to elaborate. Instead she walked away. People misunderstand my lack of response. It does not occur to them that I am simply considering, waiting a while before answering. My eyes do not light up at the sound of their voices. People don't like that, do they? They think I am cold. And so they shun me.

As I watched her close the ward door behind her, I thought of your ears, round and beautifully crafted like little snails. Mine, on the other hand, were like some hybrid vegetation, an experiment that failed. At least they lay flat beneath the dull brown hair that hid them. (How embarrassed I was when I had to be photographed for the new Identity Cards which required the subject to be seen in profile, and showing the right ear.) No one but you, Adèle, was ever moved to kiss or investigate them with a tongue. My ears have been well trained. They lie down and play dead. Yet they were ever on the alert, serving the curiosity you aroused in me. My ugly ears heard everything.

They still hear your voice — the grate and scrape of the Occitan accent when I first knew you, later oiled smooth by the English lessons you received from me and the French and voice-training my brother arranged for you with a discreet tutor called Yves Gervais whom you seemed to like. We sandpapered and polished your voice's rough edges until its weight and darkness disappeared and it became breath-light and sinuous as your walk.

In the beginning we could barely understand what you said. I could only suppose that very few people had spoken to you, your grasp of language was so primitive. Your voice made me think of the sounds of night animals, pebbles churned up by retreating waves. Though expressive, it was not a social instrument.

Since you were learning English, I guessed that it must be my brother's intent to take you to London one day. I hoped it would not be soon. Surprisingly I found I was beginning to like Paris. It is easier to be a stranger in a foreign country than a stranger in one's own. Which I had always been. More important, there was my exclusive intimacy with you. I was reluctant to surrender our sweet privacy and hand you over to my brother and to the world where you would become I did not know what. My concern turned to fear once the visitors began arriving.

My brother never shared with me his plans for you. As always, he was the master and I the servant. (I later discovered that I had been an unwitting sorcerer's apprentice.) He was loath to discuss anything other than the state of your health, the smothering of your unruly odour or your progress in languages, which were all he intended you should ever learn. But to me your welfare was essential, and I felt it my duty to question him.

'I'm sorry, dear Blanche. I appreciate your interest, but I simply can't tell you yet,' he would reply with his calm, distant manner, the one he employed with annoying patients. (The ones he dismissed as neurotic

Adèle

or hysterical. The ones who asked questions.) 'The experiments I'm conducting can't be shared even with colleagues until I've made further observations.' Here his brow would furrow with concern. 'I'm sure you understand that it would be wrong to announce conclusions prematurely.'

And I would be temporarily appeased. But soon he became exasperated by my enquiries and scolded me in his smooth professional tone.

'Doctors are not jaybirds. They don't chatter away like women or speculate openly to pass the time. Besides which, I'm not really obliged to tell you anything.' (The way he said this reminded me of his approach to urine specimens. 'Would you pass water for me, Mrs Crumb. Yes, in *here*, Mrs Crumb.') He would state only that he was keeping careful notes, writing up your case. The Strange Case of Adèle Louisante. For what and for whom? Science, entertainment, or mere self-aggrandizement?

It was a mistake to tell me about those notes. He assumed I lacked initiative, that I was purely passive. But you made me bold. Or rather my love for you did, since you never encouraged me to be anything but myself. We never tried to change each other. Change did not interest us. Only Jonas wanted progress.

Take the matter of your tooth. He was determined to remove the offending object which he regarded as the mark of your primitive nature. He also claimed it impaired your speech, preventing you from acquiring the elevated accent crucial to your advancement – and his own. He enlisted the help of the young tutor who had some talent for photography. As part of the record of your development he took pictures of you once a fortnight. Among the first is your portrait with the single tooth; followed by your smile with its painful gap; then with two perfectly fashioned incisors. This pictorial history was in turn stowed away with your hidden files.

The day after his revelation about them I went to his study. It was locked. From then on it was permanently locked, except when Madame Monmousseau came to clean, and then he was always present, supervising her work. He must have realized his error. But I was not deterred. Since I was forbidden to read his secrets, I would discover them by other means. I would will my hearing to become supernaturally keen.

At night I would creep from my room on my way to you and stop outside Jonas's door. I'd place my ear to the wood and wait while it collected sounds from the interior. So still was the house at that hour that I was able to hear the scratch of his pen. As I listened night after night, still as a standing stone, I sometimes believed I could hear the workings of my brother's brain, focused and efficient as a snake digesting a frog. He was writing your story, albeit in clinical terms. Your true story. Your past, your present, your fate. He knew more of you than you knew of yourself. He loved his knowledge of you, while I loved only you. Your breasts, your fingers, your smile. The only smile ever turned on me. Eventually I learned not to care that it was also turned on others. For your sake, I became a spy in my own house.

To this day I possess hearing of abnormal acuteness. It has served me well both in love and in my profession. When years later I worked in the veterans' hospital, I would be instantly aware of my patients' slightest movements. They writhed, dying belatedly and at length between the sheets I changed twice, often three times a day. Quick as instinct I would be by their bedsides. They knew they could rely upon me to watch over them, to tend their bodies so unjustly maimed when they were only boys. As those boys they would never have loved me. As grown men, some of them old and all in pain, it was possible. I felt almost one of them, you see. Their cries and groans were my own. I belonged among the mutilated.

I bound old wounds, the stumps of amputated limbs, long ago incinerated. I soothed nightmares and convulsions. I shifted the weight of those unable to turn themselves in their narrow beds. I pushed their wheelchairs, guided and supported them on their crutches as they stumbled and dragged themselves along that dim tunnel that led to the baths. (The underground passage had been dug when the hospital was built, in order to spare the villagers the sight of the grotesque and pitiful wounded. And to prevent any lapse of faith in the glorious purpose of war.) When we arrived at the vast vaulted hall that was our destination, I would escort them to their cabins, undress them gently and help them into the grey stone baths. There the warm sulphurous water would ease their distress as I washed them slowly and carefully as once I washed you. There is no greater expression of compassion than to bathe, with humility, another's passive body. It is a sacrificial act, a service embraced with love. I think sometimes it is even an emblem of sainthood and I remember Mary Magdalene. Then, too, it is a rehearsal for the laying out of the dead. This also I have done many times.

I eased another pain of my *mutilés de guerre*, the one I understood best, which was their longing for physical release. The practice was a kind of repeated euthanasia from which my patients continually revived. If I'd had the courage I'd have prevented this rising again from the dead and helped them to remain for good in the oblivion they craved. But I could offer only temporary comfort. (I cannot condone the taking of a life, such tenderness for all creatures did I learn from you.)

I would take their members in my mouth and, for those still able, I would bring them relief, prolonging their pleasure as much as possible, for this was more than duty. They were like you in that they never minded my face or body, grown even less attractive with ten additional years. In the dark they didn't see me and could easily imagine me as someone else. A wife, a film star, a virgin. They called out names that became familiar to me. They whimpered, cursed, cried and occasionally smiled. I was their true friend, and as I sucked them in the night I too indulged my fantasies, imagining all you and I had done together. Through their wrecked bodies I invoked your physical perfection. My life within these stone walls was almost bearable. That was before the last of my soldiers left me and I took up my other profession.

There was a multitude of sounds in the house on the Rue Beaurepaire, and I heard every one of them. You at your lessons with Jonas and the tutor, your voice striving to become another's; the tutor's clipped consonants, my brother's deceptively warm baritone. (Occasionally the tutor did not come and only you and Jonas would be in the study, you struggling with a passage from Racine, chosen for his clarity of style and the simplicity of his vocabulary. Then a long silence, during which I would cease to breathe.) The doorbell ringing at one in the morning, a quick short ring, answered immediately. Even in my third-floor room where I had been, by that time, locked up by my brother, I could hear the footsteps in the carpeted hall, then on the stairs. Voices, a man's and a woman's, young, with cultivated accents. The turning of the knob to your door, a sound so familiar. Me on my knees, my ear to the keyhole, straining to catch every clue. You. Your voice, not frightened. Your laughter. Theirs. And then the rest of it. Terrible.

Bells, footsteps, locked door. A man talking to my brother and my brother asking him to lower his voice, but I hear anyway. Hear them in the sitting room. Feet in the hallway. Bare feet, yours. Then descending the stairs and into the sitting room where the male voice murmurs. I wanting to pound the door and scream, only I must not and I do not. The front door opening and footsteps on the pavement below, only one pair I am relieved to hear until I part my window curtains and see a tall man in a smart overcoat carrying you in his arms and passing you into the back seat of a waiting car. (How wealthy or important these people must be, driving about Paris during the petrol strikes when the city's roads are quite empty.) You, wrapped in your fringed and embroidered shawl, your bare feet with their gold toenails dangling and kicking, and no, not with fear or resistance, but delight. Opening his door, the driver looks up and I see that he is wearing a pig mask. Slowly, silently the car pulls away. I hear my brother's study door closing, the turn of the key in the lock, and, finally, my own smothered weeping.

Afterwards you'd embrace me and laugh at my tears and my jealousy. No, that's wrong. You didn't laugh *at* me. You never mocked my anguish. You simply didn't understand it. You wouldn't, or rather you couldn't reassure me that it was I alone you loved. You could not make 'love' and 'alone' meet. You were merely sad that I was sad. You frowned in confusion as though I were suffering a minor illness difficult to diagnose. Such was your innocence that you offered to distract me from my misery by recounting in lighthearted detail your activities of the night. At first I said no, that I would be unable to endure it. But in the end I let you, because I realized it gave you pleasure and that your pleasure might become my compensation.

Later on I learned many variations on this theme. You helped me to turn jealousy into desire. Instead of vows of fidelity, I was rewarded with new stimulants to delight. Sometimes you would manage to visit me at five or six in the morning, dressed in the ever more expensive garments in which Jonas adorned you like a doll or a pagan statue, ready for more after a night of debauchery. You would remove the silk scarves, the satin dresses, the close-fitting trousers, the earrings and bracelets, the tiny shoes and spread yourself across my single bed, while I cleaned you like a mother cat, assiduous and joyful as you purred under the ministrations of my devoted tongue.

CHAPTER NINE

Jonas must have known that his creature was incapable of keeping secrets and that she would gaily inform me or anyone of the uses to which he was putting her. He assured me again that his interests were scientific, that his intentions were pure and that his work was of potentially great importance to medicine and biology. He was attempting to placate me, me of all people.

Adèle, he explained, was a phenomenon whom, despite the difficulties posed by what he called her 'nature', we must struggle to understand by maintaining our detachment. This was a rare opportunity, to which he was devoting his life, of exploring hitherto unknown aspects of genetics and might mean great advances in gynaecology and reproduction in general. How, I could not see. I summoned the courage to ask how he was financing his research, as well as our living arrangements, and he muttered something about a group of German doctors who had kindly agreed to assist him in his study of 'racial improvement'.

Did he mean, I asked, a new breed of human? An invented race? But he only posed another question. Didn't I think, he said, that such an outcome might be something to be wished for?

He greatly admired his Germans. They had proved a revelation, he claimed. It was so liberating to work with colleagues who practised science for science's sake; who, unlike their European counterparts, championed freedom of experiment, recognizing that research must

65

be unfettered by moral hypocrisy. He was clearly pleased.

Yet often he looked quite melancholy, as if weighed down by an insupportable burden. I had never seen my brother like that, and for a moment I pitied him. Was he, in fact, making a huge sacrifice incomprehensible to the likes of myself? He was puritanical and idealistic and had abandoned his own career to concentrate exclusively on this singular child. He might indeed be involved in a heroic undertaking. In which case he was correct to stress only the knowledge to be gained, and I had lost all perspective on the value his knowledge might ultimately have. If that were true, my emotional involvement with you was retarding progress, and it was I who was the guilty party.

But then I pictured you as you really were, a living marvel, not the subject of an experiment whose end was unclear and possibly dangerous, and I knew my brother was wrong. Moreover he had been promoting you, exploiting you to pay for this very experiment. Since he no longer practised medicine, he'd been living off certain investments whose value was since diminished by the economics of the new French government. This I had discovered by my tricks and ways. He had to make more money. In addition he'd been trawling old shops for books on alchemy, Egypt, ancient medical dissertations and other questionable subjects. And he had been such a hardened sceptic. What was happening to my brother?

With my improved hearing I soon discovered the uses to which he was putting you. His locking me in my quarters was the first clue. Then, of course, despite his swearing you to silence, you told me everything. He was prostituting you, turning you into a sexual commodity. Several men, some of them famous, you

assured me, were paying for your services. I was horrified
and very worried. He might fancy himself a modern
alchemist, but he was merely a high-class pimp. He
could not expect your clients, no matter how select
or discreet, to guard his secret. You were his ward,
a minor under his medical care. I feared someone
would talk. I feared, above all, that you would be
abused or stolen, snatched from me for ever. We
were all in danger.

He was beginning to speak like a bad actor. When
I confronted him with our untenable position, he
addressed me with perfect equilibrium plus an under-
current of biblical thunder. (I'd often thought he should
have been a preacher.)

'Blanche, you have a woman's best qualities. You're
gentle, obedient, quiet, devoted and, most important,
trustworthy. What's more, you've become an excellent
nurse. I advise you to protect and practise these virtues
because they are your only hope. Without them you
have no identity, no function. And, believe me, a
woman without her function will be, and deserves
to be, cast out. If you continue to question either my
purpose or my word, I myself will cast you out.' And
he looked at me with the contempt that had crippled
and withered me since childhood. I was afraid of my
brother.

Yet I did not abandon my efforts to find and read
the manuscript, if it existed. I was beginning to doubt
my brother's veracity as well as his state of mind. His
honour, I'd decided, was long since dead. But then,
how honourable was I, betraying my principles, my
professional ethics, spying on you, attempting to steal
the private papers of my own brother with every
intention of reading them? Nevertheless, I persisted.
I felt driven, helpless, out of control. Moreover, it had

become thrilling to defy Jonas, and I began almost to enjoy the prospect of discovery and reprisals.

There had always been reprisals, almost from the day I was born. My father, also a doctor, though not a particularly successful one, practised near Eastbourne, mainly on geriatric patients – people with just enough money left to die in their idea of comfort. They could pay their bills. It wasn't that he'd wanted me to be a boy, but I could sense that he was happier with Jonas. Not that he 'cast me out', for he was scrupulously fair and ensured that I received an equal share of his attention until at the age of nine I was sent to boarding school. He was a kind man, though, like Jonas, quite formal; and I think he loved me as much as he was able.

There were only two of us, which proved unfortunate. After my birth, my mother had a hysterectomy, but I don't think she was especially upset about it. Two were sufficient, she said. Her father, my grandfather, had been an official in Northern India, and Frederika Sylvester thought of herself as colonial, an identity which was a source of both pride and regret. Pride that she once had led a life of comfort and respect, regret for ayahs and empires. She was a vain woman who liked clothes and restaurants and was bored by her husband, her children and by a life she regarded as deprived after such former glories. We did not care for each other, and I set out to be as unlike her as I could and to disappoint her as thoroughly as possible. This did not require much effort on my part.

She made no secret of favouring Jonas, allowing him to bully me and amused by his ability to outwit me. If I cried when he broke my doll or tore to shreds the papier mâché construction I had made with such patience and care, she'd say I was feeble. She liked to behave as if Jonas could not possibly have committed such crimes without

68

either my collusion, my inattention or my weakness. If I were simply to laugh or strike him or pretend not to care, he would soon desist. The destruction of my cherished toys and projects must, by extension of this logic, be my own fault. No doubt that is why he regarded me as a poor creature, incapable of either achievement or self-defence. I was not unhappy to leave home.

I had little confidence in myself, but I did have a growing sense that I might be useful to others. I trained as a nurse at St Bartholomew's in London. That was as far away from Mother and Father as I was permitted to go. Jonas was puzzled by their parental anxiety, since he found it hard to imagine my having or arousing sexual appetites. He assumed my appearance guaranteed my protection. To him I was neuter, like a mule, the antithesis of his Creature. Yet during those years when I was in training I did have a brief taste of freedom: my own flat, mobility, one or two friends from the hospital and the acquisition of knowledge.

Then I married and put an end to what, years later, seemed almost anarchy. But it had been an illusion. I was never really free. And now I am your slave as well.

After ignoring me for so long, my family became suddenly excited at the prospect of my marriage to my brother's friend Roger. It appeared I had some value, after all. Though never as much as Jonas on whom there was no pressure to do anything but what he chose.

You were sad when I told you about my marriage and how I was more lonely with Roger than I had ever been without him. You never blamed him or considered him a wicked man. You never blamed anyone. Passing judgement didn't interest you. You processed the bad things like mildly unpleasant food and then excreted them. But you cried for me. I was astonished. No one had ever cried for me. You couldn't bear the idea of my being imprisoned in myself. And it was so easy for you to let me out. You simply turned the key which only you possessed and saved me from separateness.

CHAPTER TEN

Celia was counting her money. 'I hope tonight won't prove catastrophic.'

'Catastrophic?' Tamara opened a bottle of Minervois with a pop. 'One night?'

'The hotel's so expensive.'

'It was the only one left, we're exhausted, we had to take it, and that's that. Besides, I've got my Gold American Express, so don't panic, girl.'

Celia went to the window and looked down at the street. Lourdes was filled to capacity, which was why, when they'd arrived too late for the bus to Bez, they'd had trouble finding a room. She watched some pilgrims strolling beneath her, elderly women with crimped hair, pink cardigans, macs freshly dry-cleaned, trousers too short and sharply creased, that both hid and drew attention to their shrivelled legs, brand-new Carvels and Clark's and Hush Puppies. The evening light glimmered on their spectacles. Their faces were thin and white and their bodies fragile as onion-skin paper.

'That's what I'll look like when I'm old,' Celia reflected.

'Drink up.' Tamara held out a tumbler to her. 'It's going to be a long night.'

'Martin's already in bed.'

'The weaker sex fades first.'

Celia accepted the wine and sat beside Tamara. 'Sometimes he stays up all night with Tom so Frances can rest.'

'So he should.'

Celia paused. 'Did you see those people in wheel-chairs being helped off the train at the station? And those two Down's syndrome children? There's a special exit for them. Through that big arch that leads to the buses for the disabled. It says "Pour Les Malades".'

'I noticed. So?'

Celia stared at the mirrored armoire, the pink-shaded lamps, the pastel-tinted prints of the Blessed Virgin and Bernadette over the single beds.

'You seem distracted, my dear,' Tamara said when Celia did not reply. 'What are you thinking? Excuse me, I'm very nosy.'

'That's all right. I was thinking about Patrick,' she lied. She'd been about to mention another Mole sighting but changed her mind.

'Oh yeah. Who's Patrick?'

'He was my friend. We were together for seven years. Then he died.'

'When?'

'Two years ago.'

'And are you OK about it now?'

'Most of the time.'

'What did he die of?'

'Heart attack. It was terribly sudden.'

'So he wasn't all that young?'

'He was sixty-eight. His hair had only just begun to thin. It wasn't even very grey. Of course you could tell he wasn't exactly – '

'Johnny Depp?' Tamara smiled. 'Did you love him?'

'I did, only . . . not in the usual way.'

'You mean you didn't fuck?'

'Oh we did.' Celia looked affronted. 'Older men can still – '

Adèle

'Get it up?'

'Of course they can.' Celia thought for a moment. 'It wasn't exactly passionate, though.' She looked down at the glass which she held in her lap with both hands.

'You mean more fun for him than you.'

'Please, Tamara. I was fonder of him than anyone I've known. He was very good to me and left me some money when he died – as well as his dog. His grown-up children were completely surprised. They hadn't known I existed. He read every article and review I ever wrote and he kept them all in a special file that I found after he was dead.'

'You liked him better than Martin?'

'You know it's different.'

'I do.' She studied Celia. 'You look so young. How old are you?'

'Thirty.'

'I'd have said twelve. And you're so thin. Bet you don't pig-out on Danish pastries or Häagen Dazs.'

'Not a lot.'

'Or eat double cheeseburgers and guzzle non-diet Coke.' Tamara raised her long dark-red skirt to the top of her thighs and laughed. 'I know I'm a lard-bucket.'

'I think you're beautiful,' said Celia.

'Thank you. But the terrible truth is that I'm made of a lot of expensive slap and haircuts and jewellery and perfume. And my complexion's going.' She pinched her cheeks and chin, half comic, half rueful so that she made Celia laugh. 'Don't know what I'd do if I suddenly couldn't afford that Kanebo eye junk.'

'But you don't need any of it.'

Tamara looked at Celia as if she'd regressed from twelve to two. 'You make me feel like a games arcade – all bells and flashing lights and sirens and vulgar din.'

'You make me feel like a blade of dry grass.'

Tamara narrowed her eyes and pretended to scrutinize her. 'You look more like a wild flower to me – something blue, I don't know, a harebell or a scabious . . .'

'Do you know about plants?'

'I do, actually. But only the wild ones. Can't stand fussing with smelly manures or pots on patios. I like flora where it belongs. I have *even* been on botanical tours of the Eastern Mediterranean and China. You're surprised, aren't you?' she teased. 'Even a little impressed?'

Celia didn't ask whether the latter journey had preceded or followed Tiananmen Square. She was uneasy about Chinese tourism anyway, because of Tibet.

'I'm planning to go to the Galapagos. If I can ever finish *The Sexual Working Class.*'

'You're very adventurous.' Celia took another sip.

'But I'd never have had the guts to rob the BM. I'm too terrified of going to jail. I mean what if I couldn't get the right shampoo?'

'I didn't feel at all brave.'

'Oh give me a break, Celia. No false modesty, please. Don't you understand it's as unattractive as false pride?'

'I suppose I've got quite a lot of both.'

Tamara inhaled deeply, raised her shoulders, looked at Celia, dropped her shoulders, expelled the smoke. 'Maybe, but I confess I didn't take you for the kind of girl who just has to go down those stairs. But then innocence is often the source of audacity.'

Celia looked puzzled. 'What do you mean, stairs?'

'You know those gorgeous horror films of the thirties. Another passion of mine. I want to do a study of them. I've already talked to Martin about it.'

'Oh?'

Adèle

'Like these posh people get shipwrecked and washed up on to a tropical island and they discover a Gothic mansion complete with all mod cons owned by this guy in a tux with slicked-back hair and funny eyes. And right away there are spooks screaming and a sinister servant who's a white guy painted to look black who starts mumbling about zombies and probably is one. You haven't seen it?'

Celia shook her head. 'I don't watch television much.' She couldn't say she didn't even own one. Though she did have an Apple Mac.

'Well, the heroine and the handsome young man in plus fours realize in about five minutes that they're madly in love and have been since they left New York, but the weirdo with the house fancies her too and meanwhile all these eerie noises are coming from the basement and guests are disappearing with alarming regularity. Lots of shots of wind-blown palm trees, pounding surf under a full moon, parrots shrieking. Delicious. So the heroine's left alone with the shrieks from the cellar again and, unable to bear the suspense any longer, she opens the door on to stairs leading down to the murky depths. (Almost all of these films work on the theme of women's fatal curiosity.) Then she's cutting a swathe through fake cobwebs and bats suspended from wires that you can mostly see, and there's lots of vibrato from the string section (score probably composed by some White Russian *émigré* on the make). And sixty years later, there you are contorted on your sofa at three in the morning with a bottle of California red and a plate of Little Debbies, peeling polish off your nails you're so nervous and saying, "No, no, darling, don't do it. *Don't go down those stairs.*"'

Celia laughed. 'But she does.'

'Natch. She's the heroine.' Tamara heaved a sigh

75

and stared into space. 'Sure wish we had a packet of Doritos.'

They drank in silence, then she suddenly turned to Celia. 'So how do you find it, being alone?'

'I'm not alone.'

'Oh yeah, the pooch. What's it called?'

'Spencer. But he's hardly company. I don't really understand dogs. He seems always to need something I can't supply.'

'You have a flatmate? A boyfriend?'

'Neither. I'm on my own, but I'm not lonely.'

'Atta girl, Celia. Very healthy.'

'Don't tease.'

'I'm not.' Tamara put her hand on Celia's arm. 'A boyfriend ain't the *sine qua non,* as we are all supposed to know by now.'

Celia lifted her glass and was surprised to find it empty. 'Actually I quite like being solitary. Are you solitary?'

'Officially. I'm finished with long-term relationships. I get the feeling you're not.'

'I'm not exactly boycotting them. I just don't give them much thought.'

Tamara filled their glasses and knocked back her wine. 'Excuse me, darling, but what do you do for sex?'

'I don't think that's any of your business,' Celia bristled.

'OK, OK,' Tamara conceded. 'I didn't mean to offend you. You obviously treasure your privacy. I don't. I let everyone and everything into my life – provided I'm not working. I try to have as many lovers as I can simultaneously manage. Yup. I consort regularly with the enemy; they of the scrotal persuasion. I like living a French farce. I like it when an unsuitable suitor pops out of the armoire. But I'm not really interested

Adèle

in anyone my own age – which is forty-seven, I can
tell you're burning to know. (And you can tell Martin.
I don't care.) I think the cut-off point for men is
thirty-five max. Before they go all self-obsessed and
humourless. Sulking and stressed about their careers
and their dicks. All the sweetness goes crusty and flakes
off. Twenty-four to twenty-seven is just about right,
though seventeen to eighteen is very nice if you can
get it. For a treat, you know. Once in a while. Like
expensive chocolates.'

No wonder this woman was known as the Mae
West of East Coast academia.

'Course the boys come along less and less now. And
none of it ever lasts. But I accept it and have fun while
I can. I suppose you think I'm a paedophile.'

'I will if you want me to.'

Tamara laughed. 'Well, that's more like it.'

It was 5.30 a.m., and Martin hadn't had anything like
enough sleep.

'Don't,' he moaned. 'Don't.'

'It's me, Martin. I must talk to you.'

'Why?' He rolled away from Celia who'd been
shaking his left arm. She went round to the other
side of the bed and made room for herself beside him.
'Shit, Celia. I was dreaming of that fancy brothel.'

'Please. Just for a minute. It's about Mole.'

He opened his eyes. 'Celia, why are you doing this
to me?'

'I wouldn't do it if it wasn't important.'

'Please don't tell me you've seen him again.'

'Yesterday afternoon when we arrived. He was with
the pilgrims. He disappeared with a group that left by
way of that arch marked "Pour Les Malades".'

'Perhaps you should have as well.'

77

'He's following us.'

'Mole? Miss a day's work?'

'He could have feigned illness.'

'Celia, this isn't like you. And it's too early in the morning for words like *feigned*.'

'He wants to steal the organs back, I know it. Why won't you listen to me?'

'You made me promise to stop you fretting.'

'But there's a *reason* to fret.'

Martin sat up. 'You're really upset, aren't you? Look, don't worry, please. It won't happen. I guarantee you that I personally won't let it happen. OK?'

'Martin, what do you think we should do?'

He slid back under the covers. 'Now? Sleep.'

She continued to sit beside him, biting her thumbnail. Gently he put his hand on her neck and pulled her down by the collar of her dressing gown and covered her with the thin blankets. She lay listening to the sound of his breathing. He might chew gum, but at least he didn't snore.

CHAPTER ELEVEN

For a long time now there haven't been any mirrors. I shall never see my own face again. The nurses hide it from me the way we hid my soldiers from the villagers. They don't understand that I need no protection. I accepted myself many years ago.

You never saw what I did when I looked at the two of us together: Beauty and the Beast. Yours were the only eyes I knew that did not appraise, assess or judge. Indifferent to physical appearance, they regarded me solely with affection. The one request I ever read in them was for pleasure.

Aside from the tenderness turned on me, it was difficult to find anything in your eyes. There was only absence — of reflection, anxiety, self-consciousness. Absence of thought. Jonas said they were the eyes of a happy slave. Set wide apart, under black brows, they could turn from slate to indigo to a vinaceous brown. Untainted by discrimination or regrets, they looked permanently outwards at a limitless present. So unlike mine which were a pale filmy blue hardened to hide pain and grown sharp from spying.

At your suggestion, and with your help, I had devised a way to watch you with the others. (The testing of loose floorboards beneath the carpet, a stealthy hole drilled in the ceiling, the careful widening of that hole, the insertion into that hole of a piece of metal pipe.) With your encouragement I became a spectator as they played with your body, so small and lissom. It was so kind of you to let me do this. And my excitement was further enhanced by your awareness of my watching, kneeling in my place, both supplicant and penitent, my forehead to the floor in self-abasement, imagining your gratified smiles were turned on me in sweet complicity.

Initially I felt disgust, even rage. The sight of you caressed and penetrated by others, sometimes two or three at once, seemed a horrible betrayal. One night, the only night that Jonas forgot to lock me in, I could bear the performance no longer. I left the house and wandered for hours along the Paris streets. At last I came to the Pont Marie where I knelt, grasping the iron work and weeping. There I remained until dawn, gazing at the river and praying for the courage to throw myself in.

I don't know whether Jonas feared my knowledge or my interference, but from then on I was confined without fail to my quarters in what had once been the maids' apartment. New arrangements were clearly in progress. When you began to be taken away, mainly at night but occasionally in the afternoon, I was also locked in. (I never knew in advance. My brother would find some excuse for me to go upstairs and when I tried to leave, I would find the door locked.) You were then transported to a stranger's bedroom, carried off into the city where I could not follow, and I would be left alone, a prisoner, gagging on my own tears and vomit, until I heard the front door open and was sure you had been safely returned.

I compensated for my deprivation of you by becoming an ever more avid *voyeuse*. During this time you had several devoted clients. The ones who took you away I only glimpsed from a distance. The man in the mask, for instance. But the ones who came to the house I knew more intimately than they could imagine. Later I saw a photo of one of them in the newspaper beside an article linking him with the Croix de Feu. The Descoignes were regular visitors, young, rich and eager to experiment. Their energies were limitless. In love as they obviously were, they required another — a very exotic Other — to serve their ever renewed appetites. They enjoyed you simultaneously and at length. You also enjoyed them. There was no mistaking the willingness with which you turned from one to the other, allowing every orifice to be invaded by their greedy fingers, organs and tongues. Despite my torments, I admired the beauty of the three of you as you lay entwined, your body tight between theirs while they used you as a kind of medium through which to express their passion for each other.

They came often and paid a great deal of money for you. They brought you lavish presents and treats — ices, chocolates, eaux-de-vie (though you ate only offal and fruit), jewellery, scarves and shoes at which you would squeal with delight and which you would then put aside and forget. But you accepted the drugs that they produced to enhance the enjoyment of their exotic pet. They decorated your spare nakedness with flowers, bangles and silks, dressing and undressing you as if you were their marvellous doll. I could see how you adored it. It was play to you, your missing childhood.

There were other regulars, five or six of them, mainly men in their forties and fifties, doctors, lawyers, businessmen prosperous enough to afford you. One or two became troublesome, wanting more than their share. And though you were always accommodating, my brother was strict about payments. How else was he to finance his 'pure' experiment? But none of these lovers inflicted as much suffering on me as the woman who came in the afternoons.

Her visits were irregular, so I assumed she was trapped in a distasteful arrangement from which she escaped whenever possible. She must have been in her forties and was very *soignée* with an austerely beautiful face that would become hard with age. She was always nervous until the door closed and she was alone with you, frightened, perhaps, up to the last minute that her warder would arrive to rob her of her pleasures. She undressed as if she could not be rid of her couturier clothes fast enough. From a large bag which she brought with her she would remove a tattered cotton dress of the cheapest type and worn ugly shoes. These she would don without stockings or underwear, emerge from behind the screen and take her accustomed place on a low wooden stool. She would sit for a long time simply looking at you as you lay on the bed, your head raised on a pile of pillows beneath a spotlight Jonas had installed especially for her. The heavy curtains were drawn since she insisted that, except for the spotlight, the room be in total darkness.

She never spoke other than to order you in monosyllabic code to adopt a selection of obscene poses, as if for a camera. The positions followed each other in unvarying succession, a dance choreographed for her alone. That is how good and kind you were, giving ceaselessly of yourself. I, however, found this favouritism unbearable. During your performance she would sit leaning forward on the stool, her body rigid, her fists pressed into her thighs, her famished eyes fixed on your empty ones. What did they offer that she needed so badly? At the finale you would remove the props you had used to reveal and conceal yourself and lie naked, your only decoration your Roman purple lipstick and the gold nail varnish with which I painted your fingers and toes. Then in a harsh whisper she would order you to masturbate. How willingly you did her bidding, how at her service you were, performing your unique trick, considered such a novelty, which she relished and I loathed. She would edge forward on the stool, trembling slightly as she watched you. No doubt she was, like me, amazed at how limber you were, as if created exclusively for physical manipulation. You would lean forward, stretch your pliant back, lower your head between your legs and slowly, luxuriously pleasure yourself. Was that the best of all, I asked you. But you would never say. That was why I hated it so. I feared your lust for yourself, suspecting none of us could match that particular delight.

She issued barely audible commands – ordering you to speed up, slow down, raise your head, so she might view your swollen wet lips, your clouded eyes. What happened then I never knew. She would rise at last, walk unsteadily to the bed and turn out the spotlight. With the room in darkness, I would press my eye to the hole in vain, biting my tongue until it bled and scratching the floor with broken nails as I listened to the awful noises she made. I begged you to tell me what you did when the spotlight went out, but you always replied that it involved nothing out of the ordinary. You made love to her, that was all. I knew you were lying. Why did you lie? Was it because you did together something far more thrilling than you did with me? An esoteric act you performed only for her?

Then, to my relief, she stopped coming. About a year later I read in one of Jonas's newspapers that she had hanged herself. She was Victorine Bianchon, the wife of a politician, a supporter of Daladier. The picture accompanying the article had obviously been taken years before, because she looked much younger. The photographer's name was Gervais. Looking at her face, now dead, I masturbated violently, bringing myself to a prolonged orgasm, punctuated by cries of triumph. Never have I been so ashamed of my conduct.

Your earliest clients came exclusively from the medical profession. Jonas must have touted discreetly among associates whose tastes and bank accounts were known to him. (These included some gynaecologists who, you told me, were particularly vicious.)

I suppose they in turn recommended you to wealthy patients and friends with certain predilections, issuing the usual caution to silence. And they kept their word. No one wanted their fun spoiled either by the police or an influx of sexual spendthrifts who might drive the price of your favours out of control.

And I, the virtuous Blanche, I saw this select group at work. I knew their requirements as well as you did. I watched them, and myself, with revulsion. Their perversions became a source of gruesome titillation. Often I became so distressed by conflicting emotions that I would come to orgasm without touching myself. These spontaneous physical spasms left me exhausted and chagrined, so that I would sit for hours in dazed despair. Soon, however, I began to long for them. From the exception they became the rule. I shed my embarrassment like an old dress. I grew expert; I perfected my sin. Under your instruction, I learned to control and direct them, to make them coincide with yours or those of your clients, depending on my current preference. Afterwards I would be wretched, even consider suicide, but the practice had become an addiction. It was the only means of possessing you

84

during times you were forbidden to me. And so I returned to it, night after night.

My brother's eyes had changed. It wasn't only that he'd started wearing spectacles, the result of hours spent poring over the books he was acquiring daily and which filled his study to overflowing. His eyes revealed more than the usual contempt common to his kind of Englishman. They were filled with anger. I was shocked at times, especially when I caught him directing at me or you a look of pure hatred. I feared him in a whole new way. I dreaded what he might one day do, and this made me even more protective of you, so that I felt compelled to shadow you like a bodyguard. I thanked heaven for the many methods of surveillance I had devised.

We were neglecting your English lessons. Because I saw less of you at night, we were forced, at great risk, to take advantage of our hours alone together, spending every moment of the allotted time on the couch or the floor. I would suck you until I could wait no longer then mount you, often stuffing a piece of discarded underwear in my mouth to stifle my cries. How ugly I must have looked in the daylight, yelping like a hyena, uttering obscenities I hardly realized I knew, no better than the decomposing male bodies to whom I later brought such pitiful relief.

Jonas continued with your lessons as usual, sometimes with the French tutor, sometimes without. I listened with my practised ears − his voice, your voice, the silences between. Then one afternoon there were no voices. I was unable to find either of you. Madame Monmousseau had gone to the laundry. Had Jonas taken you to a client? Why then was I roaming the house free? I searched every room, but there was no one. I called.

No answer. I decided to exploit my brother's absence in another attempt to raid his study.

As usual it was locked. But when I tried his bedroom door I found it ajar, and so, by a miraculous mistake, was the connecting door to the study. I opened it cautiously, my touch grown cunning and precise. I peeked through the crack to see you bent naked across the huge desk, your smile vacant, your eyes fixed on nothing, while my brother assaulted you determinedly from behind.

CHAPTER TWELVE

The veterans' hospital was closed for good in 1959, the year de Gaulle became President. I found myself without employment and confronting the terrible possibility that I might be forced to sell our house and leave Bez. But thanks to the interventions of my old friend Dr Verneuil, I was appointed bath attendant at the Bez spa, and so I was allowed to remain here with you. The spa was then a shabby establishment, but boasted a variety of physical benefits and several genuine cures. Its renown was growing steadily and, over the years, more and more people, both the afflicted and the sound, came to immerse themselves in the health-giving waters.

I would find them horizontal and exposed in grey marble baths like sarcophagi, where once I'd hovered over my poor *mutilés* for whom the tubs had been originally constructed. Singly or in pairs, their toes and heels at right-angles to each other in the snug *cabines*, my bathers surrendered themselves to my care. They waited while I ran the sulphurous water, filtered for ten thousand years through the rocks of subterranean caverns. (It must fill the bath to exactly forty-seven centimetres and be no warmer than thirty-seven degrees centigrade.) I would set the timers for twenty minutes exactly. When a buzzer signalled the end of the session, I would appear with hot towels and robes and escort my clients to the wicker chairs where they reclined, dreamy, red-faced and swathed in white like new mummies. Ten minutes later I would instruct them to dress, and they would rise up and obey.

They never minded that I saw them naked, flushed, ungainly, sometimes beautiful. I was 'Ste Blanche of the Baths', and everyone knew me and was accustomed to me. I had scuffed up and down that marble hall with its Romanesque arches, dispensing brilliant white terrycloth, switching taps off and on and setting timers for so many years that they hardly noticed me. The bathers were my children. To them I was more of a nanny, a benign, neutral presence. They trusted me, just as my soldiers did before the last of them died or were dispatched to other institutions.

When I was too old to manage the baths any longer, the *conseil municipal* let me a room in the hospital, since become a home for the elderly, people destroyed by time rather than war. And here I remain in this great stone structure where I have passed nearly half my life, waiting upon you still. I seldom move. I sit by the window that faces the church. I can see your grave because the bright flowers that cover it catch my weak eyes. But when the flowers are not there, I must strain to see the tomb I may not visit until my own life has ended. Meanwhile I am absorbed in the past, remembering you as you were before he destroyed you – your eyes, your body, your smell, the serpent pattern of hair along your back. The way it shone in the light on the night of my brother's attack. The night you stopped speaking.

I bathed you in silence as you lay submerged and immobile, staring at the steamy walls. I dried and perfumed you. Anxiously I tidied your hair and applied gold lacquer to your nails. All the while you ignored me. I was as invisible to you then as I later was to the bathers I supervised with such discretion. Their distracted expression, their impersonal attitude made me think of you on that painful evening.

My brother's fear of exposure made him wary of the police. Adèle, he said, was servicing some important people, and rumours were circulating about the strange doctor, his creature and his shadowy female accomplice. He was called a Svengali, a black magician, a common pimp. One story claimed he had actually created his beautiful homunculus, fashioned her for his pleasure and profit. That she was a genie in a jar when not let loose to do his bidding, earn his fortune. That Jonas Sylvester had, by some Satanic contract, designed and made the perfect sexual object for sale to those who could pay. That was why, when you disappeared, he hired the private detectives.

You went missing four days after the event I had observed in Jonas's study. Simply vanished. We searched every room, every cupboard, under beds and behind curtains. We even questioned the neighbours, most of whom were unaware of your existence. We interrogated Madame Monmousseau until the poor woman collapsed in tears, but we failed to discover the means of your escape. We checked the *préfecture* of police, but they had no record of you. (Of course not, you didn't know your name.) At first we thought you had been kidnapped. Jonas confessed that the Descoignes had wanted to buy you and had offered a large sum of money which he'd refused, advising them loftily that the Pearl of Great Price was beyond worth. (He'd begun to say that kind of thing.) So perhaps, he reasoned, they'd stolen you, either to save money or take revenge and keep you as their amorous plaything, scented, groomed and tethered. Available gratis whenever they cared to make use of you. They were ruthless, he fumed, and had the means. Monsieur Le Page from the agency was ordered to keep watch on their house in St Germain. The other detectives were to search Paris until they found you. But how on earth were we to describe you to them? How to inform and yet deceive? Complete confidentiality was required, and my brother trusted no one. He trusted me a little, preferring to believe that I, at least, was still faithful. Meanwhile, he and I lived on the brink of madness, alternately blaming ourself and the other for the catastrophe.

'We should have left the city,' Jonas kept repeating. 'We should have taken Adèle away immediately they made that offer. We could have hidden for a while in Lyon, gone to Switzerland or Germany. The government is ruining the country, the French economy is disastrous. Everyone knows that. But how would I get the money out?' And where was this money? I wanted to ask but didn't. God knows, you had earned enough to keep us all for some time. Then he worried that his German supporters might have stolen you in order to avoid payment for his research and to carry on the 'Experiment' themselves.

As for myself, my instincts told me you had not been abducted; that you had left of your own accord, though how you'd arranged it all I couldn't think: I did feel certain of your motive: you'd fled my brother's abuse. His assaults, I assumed, had only just begun. The scene I had witnessed between you and about which I had said nothing to either of you may well have been the first of its kind. In any case, you were terrified and confused, and Jonas was to blame. He himself had driven you away.

Meanwhile, your disappearance had drawn my brother and me into a perverse complicity. We were united in the fear and pain of your loss. Barriers slipped and tensions eased. The old contempt and resentments were reluctantly stowed away in mutual efforts to regain our treasure.

For two weeks there was no sighting outside the Descoignes'. Perhaps, said Jonas, they had taken you to their country house in Burgundy. We must send another detective, go there ourselves, or I should go alone or he alone, somehow we would get into the grounds; there would, of course, be dogs . . . I suggested instead that we consider other possibilities. Was there anywhere Adèle would have *chosen* to go? The word shocked him; he glared at me.

'There is no such place!' he insisted, furious.

Yet I saw uncertainty in his eyes. He could not endure the idea that you might want to leave him. He was your teacher, father, saviour, your beloved exploiter. You could not be so treacherous as to plot escape.

'There is so much you've never told me,' I suggested gently, for now was the time. Like where you had come from and where you might possibly return. (I sensed a homing instinct in you.) 'How can we ever find Adèle,' I reasoned, 'if you don't enlighten me. Tell me, Jonas,' I commanded. 'Tell me about Adèle.'

He was so grieved by your disappearance that his defences were lowered. He collapsed into a chair and remained there, looking straight ahead, his fine hands resting on his knees. I waited, but he said nothing.

'It can only help,' I added, less aggressively. 'We must consider every possibility and close our minds to none of them.'

He nodded slowly. Then he said something he'd never said to me before. 'You're right.' He spoke quietly the words that once would have filled me with happiness. During that part of my life when I cared whether I pleased him. Then he began to talk. It was the longest conversation we'd ever had.

'You remember I spent four months in France. In 1932.'

'I do. We heard nothing from you. Father was very worried.'

'Father and the rest of you were the last things on my mind. Because that was when I found Adèle.'

'Where?'

'In a Pyrenean village.'

'How did you – ?'

'Through Cone. But you don't need to know about that.'

'Very well. Go on.'

'No one was sure of her age, because, as I told you, her name had been removed from the church registry. But she had reached puberty, if that is the correct word in such a case. I guessed she was about thirteen, though small for her age. When I discovered her she was living, or rather stabled, on the top floor of one of those old three-storey mountain houses that are used for silage and winter storage. Her mother wouldn't allow Adèle into the two rooms below which she shared with her lover and Adèle's brood of siblings. He couldn't tolerate her smell, though God knows she smelled no worse than those two rooms. Yvette seemed to be making every effort to conceal her child from the world. That is, when she was sober. The minute she and the man took to the bottle she'd forget Adèle who would run away, roving the village and the surrounding hills, barefoot in scant and dirty clothing, even in winter. She loved the mountains and forests and had great tolerance of the cold. She seldom washed and had never used a toilet. Indeed, she enjoyed rubbing herself in filth and burrowing in the hay she slept in. She rolled in the sand like the hens who flapped and pecked around the street in front of her house. Clearly she was imitating them.

'She hardly spoke, and when she did – well, you know how she spoke. Among barbarians she had become a worse barbarian. The villagers never talked to her. Many ran when they saw her coming, crossing themselves as they closed their shutters or their huge front doors. Gradually she became the focus of their fears and superstitions. It was most convenient. Curses followed her down the street and often rocks. When I first saw her she had a large cut on the side of her head which had turned septic. I persuaded her mother to let me treat the wound. Can you believe she made me pay for the privilege? As I bathed the cut, the child leaned against me like a cat, enjoying the stroking movement of the cotton swab, the touch of my fingers on her face and hair. She was completely unused to gentleness. It was then I saw, beneath the accumulated grime, that inimitable skin. Underneath the darkened surface shone a wonderful perfection. And there were those eyes, and the enormous single front tooth. (When I think of the money I spent on that dentist who removed it and gave her two like normal humans'.) But that skin! The more I cleaned of it the more amazed I was by its eerie shimmer. Which is why I called her Louisante.'

'But what was her real name? The one she claims she can't remember.' I controlled my emotions with difficulty.

'The locals referred to her as lutin or lutine, depending on how they saw her or what they knew of her. Later it became the Creature, the Thing or even the Monster. Her mother called her Jeanne.'

'Jeanne.' I whispered the name. It was unreal – of

an age, time and place before I knew you. Impossible to imagine. 'But didn't something terrible happen?'

'Yes. An attack. She barely survived it. And in the process of surviving it, she lost her memory. She was regularly going out at night, following the old trails through the mountains, sometimes not returning for two or three days. There were rumours that she lived with wild animals and even consorted with them. That the offspring of these unions had already been sighted, grotesque hybrids with enormous sexual organs. The more superstitious villagers feared they would begin to prey on the locals, rape the women and produce hideous new breeds, half animal, half human. It was a collective paranoid fantasy in which the residents of Bez made her the scapegoat for all their misfortunes.

'And yet the way she smiled' – he smiled himself as he remembered – 'as if she'd never known evil, as if she were under divine protection, an angel . . . of course she was anything but. *I* was her protection. That mob would have killed her if I hadn't intervened.'

'Who? Who were they?'

He hadn't heard or was ignoring me. 'I examined her and confirmed my suspicion that she was not a virgin. She confessed to not having been one for a long time. Men and boys in the village – as well as two or three women – had secretly taken advantage of her, though she would not have placed that interpretation on the seduction.' He sighed. 'They enjoyed her while loathing her. They weren't alone.' He sounded bitter. 'But your question – some of the older men and a couple of chosen boys formed a posse of holy avengers. The very ones who'd previously – ' He put his head in his hand for a moment then looked up at me. 'One night while, fortunately, I was in Bez, staying in the hotel, they came to her house to look for her and discovered her hiding place in the loft. Flinging her screaming mother aside, they clambered up, wild with excitement. The lover offered no resistance. According to the mother he participated, though she went on living with him. He claims he only watched and that he would have helped poor little Jeanne if only he'd had the opportunity. He was a coward, but then so was everyone else.

'The men threw her into a sack, tied it and took her away screaming in a wheelbarrow. About half a mile outside the village was a ruined château on a hill. Here they built a fire as she struggled in the sack and here they emptied her out, and by the light of the flames set about beating and violating her in the multiplicity of ways such a creature can be violated. They urinated on her and smeared her with pig manure. They stuffed it into her mouth, they burnt her with flaming sticks. Her shrieks could be heard in the village, but no one came. They would allow her to crawl away, then just as she was attempting to rise, drag her back into their circle where she would again become the focus of their attentions.

'The lover told me how they debated cheerily about slicing off her sex. One of them even began sharpening a knife and making lewd jokes. But the majority objected to this measure, wishing to enjoy her up to the moment of her death or indeed after her death, according to their tastes. Then they rested a while from their labours, inventing new amusements for the hours that lay ahead. To boost their courage and their lust, they finished off three bottles of cognac, saved for this occasion – the vindication of their manhood. Moronic with drink, they calculated she would live just long enough for each of them to indulge one last brutish fantasy. Meanwhile she was kept tethered to a stake so that they might entertain themselves by observing her increasingly feeble efforts at escape. Every so often, one of them would give the rope a violent jerk and drag her back over the rough ground so that her beautiful skin was further lacerated. It's miraculous that she has no scars. They would roar with laughter while administering intermittent kicks with their big dirty boots.

'Anxious their worn-out members might fail to perform and shame them before their neighbours, they debated good-naturedly as to the manner of death that would offer the most satisfactions. Two of them fought over who would have the pleasure of strangling and sodomizing her. They came to blows, rolling about in the darkness, while the others cheered them on. At last the fracas was broken up and the discussion of her execution resumed as she lay listening to every word. Decapitation was put forward. But who would claim the ultimate honour of performing the rite that would rid the parish of this devil and make them heroes? They were democratic and agreed to share equally in her destruction. They would take turns hacking off fingers, toes, arms, legs and finally the fearsome organ. Then one of them remembered hearing that the most painful death is empalement: a stake driven through the abdomen into the earth. And all could enjoy the spectacle of her slow death. I feel certain that not one of them doubted the justice of their atrocity, which they regarded not as murder but as exorcism. You cannot murder the subhuman. You can only exterminate it.'

I was weeping, but Jonas was oblivious to my state.

'By now their inebriation made them lax in their attentions to their victim. While a few went off to

96

fetch a branch suitable for fashioning into the murder weapon, those left to guard Adèle had discovered yet another bottle, this one the last, and were determined to consume it before their comrades returned. Their feeble wits now completely addled, they failed to notice that she was gone. La lutine had escaped them, too nimble and too lucky for such louts. With my help she had cheated them of the ultimate satisfaction.'

'You cut her loose.'

'No. She managed that unassisted. Gnawed through the ropes with her animal teeth. But she would not have got far in her condition if I hadn't been waiting by the château. Her mother had come to me at the hotel and I'd set off in the direction she'd seen the assassins go. I traced them easily by the din they made and carried the wretched bundle back to the house where her mother had by this time drunk herself into a stupor. (All the neighbours had refused her pleas for help.) Weird as her offspring was, exiled as she'd made her own child, something prevented her from abandoning it completely. If I had not been in the village, Adèle would have perished. Though I had come with her in mind, I hadn't expected such an adventure, a unique opportunity for rescue and capture.'

For a moment I hated him again. A pure, clear hatred.

'I won't elaborate. I saved her life.'

His smile chilled me.

'Without Adèle I'd have had a mediocre existence, built on the ordinary successes. But when I have finished, when they see and know . . .'

He had left me for some glorious future. 'Please go on,' I said.

He sniffed hard, and I realized he had been on the verge of tears. 'Mercifully, she'd become an amnesiac.

97

This, I assumed, would make it easier for me to create the new life I was already planning for her. I was very idealistic. (You don't believe that, do you, Blanche? But consider how I sacrificed my own career to educate and rear her.) So I decided there and then to abduct her. No, that's wrong. I came to Bez with the conviction that if she existed at all I would abduct her. I didn't know how, only that I would find a way, that I alone *could* find a way. For the first time in my life I followed a feeling. I also knew that it was only a matter of time before the villagers would find her and attempt to finish her off. The atmosphere grew uglier by the day.

'Her mother surprised me. She was loath to part with the child despite the misery she claimed it had brought her. Wisely, I negotiated with the avaricious lover, and a deal was quickly struck. I travelled to Lourdes and arranged for money to be sent from London. Naturally it was far too much, but in return he guaranteed to prevent the mother following us or going to the authorities. He would insist Jeanne had run off to the mountains. After a while, everyone would assume she had been lost, had died or was cohabiting with the beasts for good. I supposed he would accomplish this by liberal application of drink.'

(How scornful he was of indulgence, particularly women's. He hated alcohol. But then so did I.)

'After all, she was now pregnant with her fifth. The loss of a problem child in such circumstances could hardly be a tragedy. Moreover, Jeanne was not the lover's child and, even though the real father was unlikely to return (he had disappeared long ago), domestic antagonisms were bound to worsen. This she was intelligent enough to foresee, especially after I had stressed the inevitable friction. She did not wish to lose the lover either. And so she made her choice.

Adèle

'I bought Adèle a dress, shoes, a coat. I cut her hair, badly, but we covered it with a hat. I disguised her, as far as was possible, as a proper little mademoiselle. It won't surprise you that the disguise was less than successful. She adored her new garments, however, and was shortly prancing and preening before the mirror. Even then she had an instinctive feeling for clothes. Only her shoes proved hateful and I struggled to keep her from kicking them off and throwing them away.

'The lover, made ingenious by money, managed to commandeer a car and secretly drove us to Lourdes where we spent the night in a hotel. How strange it was to be alone with her in that city packed with the afflicted. I could not endure the sight of them, nor did I want her to witness such ugliness, so we kept to our room and I had some supper sent up. This she refused to eat. I hadn't yet learned her limited gastronomic preferences. I expected her to cry but she didn't. Instead she passed seven hours sitting bolt upright in her bed, staring into the darkness. I confess I was unnerved. Only when we could disappear into the city would I feel safe. In the morning we took a train to Toulouse where we changed and booked a first-class sleeper to Paris. She sat looking at me with those eyes that say nothing. She was enthralled by the train. Perhaps that's what she was trying to tell me in her bumpkin dialect. I kept the door locked during the entire journey.'

'Where did you go once you got to Paris?'

'Another discreet hotel. I called Cone and asked him to come immediately. He did and I left her with him, the only person I could trust with my precious new possession. I went to London to negotiate the removal of a large sum of money from the trust. I needed to set us up as soon as possible. You might as well know,

if you don't already, that I made an investment here
which may now ruin us – but then the government will
soon shoot itself in the foot again, at least according to
the information I've been given.'

By one of your clients, no doubt.

'That was when we last saw you in England.'

'I suppose it was.'

'And you returned and rented this house.'

'Yes.'

'And you locked her up in it.'

'I have locked myself up as well.'

'And me. What about me?'

He seemed amazed I should care. 'Looking after her
proved extremely difficult and I soon lost patience. I
couldn't cope. And then her magnetism was more
disturbing than I had anticipated. I was constantly
distracted by her movements, her glances, her craving
for physical contact. I had to put a barrier between
us. Otherwise I would lose all objectivity and my
researches would be unreliable or worse. I needed
the help of a trustworthy person. I thought of you.'

CHAPTER THIRTEEN

It was May 1936 when I set out to find you.

I told Jonas of my intentions and to my surprise he raised no objection, merely nodded agreement and continued reading one of his manuscripts. I asked him for money to pursue my plans. He opened a desk drawer, removed a wad of bills and handed them to me without looking up.

I walked all day, every day. In the evening I was only a little tired. Nevertheless I slept well for the first time in weeks. I had a purpose. I was also free to roam Paris in a way I had never done. Usually I went out only to help with the shopping or to purchase small necessities for you. Lately, of course, most of the shops were closed, even the large department stores, and so I had hardly left the house. I hadn't realized what was happening to Paris, to all of France. I'd been living a claustral existence, unaware of the upheavals around me. I wouldn't even have known about the strikes if it had not been for the lack of bread and the electricity cuts, the streets empty of cars and, most critically, the absence of fruit from the markets. (Often wizened winter oranges were all I could offer you.) We had a new government, it seemed, and for reasons I could not fathom, everyone was celebrating or brawling or making speeches or selling newsletters. I had constantly to force my way through excited and often dangerous crowds. The city pitched between fraternity and hate.

How ironic that my loss and distress had granted

me this freedom of the river from the Pont d'Issy to the Pont de Tolbiac. I inspected the narrow streets of the Marais and the boulevards of Montparnasse, the markets and restaurants of Les Halles, wandered the Bois de Boulogne and the Luxembourg Gardens where I would stop to rest beside the Medici Fountain to stare at the embracing couple in their damp cave and the gigantic Cyclops watching from above. I knew his anger and his anguish. It was my sole erotic adventure during my daylight excursions.

I imagined catching a glimpse of you in that smart car into which I'd seen you bundled one night the previous winter. I scoured the 1st and 4th arrondissements for a glimpse of Madame Bianchon. I searched for the Descoignes in St Germain and for the other clients whose names I was not permitted to know. Faces the detectives would not recognize. Faces I knew intimately, bodies that had been the unwitting stimuli to my desolate pleasures. With which of them were you now consorting? Not to know, not to be present during these couplings, even as the despicable *voyeuse*, was a torment which I burnt up in the hundreds of urban miles I trudged in my search for you.

One afternoon I found myself in the midst of a riot. I passed between two groups of newspaper vendors who were shouting at each other from opposite sides of the street. Within seconds they had been joined by mutual supporters, and the effect was like a sudden gale at sea. I clung to the side of a building, inching my way towards safety as the bodies surged around me. The struggle was so dense that I gave up trying to push my way out and could only stand, paralysed, my back to a café whose windows were shortly broken. Then the police arrived. I crouched and covered my head to escape the rocks and bricks and the ugly male voices raised in fury.

Adèle

Finally everyone dispersed and I was left squatting on the pavement, trembling. Copies of *l'Humanité* littered the street. Hundreds twitched and fluttered in the wind, many of them stained with blood.

Guerrilla warfare was becoming common. Strikers' processions criss-crossed the boulevards of the feverish city. Every Saturday there were demonstrations on the Champs-Elysées and in the Latin Quarter. The Gare St Lazare was a regular battleground for the Fascists and the Left. None of this deterred me. I even had moments of joy when the wide Paris sky, full of light, threw its reflections on to the windows of ornate blackened buildings. In the wealthier arrondissements many of the balconies were adorned with the tricolour as if for a holiday or a parade. (In fact they were a riposte to the red flags planted at the entrances to occupied factories.) Some of the French flags flew little blue-and-white streamers, the colours, I was told, of the deposed monarchy. Even so, they looked lively and gay. After three years of confinement, was it surprising that I relished colour and mobility? My flaccid arms and legs took flight, and I walked as I had never walked before, propelled, it seemed, by some superior force. I wanted to greet the world I had forgotten and with which I must now form an alliance.

I scanned doorways, inner courtyards, restaurants, certain that I would see you there and that you would turn and smile at me. My faith was unaffected by disappointments. Still, reason argued that my daylight excursions were fruitless, and that if anything held you it was the night.

So I began with the brasseries in Montparnasse – the Select, the Globe, La Coupole, making circuit after circuit of them. Unrewarded, I moved on to less elegant establishments. I had continually to overcome my fear. I was unnerved by the dark streets and the slums of unexplored arrondissements where I was convinced you had fled. I resolved to seek you in the dim corners, amidst the ruin and the squalor which Jonas swore was your natural element. You had not run from me simply to take shelter with your wealthy clients. Their money meant nothing to you, and anyway you never saw a penny of it. I hadn't known you to make even the smallest financial transaction. How were you living? I shuddered to think of you as the victim of some brutal patron.

Perhaps my brother was right after all, for it was in squalor that I found you. For four months I left the house at 10 p.m. to investigate the bars, *caveaux*, night-clubs, bordellos and opium dens which were to me an alien world peopled by those I'd once considered scarcely human. I forced myself to follow certain streets, descend certain stairs, open certain doors. I visited at all hours the streets notorious for their prostitutes. I loitered around the *hôtels de passe* in Les Halles and the Rue des Lombards. The pavements were crowded with what seemed to be whole families of women, competing sisters, companions, colleagues. Later you confessed that you'd once tried to work that very street, but the whores had turned on you, driving you off into even worse territory. Once they even summoned the police and you were confined to La Roquette in a communal cell where the other girls tormented you as you shrank further into your corner against their blows and abuse.

I would continue my search until 4 or 5 a.m. Sometimes I would come upon the cess-pool cleaners with their noisy machines juddering beneath the streetlamps and gulping the filth that was their food. I'd heard them pass in the street below on mornings when I left you to return to my own room. I associated them with these sad departures. But I had never bothered to look out the window at the source of the racket, never given a thought to those who performed this scorned, essential task. They were something to be avoided. But now I didn't even cross the street or put a handkerchief to my nose to muffle the stench. I grew accustomed to it. It was almost friendly. And the men spoke kindly to me, not like the brutes I had imagined, though their accents were rough and I had to listen hard to catch their words. If they thought it strange that I, a plain drab woman, clearly respectable, should be walking alone in the small hours of the morning, they never remarked on it. After a while I returned their greetings. I thought of them as guardians of the underworld into which you had vanished. I fancied they held the key to that mysterious kingdom, and that they would show me the secret door, the steps that led down into the darkness where you hid from me.

So I sought the guardians' advice. They were helpful and expressed no curiosity about my motives. But I was unprepared for their suggested establishments. I tried the most expensive and fashionable houses first. You were a luxury after all, and I naively assumed that any Madame would be delighted to offer you as an exotic morsel to a favoured client. The Montyon, the Chabonnais, the Colbert – I trembled before every door. The famous Acropolis refused to admit me, so I stood outside on the pavement watching the splendidly dressed clientele alighting from their beautiful cars – Hispano-Suizas, Bugatis, and something new called a Buick – and hastening out of the rain towards their elite diversions. Industrialists, politicians, actors, gangsters. Not one of them noticed me. But I recognized many of them.

One, a champagne manufacturer, had had his photo in the paper with Colonel de la Rocque. Another had been a frequent visitor to your bedroom. You had told me, with a little flash of pride, that he was a leading member of the Parti Social. Neither of us had any idea of that organization's origins or intent.

The doormen at the Acropolis grew used to me and stopped telling me to move on. They tolerated me and let me wait. That is how I managed to catch a longed-for glimpse of you, though not in the flesh. I slipped past a distracted attendant and got as far as the main hall, a glare of marble and glass, before I was accosted and ejected. Afterwards I was unwelcome and no longer permitted to occupy my place by the entrance. But I had seen something just before my arms were seized and I was lifted off my feet by two large men in dinner jackets. It was a photograph taken at what must have been a ball given at the Acropolis by some magnate who patronized this grandest of brothels. The photo was of several girls during a high point in the festivities. And there you were. Among them. Even partially veiled, I knew you.

Outside I stood and wept. I begged the doormen to let me speak to the manager, but they were adamant, they had their orders. Finally they threatened to call the police, and I was forced to leave. But here, at least, was something tangible, evidence that I was on the right road.

(Months later you told me you had indeed worked in the Acropolis, but only twice, hired out by my brother for special events and customers. But he quickly became paranoid about your relative freedom within such an ambience. The money wasn't worth the anxiety. Besides, the other girls hated you. The photographer, your old tutor, Gervais, had been present. It was he,

106

you said, who took the picture, and yes, he was the same person who had photographed the deceased Victorine Bianchon.)

I went on to the more modest houses like Suzy in the Latin Quarter. The place advertised girls in gossamer tunics lounging about and chatting with the clientele. A friendlier brothel by all appearances. The Madame knew of you. I offered her money, as I had in so many other houses, but this time I bought myself information, however flimsy. You hadn't worked for her, she claimed. You were too bizarre for the tastes of her conservative customers who were mainly family men. But yes, she believed someone had said something, one of the girls, perhaps, she couldn't remember. This person had seen you on the street, though in another arrondissement. Perhaps the 18th. Again she was unable to remember. I was excited, but the lead was a mere thread, cut too soon. At least you were out there in the city. And so our meeting was inevitable.

I would nearly lose heart, then some chance encounter would cheer me. Several times I passed occupied factories, hotels or stores. The man guarding the entrance would salute me and smile and I would pause to watch the workers eating together their suppers brought from home by children or wives, entertaining themselves or being entertained by professional actors and musicians who volunteered their talents to relieve the tedium of the strikers' long days and nights. Laughing and singing, they seemed happy, united. I envied them this communal strength and wondered what it must be like. To an isolated woman like myself it was mysterious and wonderful. It also increased my pain.

Night-time Paris was now more familiar. The working-class girls with their exaggeratedly painted bow lips and kiss-curls, their T-strap shoes and pencil skirts held up with braces and worn with the little satin blouses that were so appealing; the young men in caps, many of whom were in the pay of gangsters, gave me hints and occasionally an address. I knew the cafés and dance halls in Montmartre and Montparnasse where I could not go, as well as those that would tolerate me. I spent the money given me by my brother sitting alone, pretending to sip some pink or green drink while I watched and waited for you. The customers in these places never disturbed me, absorbed as they were in each other. I even went one night to the Bal Nègre where Parisians and Africans danced wildly together. The charming mulatto girls in crocheted hats or bright scarves wrapped round their heads reminded me of you.

But it was not as a female that I found you. On the advice of the Madame at Suzy (to whom I returned and to whom I gave even more money) I visited some of the 'special' night-clubs. The look-outs poised to spot the vice squad were sometimes suspicious of me. I was hardly a typical patron. Perhaps they assumed my dress was a costume, signalling some arcane predilection. I spoke to no one. I had learned that questions only bred hostility. Better to fade into the background, staring from my perch at the proceedings, a drab bird with one eye fixed always on the door.

Although these clubs were filled with couples, it seemed no crime to be alone, and after a while I actually felt comfortable in these 'temples of inversion' where women partnered with women and men with men waltzed and javaed with impunity. I was approached a few times, but my fear was apparent and I was ridiculed, though not cruelly, and left to myself. 'Je ne sais pas danser,' I would mumble, wishing to sink through the cigarette-littered floor. If they persisted,

I would turn away. My coldness was an advantage in these circumstances. Later you asked me why I did not enjoy myself and make a friend for the night. You never understood that for me love and sex were inseparable and for you only. As far as other bodies went, I was still the frosty Englishwoman who shrank from the touch of my own kind, male or female.

I watched couples of all classes laughing, clinging together, dancing or simply sitting and holding hands, their pupils dilated by belladonna. Some argued, smashed glasses, stormed off in inebriate rage. It amazed me that what they felt for each other and did together might be similar to our own intimacies. Despite their so-called deviance, they seemed almost normal compared to you and me. For it was we who were monstrous, we who were the freaks.

No one else would have recognized you the night when, after more than a year, my patience was rewarded. Your disguise was complete, a young man from the streets, Algerian or Corsican maybe, with all the transient grace of an Arab boy. You wore loose trousers belted tightly at the waist, an old tweed jacket, a battered cap tilted at an angle. Your skin was very brown. You'd darkened it somehow because its scintillation was gone, smeared by make-up or grime or exposure to the sun. A tall man stood next to you, his arm around your shoulders so that you were tucked under his armpit. He talked in a bass voice to some other men who stared at you in admiration, flattered or insulted you as they felt inclined, because you were there to be treated that way. I could not hear properly for the music and the din. It was difficult even to see you through the fog of tobacco smoke. But there you were, unmistakable. Why was I so sure? Because of your smell.

Even through the smoke, hair oil, perfume, sweat and alcohol I detected it the moment you entered, sheltered by his male body, a pearl in an oyster. He was so big. How could he not hurt you when he did what he did when you were alone? But perhaps you had never been alone. Perhaps he was only for the night. What did he make of your ripe scent? Did it repel or excite him, or both? Obviously you no longer wore the perfume I had purchased for you at such expense. You'd left the bottle behind by the bathroom mirror.

With the money that would have been spent on the perfume, the dresses, shoes and bangles, on the offal and fruit and milk which were all you would eat, though in vast quantities, I bought untouched drinks and useless information, admission fees, taxis home. I paid the detectives in whom Jonas still placed his faith, perhaps because they were men. But now I had succeeded where they had failed. They lacked the mad persistence with which, for better or worse, love endows one.

I had no intention of confronting you. Not then, not in these surroundings. I had thought a great deal about this meeting and decided that directness would not be advisable. Who could say if you'd even remember me? Your mind had lapsed before. I would wait, immobile, watching your every move to see if you recognized me. Unlike you, I wore no disguise. Even so, you might not notice me.

In fact you did. You looked straight at me, stopping my heart. At me, through me, past me, making no distinction between myself and the other customers. Your eyes were blank, though they showed the effects of some drug. Minutes later, the tall man led you past my table. I thought I could detect a flicker of disturbance on your face, but I wasn't sure. You looked thin and used. The black rings under your eyes made me anxious for your health. It was all I could do to sit still and appear indifferent. I held my static pose, fighting the impulse to seize and abduct you. I felt an enormous physical strength by means of which I would attack and grapple with the tall man who treated you as his possession. I would kill him, carry you off, escape through an astonished crowd powerless to stop us. Instead, by means of a greater strength, I acted according to my plan. I did nothing.

You sat down at a table full of men, most of them Parisian and young, though a plump older gentleman kept trying to fondle you. I could see his hand beneath the table making its way along your thigh. You smiled sweetly at him. I could sense the others longing to do as he did. One snatched your hat and ruffled your curls. You had cut off your hair. You were bangleless and your breasts had been bound flat. You sat and let the two men caress you, not reacting but smiling at them occasionally. Clearly the tall man was showing you off and putting you up for the highest bidder. He spoke with a strange accent and was much older than I had thought at first. The men went on smoking, drinking, talking. But their eyes were riveted on you.

The four-piece band began to play and you danced with the man beside you. When he put his arms around you I looked down at the floor. Otherwise I watched you undistracted for two hours. Then you left with the tall man who was by now quite drunk. You looked barely alive, an exquisite little zombie. Again the ripple of possible recognition when you passed me. But no gesture, no complicitous split-second glance. You had forgotten completely.

No matter, I told myself. Jonas had raised you from

the dead before. Together we would manage it again.
I made myself count to sixty, paid the bill and moved
with painful restraint towards the exit. When I reached
the street I could contain my tears no longer, and they
spilled over, blurring my vision so that I nearly lost
sight of you.

I followed at a distance, cursing my heels as they
clicked on the pavement. But no one seemed to hear
me. Did you hear? Were you aware all along of my
presence? The two of you were drifting towards the
labyrinth of dark streets behind Pigalle. Twice you
disappeared and I panicked. I had no idea which way
I had come or how I would get back. I was mapless,
but I went on with nothing to guide me but the traces
of your smell.

You entered a house with a scarred front door and
rubbish heaped around the steps. Laughter and male
voices came from an upstairs window. I crossed the
street and waited, invisible under a tattered awning.
Arab music issued from several of the buildings. I
waited until I saw the large man at the window. He
looked down at the street then closed the shutters. I
remained where I was.

After a while I tiptoed to the door. No number.
I felt for any marks of identification. I touched a
door-knocker and recognized the shape of a female
hand. I was paralysed. I had no idea what to do. My
plan had not included being stranded in such a place.
And it was far too dangerous, I knew, to open the
door and go up. But soon a couple approached me.
I could see the glow of their cigarettes as they turned
the corner of the street, two tiny stars in the depths of
space. I coughed in advance so as not to startle them.
Where was I, I asked. They were surprised to find
me and at first suspicious. The man flicked a cheap

cigarette lighter and held it up to the street sign. Rue
de Sofia. I offered money and asked them to escort me
to the nearest boulevard and he nodded a reluctant yes.
In the lighter's flash I saw that he was a foreigner. Dark,
close-cropped hair and eyes that squinted like those of
your protector. Eyes exposed too long to the sun. As
we walked I tried to remember landmarks by which
to steer the course of my return.

A block or two before Rochechouart I noticed
some graffiti scrawled across a wall: 'Mieux Hitler que
Blum'. Even in my distracted state I was shocked by the
sentiments. All of a sudden I grasped the significance of
what had been happening in Paris and felt an alarm
which was, however, quickly swallowed up by my
stronger personal fears, my desperate concern for the
welfare of a beloved individual.

I said nothing to Jonas. He was awake reading, but
I did not look in on him and went straight to my
room where I lay without sleeping until eight the
next morning. I dressed, went round to the Café
de la Poste and drank a *grand crème* then went to
the bank from which I was temporarily permitted to
make withdrawals. There was a bad atmosphere in the
district. Demonstrators had been shot and wounded
by the police at Clichy and everyone was frowning
over their newspapers. New anti-Blum posters had
been pasted up across the street. Why, I wondered,
did they hate him so? What had he done to incense
them this way? Then I set out my plan, on which I
concentrated exclusively.

I alighted at Rochechouart, and after some false starts
I came to the Hitler–Blum graffiti and from there to the
house with the hand on the door. A bright sun exposed
the ugliness and the detritus in which I had trodden the
night before. The confusion of smells made tracking

the ghost of your scent impossible. I was anxious and frightened carrying so much cash, yet I felt lucky. And I could not afford to hesitate. By tomorrow you might be gone. Even now that upstairs room might contain only the remains of your presence, a lingering putrid odour. There was no sign of life in the house. The drone and whine of Arab music was all around, hypnotic and heavy and full of sexual menace. Across the street a small bar was open so I went in. The patron read his paper and fiddled with his beads. The walls were patinaed with tobacco and kif smoke. I ordered another coffee and resigned myself to waiting.

Men passed dressed in jellabas and laughing children threw stones. An hour went by. Eating was out of the question so I ordered a brandy to settle my stomach. Suddenly my body began to heave with dry sobs. Nothing would happen. I would never find you and so my life was ended. I knew I should go to the WC to try and calm down but the thought of its condition made my stomach heave. Besides, I did not dare leave my post. I drank another brandy and went out into the street. The shutters in the second-floor room were still closed. I seized the door-knocker and banged as hard as I could. No more waiting. I had reached an emotional barrier and must either smash it down or retreat. I waited, knocked again, waited on the filthy stone step, ankle-deep in rubbish. Then I touched the door. It was open.

CHAPTER FOURTEEN

'Dumpsville!' Tamara set down her bags and surveyed the village of Bez.

'It's a very pretty river,' Celia offered. She was leaning over the stone bridge watching the rushing water foam and churn beneath her. 'And very clean by the looks of it.'

Their bus pulled out of the car-park, inched its way up the steep main street, turned right and disappeared, trailing clouds of noxious fumes.

'Good riddance,' said Tamara to the bus. She glanced at the bags. 'I knew I brought too much.'

'Come and see the river. The bridge must be ancient.'

'1967 at least.'

The three of them looked down into the water which was indeed very clean. On either side of the valley the mountains rose dramatically, their peaks lost in mist. The snow flurries persisted, becoming neither better nor worse. On the opposite bank wood anemones and hellebores grew from dead leaves around the roots of trees and mossy stones.

'Look,' said Celia. 'Aren't they lovely.'

'I suppose the nature's OK.' Tamara turned to the parade of poky shops that lined the main street. 'Anyone see a bar?'

'What's eating the nutty professor?' Martin asked Celia as Tamara strode on ahead, despite the weight of her luggage. 'PMT, do you think?'

'I expect she needs a sugar fix.'

'Ah.'

How could she gorge that way and have such lovely skin? It couldn't only be the make-up, and there were no signs of surgical intervention.

They checked in to the better of two hotels.

'Est-ce qu'il y a beaucoup d'eau chaude? Est-ce qu'il y a un radiateur dans la chambre? Electrique ou soufflant?' Tamara grilled the woman at the desk who promised her all she desired and more. 'Avec douche . . .' she was insisting as Martin and Celia entered and stood behind her.

'D'accord, Madame. Bien sûr, Madame. Pas de problème.'

'And what do you two want?' Tamara turned to her friends. Evidently she was determined to have a room to herself. Celia was a bit hurt. Nevertheless she agreed to share with Martin. After all, she'd done so before.

Once installed upstairs, she had practically to drag Tamara back outdoors.

'We really must have a recce before the light goes,' she pleaded, standing in the open doorway.

'Come on, Tamara, we need you,' said Martin, appearing behind Celia.

'All right, all right.' Tamara was unpacking, hanging some items in the wardrobe and flinging others into the far corner. Already the tiny shuddering heater was operating at full blast.

'For Christ's sake, close the door.' They did as she asked. 'I didn't say come *in*.'

She was not, she fumed, in the habit of undressing before strange men.

'Well, if you believe that, you'll believe anything,' Martin whispered as they waited outside in the hall. 'Know what? I've figured out who she looks like:

Rhonda Fleming in *Out of the Past*. I knew there was something familiar about her. Of course, a more mature Rhonda Fleming.'

'Shhh,' Celia warned. Tamara's mood was black enough. But it could not spoil Celia's excitement, and she was feeling quite indulgent towards Dr Sass.

'You look like bloody Bambi when you smile like that.'

'Was I smiling?'

Martin kissed her on the forehead. She started, drew back, blinked at him.

They set off up the steep main road towards the church, their calf muscles straining. The first turning presented them with a view of the church tower. Celia stopped to admire it and Martin took a photograph. Tamara lagged behind, her hands deep in the pockets of her coat. When Celia and Martin turned to check her progress she had disappeared.

'Where the hell is she now?' asked Martin, exasperated.

'I think I know.'

Suddenly Tamara emerged from a patisserie halfway down the hill. She caught up with them, her teeth bared, about to be sunk into an *amandine*.

'That's more like it,' she said, her mouth full, bits of pastry catching at the corners of her lips and in the strands of her hair. 'Want a pain au chocolat?'

Martin helped himself and they stood munching happily.

'I found this brochure.' Spitting crumbs, she rifled her enormous shoulder bag, extracted a shiny leaflet and waved it at them. 'A potted history of the village.' She wiped her mouth on the back of her hand. 'Some architectural tit-bits, the mandatory martyred Cathars and a map.'

'What does it say about the church?' Celia asked.

'Ummm, let's see: twelfth century, site of an older structure, unique heptagonal tower of outstanding interest,' she translated as they walked on. 'Messed around with over the centuries, your usual aesthetic travesties. No one's quite sure what the original layout was like, where everyone sat, etc. Couple of classy carved thirteenth-century capitals, nineteenth-century red marble baptismal font. Help. And *that*' – she pointed to a grey stone building on the right set into the side of a mountain – 'is a kind of rest home or sheltered housing for geriatrics. Built by Napoleon III – well, well – as a veterans' hospital. Listen to this. Originally an underground passage linked the hospital to the "world-famous", if you please, sulphur baths so that when les mutilés de guerre were escorted to the bath house the locals would be spared the sight of them. Tunnel now blocked up. The place remained a veterans' hospital, though much reduced, until the fifties when it became briefly a hotel attached to the baths. They were hoping to make the place a spa town but obviously it didn't work out. Then the building was empty for a while, fell into disrepair, finally renovated with a government grant as a sort of fifth-rate national monument then reopened as a home for the elderly. Meanwhile the baths have been given a facelift and are now used by the locals and by skiers to ease their aches and pains. Supposed to have marvellous healing properties. And there they are! Hooooow hideous.' She pointed to a seventies stressed concrete structure towards whose grim façade several people were making their way. 'Never mind, things are looking up. The Great Hall has been restored to its former glory, with Romanesque arches, reclining wicker chairs, potted palms, the works.' She showed them a blurred photograph of people resting in the chairs and wrapped in white. 'Don't know about this water. They look more like it killed them. Anyway, I'm heading for the Great Hall and whatever lies below as soon as our mission is accomplished. At least it'll be warm.'

'And what's that?' Celia pointed to a complex of more grey stone buildings, not unlike a prison.

'Barracks. Training on the left, departure platform on the right.'

'Of course. And still active. Look at the soldiers. Didn't you say Adèle's father was a soldier?'

'That's one theory.'

'Then it's more than likely he'd have been stationed right here.'

'Could be.'

And if he had been. And if he had seduced other women, or even given Adèle's mother another child, providing Adèle with brothers and sisters who might still be living in the village. Everyone in Bez must be related, so why not to Adèle? Why shouldn't there be another pair of eyes like those in the Acropolis photograph?

They reached the church to the accompaniment of yet more reportage from Tamara's brochure, which concluded with the optimistic prediction of Bez's future fame as a sports centre. (They had just passed the town's first ski shop, empty of customers.) She was about to enumerate the mayoralty succession when they arrived at the church.

'Not in great shape,' she said.

'But still beautiful.' Martin looked up at the gouged and pitted façade.

Celia headed for the cemetery.

It was a wonderful site, perched on the rising edge

of a cliff which dropped hundreds of metres into the valley below. Another village was visible on the mountain opposite. What a vision it must be when the mist cleared; what perfect surroundings for eternal rest. Celia felt an uncharacteristic envy for the beauty, security and continuity the church and cemetery seemed to embody. Rubbish, she thought, sentimental rubbish.

'Have you found it?' Tamara joined her, breathless with glowing cheeks and eyes.

'Help me look.' Celia took her hand.

Then Martin called out and they ran to him, tripping over the remains of ancient graves.

The plot that contained the incomplete remains of Adèle Louisante was close to the west wall. An unadorned headstone of rose-red marble bore her name, the date of her death, 12 October 1941, and the words '*Enfant Aimée.*' Small yellow narcissi covered the grave and around the base of the headstone a cluster of white violets was beginning to bloom. Before the stone was a vase of ferns and hellebores, fresh yesterday by the looks of them.

'*Pseudonarcissus lobularis*,' whispered Tamara.

'Someone's looking after your Adèle,' said Martin.

'But who?' Celia felt an impulse to sit on the grass but remembered her troublesome kidneys and refrained.

'I didn't think anyone else – ' Tamara broke off.

They stared at the grave and the flowers, not speaking.

'It's getting dark.' Martin broke the silence. 'We'd better have a look around. It might be nice to start with a shot of the church. First the tower with the mountains then track to the cemetery. Shoot it so it's like the edge of an abyss. Which I guess it is.'

'Yes, yes.' Celia was mesmerized.

Adèle

When they entered the church they could barely see and could not locate the light switch. But as their eyes grew accustomed to the darkness they could make out the seven-sided tower in the centre. 'So clever,' said Celia. 'You'd never guess from the outside.'

They squinted at the capitals with their exuberant foliage, traced with their fingers the drapery of eroded stone saints, craned their necks to gaze up into the tower. There was a sudden movement from one of the many dark corners: the scrape of a chair, the rustle of a coat and then a light tread magnified by the heels of heavy boots. They turned in the direction of the person who must certainly have been present since before their arrival and heard every word they'd said. They sensed, rather than saw, his tall form move towards the doors and open them. For less than a moment he was silhouetted in the archway. Then he was gone, letting the doors close with a bang and leaving them in blackness.

'Who was that?'

'A penitent?'

'Don't think so, somehow. No one's hearing confessions. Where are you two? Take my hand, someone.' Tamara groped her way to where she remembered Celia was standing.

Then the lights went on. In bustled the sacristan, who seemed unsurprised by the presence of three strangers in his cold dark church. Everyone uttered a simultaneous 'Bonsoir'. The man performed a deep genuflection before the altar and disappeared through a side door.

'Let's ask him about the grave,' hissed Tamara not very quietly.

'No.' Celia was firm. 'We mustn't make ourselves conspicuous.'

'She's right,' Martin agreed. 'We're just normal tourists. Look at that vaulting.' He pointed at the roof as the sacristan re-entered. They gaped at the stonework until he was gone.

'Strange,' mused Celia, 'that she should have been struck from the birth register then buried with all due Catholic ceremony in the churchyard.'

'I'm not too sure about the "all due" part.'

It was night when they left the church. At the end of the path Martin held the gate for the women and closed it behind them.

'How did you find out where she was buried?' he asked, lowering his voice.

'There was one reference, early in the correspondence, to Bez. I took a chance, wrote to the mairie and voilà!'

'Brilliant.'

'Listen, I'm freezing. And I feel weird. Why don't we go take a bath?' she suggested, tilting back her head, opening her large mouth and catching snowflakes on her tongue. 'Delicious.'

'So what happened to the other two?' Martin went on as they mounted the steps to the baths. 'Sylvester and Jessel, I mean.'

'The good doctor died of liver cancer in 1961. Cone mentions the death in a letter to another colleague. Didn't seem deeply grieved. Just the facts, ma'am.'

'And the sister – Blanche.'

'Elle a disparu.'

CHAPTER FIFTEEN

I brought you home. Though the house on Rue Beaurepaire was anything but a home. It was a fortress where my brother ruled and where he was in turn imprisoned. But I had nowhere else to take you and no money. And I confess I had panicked. I was so concerned for your safety that even that terrible place was sanctuary of a kind.

Moulay, the tall man who was your protector, wanted more money than I offered him. I suspected he would. And so I was forced to turn to Jonas. I telephoned from the café (the phones were working that day), terrified you would disappear in my absence. Send the cash this minute, I commanded. In a taxi. Send the housekeeper. Tell her to come to this address and hold the car. It did not occur to me until later how humbly he did as he was told.

The three of us waited in the dank hot room where you'd been staying, I assumed for some time. I refused to sit. There were no chairs, the floor was stained and sticky and had not been swept for weeks. In a corner, you huddled on a torn cushion that was spilling its stuffing like a gutted animal. You seemed unaware of my presence. Wrapped in a filthy blanket, you leaned your head against the wall and stared at nothing. You were unwashed and your smell was sickening, even to me. I presumed your condition was due to the drugs which this man you called your father no doubt sold and administered to you to keep you docile. In mangled French he asked me to be seated and offered me a cushion. At last I sat, my back to the wall, my legs in pale stockings, my feet in English shoes straight out before me. I crossed my ankles and pulled my dress over my knees. I longed to gather your wasted body in my arms and fly out of the window with you. But I knew I must wait and appear calm.

Moulay smiled at me, showing his blackened teeth. I nodded. We'd communicated well enough to seal our bargain. But I didn't ask him who he really was – since he could not possibly be your father – or how he had found you and persuaded you to come to this room and let him keep you here in near starvation. I wondered whether he was simply a brute or if he too had fallen under your spell and now loved you or, like many others, was addicted to you.

I thought it would be easy, apart from any last-minute aberrations on his part, to whisk you from the flat and into the taxi. You were so passive. (How willingly you allowed yourself to be carried off.) But when Madame Monmousseau arrived and the money had changed hands and she and I bent to lift you, you came suddenly and horribly to life. You looked at me with confusion, then with terror. You squealed and kicked and wriggled. The resistance put up by your slight form was amazing, and I later found my arms and legs covered with bruises and scratches, some of which turned septic. You even bit my hand. In the midst of our struggle I remembered Jonas's opinion that you weren't human and thought he might be right after all. I recalled your time in the forests and what the villagers had said about you. Yet all the while tears, real tears, were running down your face. Moulay was highly amused. Laughing, he rose in his dirty white robe that nearly covered his enormous bare feet, extricated you from our grasps and lifted you, blanket and all, in his arms. What was he about to do? I had bought you back. I had paid for you. I would have to kill him if he tricked me now.

As he moved towards the door with you, you clung to him, screaming 'Papa, Papa'. But he went on laughing and opened the door. Then I saw him hesitate. I saw him look at you, at your wet open mouth which he silenced with kisses. He thrust a large purple tongue deep into your throat and you kissed him avidly as he caressed you under the blanket.

'Allons, allons!' I shouted and he smiled, his wide mouth gleaming with your saliva. I rushed at him and pounded him on the back, but this only increased his merriment and he carried you briskly down the stairs. The heart-broken screams began all over again. Madame Monmousseau was mumbling and crossing herself. How we ever wrenched you from your 'father's' arms and locked you between us in the taxi, I don't know. You wailed like a baby weaned too early, like an animal torn from its natural habitat and bound for the laboratory. We pinned your arms and legs to the seat as the taxi drove off. I looked out of the back window to see Moulay in his white gown and bare feet sauntering towards the café. He had money to spend.

Madame Monmousseau was sent home, not even permitted to cross the threshold. Jonas snatched you from me. Exhausted by the past twenty-four hours, I could not resist him. He treated you with laudanum though I asked him not to. I was convinced that if only you and I were left alone together, I could heal you myself.

When we'd settled you and you were at last asleep in your bed, Jonas insisted I join him in the study. All

I wanted was to be with you, to take your limp hand and rest my head on your heart to assure myself that it was still beating. I wouldn't have done anything else, merely watched over you, a chaste nurse, while you slept. But it seemed unwise, just then, to contradict my brother. And so I followed him along the corridor. He opened the door to his study and went to his chair, motioning me to take the one opposite. We sat facing each other across his large desk.

He expressed no joy at your return. There were to be no congratulations, no gratitude for my persistence and my valour. Instead he delivered the oddest diatribe I've ever heard. I'm still not sure of its meaning. (Ideas muddle themselves in my damaged brain. I remember only feelings and events.) He began by opening an old book which he pushed towards me for my inspection. Some of its imagery still flits across my mind, shadows on a screen.

I saw a medieval woodcut with a caption describing its subject as 'The brother and sister pair in the bath of life'. I was alarmed. Was he using the picture as a warning that he knew about you and me? His eyes told me nothing. He informed me, his finger still resting on the picture, that it represented the process by which the alchemists sought to marry the masculine and feminine elements through immersion in the alkahest, that is, liquid, pure spirit.

'The couple symbolizes the attempt to resolve an inner struggle, the unification of opposites for which man has always longed.'

I supposed woman did not.

He gravely explained how the alchemists, as well as certain Eastern religions, believed that the creator of the universe was both male and female. The

Primordial Father — that's the expression he used — was hermaphroditic.

I didn't answer. I'd always assumed Jonas was an atheist.

He turned to another page marked with a dark-red ribbon. This time I saw a dragon in the process of devouring itself. The repulsive creature was described as follows: 'Mercurius manifests as the Worm Uroburos, a double-sexed dragon who swallows its own tail, fertilizes itself, kills itself, then gives birth to itself once more. Like the Creator, the Spirit Mercurius has a double nature. It too is composed of opposites — masculine/spiritual and feminine/corporeal, darkness and light, good and evil.'

I said I was confused. I thought the spirit was liquid. His mouth twitched in irritation. He couldn't be bothered to answer.

'This paradoxical being is the Saviour. It is also deadly poison. They called it "monstrum", "rebus", "thing".' He stressed the last word and looked up at me. 'You think this is mere fantasy, don't you?'

I replied that I felt unqualified to comment on the matter.

'I too dismissed these ideas at first. But in Adèle I find I have made a being — perhaps the only being — in whom the polarities incarnate themselves like God in Christ.'

How blasphemous, I would have thought, had I remained the devout Christian I'd been raised to be. And what did he mean by 'made'? As if he, not your mother, had created you. This was obviously the fruit of his recent reading. I wasn't sure whether he was attempting to clarify the discoveries to which his researches had led him, whether he was wielding arcane philosophy to justify his exploitation of you or whether he was mad. How ironic that when at last he chose to reveal himself and his motives to me, as I had begged him so many times to do, he did so in terms that were incomprehensible.

'Do you understand, Blanche?' he enquired, as though he had read my thoughts.

'Yes,' I lied. What did he care if I understood?

He looked at me, surprised. Then he stood up and began to pace.

'Because she is a binary, she is by nature untrustworthy, a slippery substance, as we know too well. She'll always vacillate between extremes and rest nowhere. Always compromise herself and everyone around her. Her behaviour and her attitudes are those of a thief and a whore.'

I opened my mouth to speak in your defence, but he went straight on.

'Adèle Louisante is an abomination.' He stopped. 'Yet she is also wholeness and perfection. Can you comprehend any of this?'

'Jonas,' I said gently, 'why don't you sit down, dear?' He'd become so agitated I feared physical collapse, a stroke even. 'It's time for tea. I could bring it to you.'

He wasn't listening. He was tossed by the storm inside his head. The ensuing silence must have lasted twenty minutes. Finally he dismissed me. He appeared calmer, so I went with relief.

He didn't speak of these things again for several months. In fact, he hardly spoke at all, save during sessions with his Creature. He was trying to revive your memory, or at least to make you speak. But, though your health improved, you showed no desire to communicate or to get out of bed. You had retreated to an inner world where even my entry was barred. As

I continued to nurse you, you did sometimes smile at me, but not with recognition. You had simply regained your customary sweetness and good humour. And so the house was silent for most of the time. On only one occasion did I find my brother in an expansive mood. I met him at breakfast absorbed in *Le Temps*. He looked up as I entered the dining room, his expression almost benign. He informed me, without any preliminaries, that because of the new government there were to be no more taxes on investment income or capital.

'And is this beneficial to you?'

'It is beneficial to us all,' he said and returned to his newspaper.

You continued to progress but not to remember. (I did often wonder if you were feigning amnesia. I had wondered before, when I first knew you. Of course I shall never know.) It was not until late August, 1938 that the momentous events occurred. Not only the threat of war and the universal tension it generated, but in the house on the Rue Beaurepaire.

It began with the books. My brother's sense of isolation must have been extreme since he summoned me for a conversation which, once again, was more lecture than dialogue. Immediately I entered he began to talk about the Stone. He asked if I remembered our previous discussion. I said I had thought of it often, which was true. Ideas that had been obsessing him and for which he'd had no outlet but his journals emerged in a hail of verbiage. He informed me that finding the Stone was considered to be the most difficult task on earth, and that he had discovered it, not realizing what it was. Even the great Cone had lost patience and abandoned the search. Jonas went to the desk and opened yet another of those volumes that made me so uneasy. He turned to a page near the end from which he read, translating from the German.

'"For the Stone is underfoot, unnoticed, kicked aside like rubbish. It is 'exilis', ugly, despised, born of the gutter and the dunghill. The Stone is an orphan who resides among the poor, the sick and the homeless, with prostitutes and thieves. Which is why it is always passed unnoticed by the worldly-wise."'

He seemed under a great strain. I had no idea what he might do next and sat stiff with anticipation, my hands gripping my long shapeless thighs.

'"The stone that the builders rejected, the same is become the headstone in the corner,"' he quoted. And when I thought of your origins, your childhood, the hatred you inspired, I understood the meaning of the prayer.

'Remember,' he intoned, as though warning me personally, 'that the Stone is not only the goal. It is the end but also the beginning.'

'The beginning of what, Jonas?'

'The New Mankind.'

'Excuse me, I don't — '

'It's not the culmination of a selfish quest, something to be found and kept as I had imagined. It redeems the light fallen into matter. For the benefit of humanity.'

I was glad to hear it.

'Great sacrifices will be involved, but our success is inevitable.'

'And what are these new beings?' I was wondering what he had in mind for the rest of us.

'A perfected race, powerful but pure.'

My discomfort was extreme. Even my limited experience had convinced me that power is never pure.

'This race has been written about and discussed for

centuries. But now its time has come. I believe Adèle is its avatar.'

'Is this what you've been writing about?'

'Recently, yes.'

'Will anyone publish it?'

'A German company is interested. The scientific group subsidising my work has been very helpful. Cone is also negotiating with an interested party in London.'

'Well. Congratulations.' I was about to suggest bed and a tisane when he moved to the window and faced me, lit from behind.

'What regret Cone must feel, and yet he assists me.'

'Why regret?'

He didn't answer. His gaze was fixed beyond me. I turned to see you standing in the doorway. If you had heard what Jonas was saying, you gave no indication. You smiled at us. You seemed anything but demonic, more a drowsy adolescent. You looked well, though you'd been in bed for months, hardly waking or eating apart from a little milk or a segment of orange. You'd even rejected your adored offal, after I had gone to such lengths to procure it. Did your smile indicate recovery? I crossed the room and knelt before you. Slowly I extended my hand as one would to a wary dog. You took the hand, raised it to your nose and sniffed it. Recognition filled your face, and you grasped my hand in both of yours and joyfully licked the palm. Then you slid it down the front of your body and placed it on your genitals.

My brother was quick to intervene. He snatched away my hand, thrust himself between us and commenced a bizarre pantomime of a medical examination, shining a light in your eyes and ears, applying a wooden tongue suppressant with trembling hands, checking your heart rate. Then he dropped his instruments and clasped you in his arms, swaying and moaning, burying his head first in one side of your neck then the other. Rocking you back and forth, he cried and sobbed as you stood passive in his embrace.

I nearly dragged him off you, but waited instead for the fit to end. I couldn't bear to watch, but neither could I look away. As his emotions subsided, he drew back to look at you, to feast his eyes. He had torn your nightdress, unveiling the brown nipple beneath. At the sight of it his mood altered completely. All at once you were the enemy. Victim and exploiter changed places in his mind, and he attacked you as though he were defending his life.

He struck you across the left cheek. You staggered and I ran to catch you, but he hit you again, gripping your hands behind your back as he flailed distractedly at your breasts, shoulders and head. He was punishing you, you who were incapable of violence. He shouted that you were filth, poison, that you should have been strangled at birth rather than set free to corrupt unwary humans and infect the world with your monstrous sex.

You were hysterical. Little animal squeaks came from the back of your throat. He threw you on to the carpet and made for the poker. Convinced he meant to murder you, I scanned the room for a weapon. I spied his letter opener, snatched it from the desk and rushed at him, stabbing him as hard as I could in the upper arm and leaving the knife protruding from his expensive jacket. (How well he'd been living. How he spoiled himself while paying me a subsistence wage.) He cried out and released you. I did not wait to see what would happen next, but left my brother to cope with his injury and dragged you to the door which I quickly shut, taking the key and locking it from the outside.

I tried to make you stand but your knees collapsed. I lifted you in my arms, staggering under the weight of you but animated by a strength which I'm told mad people feel, and carried you upstairs to your room.

I barricaded us in by means of a chest of drawers and did the same with some chairs to the entrance of the *en suite* bathroom. I bathed your wounds. Already your eye and cheek were bruised and swelling. What would I do if you had concussion? How could I get you to a hospital? I was penniless. But as usual I was stern with myself and forced myself to think calmly. I saw that I had foolishly made us prisoners in your room, cut off from food, money, transport. Left us, in fact, at the mercy of Jonas who could now lay siege to us at his leisure, taking his long revenge until the inevitable capitulation.

A few minutes later I heard him leave the house. Probably to see a medical colleague. Then to visit the bank, in order to cancel my authorization to make withdrawals. I waited until I was sure that it was not a ruse, then went cautiously downstairs where I took the dismissed Madame Monmousseau's shopping bag and filled it with fruit, milk, bread and some clean glass cloths to serve as bandages. At least you wouldn't starve. I myself had no interest in food. Only in purchasing a day or two in which to nurse you and devise a plan of action. I returned to your room and secured our fragile fortress, sufficiently, I hoped, to prevent Jonas assailing it that night. At ten I got into bed with you.

When I woke there was a sharp line of light between the heavy curtains. I was aware of your fingers delicately exploring my anus. Slowly, gently, they inserted themselves in the opening – one, two,

133

three. I gave a violent jerk and you giggled. You moved closer and lifted the front of my slip. With your left hand you teased open my lips. I wanted so much to extend the delight of all this, but, starved for the long-lost food of you, I surrendered too soon to the spasms that galvanized my body. Then I embraced you, eager to gorge myself. You lay on your back with your legs spread, and I grasped your knees, pushing them further and further apart. You were so limber that both of them came to rest easily on the mattress, and I lowered my head, mouth open, tongue protruding. It was as I tasted you at last that I knew my brother was in the room.

I feared he would kill us where we lay, yet the possibility we might die as I brought you to orgasm was thrilling. Then I froze, feeling suddenly, of all things, embarrassed.

'You needn't stop on my account,' my brother said.

But we were now beyond stopping. And so he watched us until the end.

CHAPTER SIXTEEN

'Celia, move to the right, will you. You're in Tamara's shadow.'

Martin waved her aside, moved forward with the camcorder then back again, bumping into a low gravestone.

Tamara giggled. 'Isn't this incredible. I mean after talking about it for months we're actually here. Doing it. Mission accomplished.'

'Could we test for voice now?' Martin was serious, in control. The women, however, were skittish.

'Please stand still and speak up. Remember there's no mike.' At least the light was good. And it had stopped snowing.

The sacristan emerged from the church door with his quick pious walk. 'Bonjour, Monsieur/Mesdames,' to which they replied in unison like a class of six year olds, 'Bonjour, Monsieur.' Celia liked the way the French made a point of addressing each other, instead of scuttling past with averted eyes like the English. He moved briskly to the north wall where he proceeded to inspect a drain. Celia placed a restraining hand on Tamara's arm, guessing she intended to ask him about the flowers, but she escaped Celia's hold and made straight for him.

'Honestly,' Celia sighed. But Dr Sass returned with some interesting news.

'Guess what.' Her eyes were alight. 'Monsieur Bridau knows the flower boy. His name is Marcel and he works as a mechanic at the garage down the hill. Says he comes twice a week and that a woman pays him to do it. Apparently this Marcel isn't very forthcoming. Anyway, he changes the flowers and tends the grave. Monsieur Bridau's happy as long as his graves look smart.'

They sat on the wall, pretending to admire the view, and waited until the sacristan, satisfied with his drain, climbed into his old blue Renault and drove off with a wave.

'Nice little man,' said Tamara.

'The people are nice here. But what about this Marcel person? We should find him as soon as possible.'

'Shouldn't be difficult. We'll go to the garage and ask.'

'No, no. Too obvious.'

'Then what do you suggest?'

'Right, women,' Martin interrupted. 'Shall we try again?'

'What if Marcel has new information? We might have to alter our lines,' Celia pointed out.

'We can still rehearse,' he pleaded. 'We can shoot the grave and the mountains and you two conspirators doing your stuff.'

'OK.'

The mountains that morning were blazing white against a blue sky. Tamara had to be persuaded to remove her sunglasses.

'*Please.*' Martin was losing patience.

The women resumed their positions on either side of the grave.

'We've come to this remote Pyrenean village to right an old wrong,' Celia began, her voice high and nervy. 'Even as we speak, Harley Street doctors are performing the same operation for large fees . . .'

Martin tracked slowly past the pair to get a better shot of their glorious backdrop. 'Celia,' he stopped them. 'Do you have that trowel?'

'You mean bury the box *now*?'

'Just practise. We'll try a close-up of the grave. You digging and Tamara standing over you. Let's just see how it looks. OK. Anybody around?'

They were worried about interference from God-fearing upright locals. Were there laws in France, they'd wondered, against putting something into a grave as opposed to taking something out? This was, after all, hardly defacement. The *Pseudonarcissi lobularis* would continue to bloom undisturbed.

Celia knelt by the grave. The grass was damp and cold under her knees. She plunged the trowel into the earth, still hard from the winter. She thought of the woman whose remains lay beneath and the unknown person who had buried her here and was responsible for such tender care.

'Terrific, Celia. Now, Tamara, you kneel beside her . . . Well, then why the hell did you wear a skirt? . . . oh come on, try. Do it for Martin, Doctor . . . no, no, don't look at me, for Christ's sake. Celia, why are you gaping like that? Oh shit!' He switched off the camcorder. He heard the crunch of gravel behind him and turned to see the focus of the women's attention.

All four of them stood frozen in their places, embarrassed, curious, apparently struck dumb.

'Bonjour.' The young man spoke first. His voice was a pleasant growl, his accent thick with rolling r's and stressed vowel endings.

'Bonjour,' said the English in unison.

Tamara addressed him cheerily in French. 'We're filming,' she announced. 'Would you like to be in the movie?' From a distance he looked quite photogenic, slender with regular features if a longish nose, and shiny black hair which he wore well over the collar of his worn leather jacket. His eyes were deep-set and brown, his face scarred by old acne. He carried a large basket from which emerged diverse leaves and buds. His hands and jeans were smeared with engine grease. He looked an unlikely gardener. Yet this had to be Marcel.

He shook his head in answer to Tamara's question. Serious but not hostile.

'Ils sont anglais. Je suis américaine,' Tamara informed him, as though the knowledge would assure him that nothing bad could possibly happen. He was unimpressed.

'Vous voulez une Gitane?' She held out the pack and he came towards her. She produced a lighter, lit his then one for herself. She looked, thought Celia, as though she was taming an animal.

They continued to assess each other and smoke. Then he pointed to the grave and to the camcorder and said something Celia found impenetrable but which Tamara managed to grasp. She responded in her unselfconscious American French.

'He wants to know why we're taking pictures of the grave and says we mustn't dig it up,' she translated without turning. 'I told him we have no intention of digging it up. How do I explain the trowel?' When there was no quick response, she just went on. 'C'est vous qui a repiqué les petites fleurs?'

He nodded.

'Très jolies.'

He stared at her.

'Comment vous appelez-vous?'

'Marcel.'

'Moi, je m'appelle Tamara.'

138

'Comment?'

'T-A-M-A-R-A.'

'Ah oui.'

'What do I do, darlings,' she called. 'He's the one!'

Martin came forward, followed by Celia. Missionaries confronting their first savage. In slow careful French Celia explained that they were making a short film about the area around Bez. Monsieur Bridau had no objections to their being in the churchyard. She hoped he, Marcel, had no objections either, but if he did, she hoped he would say so.

Marcel shrugged again. Celia doubted he'd understood much of what she'd said, but thought she had better introduce herself and Martin. She was desperate to keep him there. They all shook hands solemnly.

'Ask him if he tends every grave,' Martin suggested.

Tamara complied and Marcel shook his head. 'No,' she translated, 'only this grave.'

Then she risked it. 'Mais, pourquoi?'

Celia winced, frightened Tamara would drive him away with her bold curiosity. But he answered immediately.

'Parce qu'elle me paie.' Suspicion was in his eyes.

'Do you know anything about the person who's buried here?'

'Elle est morte.' He stubbed out his cigarette on a stone and dutifully put the butt into his jacket pocket.

'But who is she?' They were all three smiling rather stupidly at him. He glanced at the camcorder.

'Want to have a go?' Martin handed it to him and for the first time Marcel smiled. They walked out of the shadow and into the light where Martin showed him how to film the glistening mountains and a goat in a nearby field.

'Good ol' Martin.'

'Mmmm,' Celia mused. 'Men *do* love gadgets. Isn't it funny.'

Tamara smiled. 'Maybe it's not a gender myth after all.'

They watched the men have fun with Martin's toy.

'Should we offer him money?' Tamara asked.

'Definitely not,' replied Celia, her eyes wide with horror at such American vulgarity. She detected pride in Marcel and not a little touchiness.

By the time Tamara had smoked another cigarette, Martin and Marcel were returning.

'Please, God,' she whispered, 'let them have deeply bonded.'

Marcel certainly looked more relaxed and Martin was grinning.

'Martin, what's going on?'

'Ask him.' He indicated Marcel whom Tamara was now plying with Toblerone.

'It's OK?'

'Seems to be.'

Celia gathered up her vocabulary like long unwieldy skirts. 'I hope you don't think I'm being rude,' she began, 'but I'd be very interested to know who employs you to look after Adèle Louisante's grave.'

'La vieille.' He pointed to the hospital on the opposite slope.

'And what's her name, this old woman?'

'Madame Jessel,' he replied.

CHAPTER SEVENTEEN

I expected my brother's vengeance to be immediate but it was not. I sat on your bed in my slip and stared at him. You, meanwhile, rolled over and fell asleep. I confess I enjoyed watching his thoughts reveal themselves in his haggard face – in particular the recognition that his plain and devoted sister was far from neuter. Though I knew I would pay dearly, my momentary satisfaction seemed worth the punishment. How brave I felt, smiling at my executioner, for I was smiling. Jonas's looks mixed hatred and disgust with shattered confidence. How could he have been so wrong about me? He left the room.

I tried to wake you but it was no use. I dressed and collected a few belongings. The room was suffocating with the smell of you, so I opened a window. It was a cold sunny morning inviting escape. How this was to be accomplished I had no idea. I was without funds, and as far as I knew, you were penniless. Moreover, I had no friends since my life in Paris had been centred on you alone and I'd hardly left the house except to buy necessities. Nor was there much we could sell besides your jewellery – gifts from clients which Jonas kept locked in his study safe.

At last I managed to rouse you. I explained that we were in danger and that we must leave at once. You smiled and nodded like a child, happy to be setting out on an adventure. I wondered if you were still mute, but this was not the time to test you. How we'd even reach the front door I didn't know. I was simply proceeding, animated by will alone. An engine was turning inside me, blind to obstacles, and so all else in the world would have to make way for our exit.

We each took a small suitcase and went quickly down the stairs, expecting at any moment to encounter Jonas. Had he assumed we were paralysed with fear and incapable of action? More incredibly, did he want us to go? We made no attempt at concealment. It seemed absurd after our shameless performance of an hour before. We passed the study door which was closed and hastened along the corridor to the front door.

It was locked of course. He wasn't a fool. But a lock was insufficient deterrence. I went to the sitting room and took the poker Jonas had intended to use on you. It had been returned to its stand by the fireplace, where no fires were ever lit save for prospective clients. With it I smashed the street-facing window, knocking out any remaining shards around the frame. Being the more agile, you went first, slithering through the open space on to the courtyard. I threw the bags after you. Then, for the first time, I balked. A sill, such a simple easy thing, but I felt stiff and wooden, a marionette without its puppet-master. You held out your hands to me as I heard a door opening upstairs. I removed my shoes, lifted one leg over the ledge then the other. Despite your assistance, I stumbled and fell to the ground. When I rose to take my first step, I collapsed in pain. I knew I had sprained my ankle.

My brother stood framed by the empty window. Then he jumped out and followed us to the street entrance as we climbed into a taxi and drove away. I expected him to shout to passers-by that we were thieves and must be stopped. Well, I was a thief. I was robbing him of his precious Stone, his pearl of great price, and I exulted in my daring and my success. But as soon as we were out of immediate danger, I was gripped by the terror I had suppressed for the past twelve hours, and I trembled.

The throbbing in my ankle was excruciating, and I had no money to pay the taxi. But you did, and handed him a ten-franc note. You saw my surprise, but as always you smiled and did not explain. You were looking especially androgynous that afternoon: trousers and a boy's jacket and shoes. But your hair had begun to grow out and hundreds of springy curls fell over your forehead and on to your neck. You wore a little gold stud in each earlobe, and the thinnest green leather gloves on your hands. Whenever you moved the jacket opened to reveal nipples pushing against the weave of your jumper.

'Button it,' I hissed then clenched my teeth as a current of pain shot up my leg. It occurred to me that we looked too eccentric to get very far and badly needed an incognito. You looked so foreign that if we'd been stopped by the police they'd certainly want to see your identity card. You, however, were unconcerned and seemed to know exactly where we were going. Preoccupied with my ankle, I had missed your instructions to the driver. You must have spoken to him, but when?

I should have guessed you'd take us to Moulay's. To whom would you turn in trouble if not to your 'father'? Audacious as I'd lately been, I now felt powerless. Control had passed mysteriously to you. When the taxi stopped outside the house I'd hoped never to see again, you hopped out, paid the driver, and motioned me to wait in the car while you removed the bags and carried them to the doorway. Then you returned to help me up the rubbish-littered stairs.

The flat was empty. I sank on to a cushion, grateful simply to be hidden and physically still. You produced a jug of cloudy water which you handed to me without a glass. Even in my discomfort I basked in your solicitude. I was almost happy, drunk with our accomplishment. Then I asked you was I really drunk and was that why my head felt light and the room kept spinning? I was wet and I wondered if I'd spilled water down the front of my dress. But when I touched my face and chest, they were covered with sweat. All of a sudden I knew that what I had just done had proved too much for me and that I was going to be very ill. I panicked. Ill – here in this place without a bath or a toilet, where cockroaches scuttled and the rats pursued their vicious intents. I tried to rise, but you held me down, gazing at me as my head rolled from side to side, concern in your brow if not your eyes. Already the rats had arrived. They were banging at the door. I saw them enter in the suave and glittering attire that hid their mangy fur. I knew these rats, recognized each one of them. The Descoignes, Madame Bianchon, the tall one in the pig mask. The rats were your clients come to fetch you back. And I was too weak to protect you.

I still retain some blurred impressions of the following days: people entering and leaving the room, wearing strange clothes, speaking a foreign language. The rats appeared in their finery and I would struggle and scream for help, or at least I thought I was screaming. No one paid any attention. Occasionally your face floated above me like a protective spirit, arching over the city, filling the Paris sky with your angel smile. Then the image would dissolve, and I would fall back into a colourless world without boundaries or time, a vast prison of boredom and anxiety.

Then one day I woke up. I blinked in the morning

144

light, aware that my mind was clear and that I was hungry and, above all, that I was alone. Then I saw Moulay stretched out on the mattress, covered with a blanket and snoring loudly. I tried to stand but couldn't. I called your name, and you rose up from behind his huge body, your shoulders naked, and stared at me with sleepy eyes.

'Come here, come here,' I mouthed.

You rose, dressed in one of your expensive nightdresses, now stained and torn, and crossed the room. You sat by me. You held my hand and kissed me. I asked if you were speaking yet, but you shook your head. You pointed to my ankle which had been neatly bandaged. You patted it with a dirty hand and smiled. It was better. I would be all right now. You put your hand on my forehead and frowned. I had been very ill.

'Who looked after me? You?'

You nodded.

'But the ankle – '

You pointed at Moulay, still snoring. He must have found a doctor who'd agreed to treat me.

'Thank you,' I whispered and pressed your hand and kissed it. Then I enquired if there was any food.

You clapped, delighted my appetite had been restored. You dressed and went out. I lay down, exhausted from our brief exchange. You returned with a baguette, a packet of rancid butter and some milk. You made me eat slowly, wisely removing the food before I ate too much. Unable as yet to speculate about where the money for the doctor and the food had come from, I fell asleep.

Another week passed before I could walk. I had lost a great deal of weight (I must have looked grotesque) and wanted to eat all the time. Food was always provided by you. I devoured it, slept and woke again, usually to find you and Moulay gone.

At first I was terrified alone in that cold dark place with its stink of urine and rotting vegetables that smothered even your pervasive scent. Each time I woke I was certain you'd never return. But you did, with Moulay, just before daybreak, and the two of you would sit and smoke kif or consume chunks of glutinous black majun before collapsing on to the ragged mattress, not bothering to undress. The smoke made me nauseous. Then I was forced to listen to the sounds of your love-making as the room filled slowly with grey light. Too exhausted to practise my old solitary rites, I lay in tears until you had finished.

I feared you might never leave him. Having rescued you from one slavery, I had thrown you into another. I did not dare mention departure. I didn't want to alarm you or pressure you in any way. I waited to be alone with you to discuss our future. I also needed a bath. When you offered, once I could walk, to take me to the hammam I agreed.

'Don't go in there,' Moulay shouted after you. 'When they see what you are, they will chop you up in pieces and turn you into a bastela.' He roared with laughter.

On the way to the baths I asked if Moulay had given you money and you said no. Then how did you buy the food? You removed from your trouser pocket (you now dressed permanently as a boy) the notepad you carried with you. In crude capital letters, you informed me that you earned the money yourself.

'As before?' I was unable to conceal my jealousy.

You shook your head proudly. 'Moulay m'a dit non,' you wrote.

'Then how?'

Adèle

You passed me the notepad on which I read: 'MOI, J'AI TROUVÉ DU TRAVAIL.' And underneath: 'VIENS ME VOIR DEMAIN SOIR.'

Funfairs depress me. The music and laughter and flashing lights, the haunted castles and rifle ranges and tawdry entertainment seem sinister and toxic. The greasy atmosphere makes me loath to touch anything for fear of contamination. So I approached the Foire de Trône, which was making its St Anthony's visit to the Cours de Vincennes, with my nerves strung tight, wary of everyone, dreading to discover what your 'job' might be. Even the smells of smoked ham and gingerbread repelled me. I felt an alien among the working-class families with their ungovernable children, the cocky young men who presided over the games, the couples embracing in the tent shadows. The coloured lights threw sickly tints across excited faces. From all sides I was importuned loudly in coarse accents. People were enjoying themselves in a rowdy human way from which I felt permanently excluded. I was too self-conscious, too fearful that joy and abandon would render me even more ugly and ludicrous than I already was. That I would suddenly catch sight of myself in a mirror and see myself the way others must see me and be filled with shame and revulsion.

To me the fair was eerie and sad, the music from the hurdy-gurdy lending a lugubrious accompaniment to the shabby scene. Into this labyrinth I went in search of the tent where you worked. You still had not told me of what this work consisted. You wished to surprise or horrify or delight me, possibly all three. The only thing of which I felt certain was that Moulay was involved.

A voice barked through a megaphone, summoning

customers to witness 'spectacular tableaux vivants' enacted by some girls lined up along a raised platform. Behind them was a green shade which obviously had witnessed hundreds of such performances. They wore half-masks and sequined dressing gowns which they clutched to their bodies. Their shoes were old and worn, each pair different from the rest, and all had kiss-curls plastered coquettishly to their foreheads. As each of them was introduced by name, they stepped forward and smiled – shyly, brazenly, cynically, coyly. The crowd of men grew larger. I watched cloth caps, felt hats, soldiers' and sailors' hats swaying this way and that as their owners strained for a better view. This spectacle of degraded innocence depressed me even more.

The fat barker had a glistening pock-marked face and a roseate nose bulbous from drink. He leered as he promised his audience the delights of Leda and the Swan, a Sapphic Orgy, Salome and the Seven Veils, a dance with an anaconda. He assured them the ladies would be fully undressed for their entertainment. I looked for you among them, but you weren't there. I walked on, wishing I hadn't come. And then I saw you, or rather a gigantic image of you, painted on a banner that swayed in the breeze. The banner, which was surrounded by a frame of electric lights, bore the advertisement: 'Adolphe – Freak or Fraud? Let the People Decide.' At first I thought the show involved you alone. But in fact you were the star turn in a varied array of mutants: a man with an obese body and a tiny head, a pair of Siamese twins dressed as bellboys and joined at the waist, a woman covered with fish scales, a young man whose fingers grew out of his neck, another who appeared to be a talking torso wearing a crown and seated on a tiny throne, a child with a head the size of a medicine ball, a woman with five breasts.

Your picture exerted a magnetic effect, for the barker was having no difficulty summoning large numbers of both men and women to his tent. Despite my horror, I found that it also excited me, and I was all of a sudden as impatient as the others to witness this bizarre spectacle. I joined the queue and paid my entrance fee.

Since you were the *pièce de résistance* and therefore appearing last, I was forced to endure the lurid pantomime to the end. (The most tragic specimens were the Siamese twins who, as they smiled and simpered, really did appear to be physically linked.) I feared I might be sick and have to leave the tent before your act. At last the ordeal was over, though I knew a worse was only just beginning.

'And now, ladies and gentlemen,' boomed the master of ceremonies, a repulsively handsome man in his mid-forties, 'the most amazing of all the phenomena you have just witnessed – ADOLPHE, THE LITTLE LADY WITH A LOT TO HIDE.'

The ragged curtains parted to reveal you standing upon a platform which seemed to be made from a collection of painted orange crates, naked except for cascades of barbarous bangles, a necklace made of skulls, a belt of teeth and a feather head-dress atop a gold wig. A little apron of parrot feathers covered your pudenda. Your skin had been darkened, but it still shone under the lights as you descended from your dais. With customary grace and agility you then performed a lewd jungle dance at the climax of which you removed the feather apron to expose your astounding genitalia. The audience gasped, heckled, cheered, laughed in hysterical disbelief. At the MC's request you walked to the front of the stage. Everyone was suddenly quiet.

'Now turn around, Adolphe,' he ordered, 'and show the people your delectable backside.'

The swirl of black hair on your back glistened in the spotlight.

'Adolphe doesn't talk so good, you know.' The MC pointed to his head. 'She's a bit slow. Her maker put so much energy into the body, there wasn't any left over for the brain.' He roared at his feeble joke and the audience followed suit. 'But her little boyfriends and her little girlfriends don't mind at all. They'll be happy to testify that she's got *other* strengths.' More laughter. 'Even if she is – what would you say, folks, a bit dusty, a bit musty.' There were hisses and cheers. 'Adolphe was discovered and captured in the jungles of a remote island in the Pacific. Living alone with animals in a primitive Eden. She must have dined well because, as you can see, she's in pretty fine shape for a freak.' Everyone laughed. You stood absolutely straight and relaxed, smiling without embarrassment.

'Now I know what you're all thinking. It's just not possible that such a creature can exist, and Adolphe and I and the management are playing a clever trick to relieve you of your hard-earned cash. Well, good people, I intend, with all due respect, to prove that you're mistaken. My little friend and I will convince you that she is indeed a biological marvel. Then *you*, honoured guests, will be given the opportunity to prove it to yourselves. I guarantee you this is no swiz and that you will leave our humble establishment amazed and convinced. OK, sweetheart, show them you're not just a pretty Mademoiselle with a dildo.'

Obediently you placed your hands on your hips, spread your legs, leaned forward and looked down at yourself. Your penis twitched, began to swell, then slowly raised itself until it stood erect.

The silence was complete, the audience stunned by your dimensions, larger, no doubt, than many a man's present. Then came bravos mixed with cat calls, the stamping of feet, hoots, obscenities and demands for verification and money returned. You'd transformed everyone into the wild brutes among whom the MC claimed you'd lived. And I could tell you were enjoying their behaviour.

'Quiet, please,' roared the MC, attempting to restore order. 'Now is your chance to play a part in this unforgettable evening.' (Cheers.) 'Prove to yourselves that Adolphe is no fraud, that your eyes do not deceive you. Volunteers!' he shouted. 'I need volunteers to come forward and confirm with your own lily-white hands that Adolphe is a bona fide hermaphrodite.'

There was a general rush towards the platform.

'Now, now!' He held up his arms to the impatient queue of men and women. 'I want the real doubting Thomases, the hardened cynics, those of you who've been telling yourselves you don't believe this codswallop for a minute. You're the ones we're determined to convince.'

Four of the largest men pushed their way through the crowd and climbed on to the platform. They were followed by a fat woman with bright-red lipstick and a black-and-white-flowered dress that barely contained her wobbling bosom. Her appearance prompted a deluge of rude remarks which she returned in kind.

'Now, no monkey business,' the MC admonished. 'Remember this is purely scientific.' The spectators shrieked with laughter. I leaned against a post to keep my balance.

One by one the volunteers came forward to examine you, feeling the weight of your testicles, stroking the erect penis, searching for the glue, the clever attachment, the loose connection they were sure they'd find. As they inspected and fondled you, you gave them smiles and sighs of delight. In each case the encounter would become overheated and the Thomases would be driven off the stage by the MC, wielding his cane in farcical indignation at such breaches of conduct in his respectable establishment.

The audience was wild. The howls and hoots and applause drowned out the MC's disgusting jokes. People pressed closer to the stage, drawn to the spectacle of this loveliest of freaks. The tent swayed, and I was afraid it would collapse, but no one seemed to notice or mind. You continued to flirt and pose and allow yourself to be 'examined'. It was unbearable. It was also dangerous. I had to get you out. But I was unable to push my way through the dense crowd you'd aroused so successfully and which seemed on the verge of riot.

I feared a police raid (apparently there had been one already), our discovery, capture and ultimate return to the Rue Beaurepaire. But the MC was accustomed to dealing with debased humanity and brought the show to a speedy end. There were vigorous protestations, and the furious customers who had not yet got their hands on you vented their frustration by shaking the tent poles. These malcontents were escorted to the exit by several enormous men who suddenly emerged from the crowd. Fights broke out and were brutally suppressed. By the entrance, queues were already forming for the next show. Your secret was out for all the world to gape at, no longer the occult toy of a perverted elite. How could I rectify your mad mistake? But I knew it was already too late. Your notoriety would attract the detectives I was certain had been looking for us. You would be discovered, recaptured, and what would become of us then?

Adèle

I was not wrong. It happened a fortnight later after one of your performances, all of which I attended since, despite my revulsion, they excited me horribly so that I could not keep away. Hired thugs snatched you as you made your way between the show tent and the hovel – lit only by an oil lamp – that was your dressing room. Moulay, who always waited there to protect you from those who might wish to harm you – men who hate the beautiful and the marvellous and are driven to destroy them – was quick to the rescue but not quick enough. He heard your sharp little screams and ran to your assistance, but he was too late. You'd been slipped into a hessian sack and carried off by two faceless men. He caught only a glimpse of your feather head-dress as it vanished into the night.

My brother was the prime suspect, but any of your former lovers might have got word of your whereabouts and dispatched their henchmen to abduct you. You were a magical charm none of us could resist, the jewel we were all compelled to steal.

Not knowing where to turn, I could only wait for a summons or a clue. I remained alone with Moulay, that strange man whom I had always regarded as vicious and ignorant. Those nights in the room waiting for news of you, waiting for him to come home, I spent curled up under my dirty blanket, listening to the sounds of the street. I expected him to throw me out, but he didn't. He even spoke to me, sometimes kindly. Smoking a soupsi of kif he would ask me about you, your past, where I thought you might be now. Once I heard him – he who had been happy to sell you to me and to many others less concerned for your welfare – sobbing in his bed. Knowing I was without money, he brought me food which we ate together, and I almost forgave him his callousness. On several occasions we smoked opium, sedating our pain in silence. But when my mind was clear, I became once more incensed. What had he done with your earnings from that vile street fair? Spent them on drugs, no doubt, on the daily habit I now shared with him. Yet he was clearly bereft, and I could not help but pity him.

Three weeks later, the message arrived. My brother demanded my immediate return to the Rue Beaurepaire. We had much to discuss, he implied. You were very ill, and he was keeping you under lock and key for your own protection. I was not to fear for my safety, since we shared what he called common interests — two enemy nations uniting against a third. All was negotiable. He knew my anxiety for you would guarantee my obedience.

I considered asking Moulay to assemble a mob to storm the house and retrieve you by force, with no restrictions imposed on my brother's treatment. But the result would be mayhem, even death, and you and I might find ourselves not only at the mercy of one of your 'fathers', but the law. I decided I must go alone, whatever the consequences. At least I would see you again. Jonas was my brother, after all. Surely we could reach some agreement now that we had no secrets from one another, now that he again held all the cards. And so I walked the entire way back to the Rue Beaurepaire, leaving Moulay in ignorance of our whereabouts, to weep and smoke his kif and find another freak to love.

CHAPTER EIGHTEEN

This is what I do all day, every day, since I have been a patient here where once I tended patients. I perfect the system I have developed over decades of life without you. Methodically, and with the utmost attention to detail, I invoke your smell, your voice, your taste, your touch, using each separate sense as an *aide memoire* to recapture the whole.

I have practised so hard and so long this work of memory and reconstruction that my fantasies have put on flesh. Their action no longer transpires in a haze – glimpses of bright fish under water – but in clear light and air. More real than my life in this room, so that I often wonder where I am, what year it is, or whether I am alive or dead. This afternoon I have been conjuring the feel of your body under my hands: your breasts with their pert brown nipples, the delicate bones of your knees, the belly a moon irradiating thin clouds, the gleaming buttocks (what life beneath to make them swell that way), the backs of the knees, sturdy yet vulnerable, the tiny ankles I can grip within the bracelet of my thumb and middle finger, the feet with insteps high as hooves. And then your sex, the shocking strength of it. After stroking you, my hands felt covered with a fine metallic dust. You were a treasure worth more than all the world's gold.

When you embraced me, your touch was feather-light, a thousand teasing tongues that searched out each of my fault lines, setting off earthquakes inside me. If my self-hypnosis is particularly successful, I can feel them again. You see how sex transcends the physical, binding two humans even in the most terrible circumstances, stronger than death. Had I been merely your nurse, your nanny, however devoted, we would never have survived our catastrophe. Sex united us long after sex had become extinct.

The fantasy progresses to the very end. I do not omit from it the feel of your body when I cared for you in your last and most pernicious illness. I bathed you as I had when I first knew you. Only this time your response to my ministrations was simply gratitude. You'd developed a wasting disease, growing thinner and thinner, so that your tiny bones almost pierced their veil of skin. Your clavicles were practically fleshless when you coughed, which you did continually. I diagnosed emphysema but later thought pneumonia. Your thick skin withered and your breasts collapsed as your body's protoplasm was drained away. But what was draining it, and where did it go? The beautiful rounded parts of your anatomy sagged like ragged tapestries that, when new, had decked a palace. The place between your thighs was now a ruin. Your smile daily revealed more of teeth and gums, the skull lurking beneath the still-sweet face. Your eyes, once blank, now picked out every distant detail on the road to death. Your skin, your glory, turned grey-white, flaking from the sporadic and painful rashes which were unresponsive to medication. I often despaired in that Toulouse hotel room of our ever reaching Bez.

It was because of your illness that, at the time we left Paris, I could do nothing to punish my brother's crime. All of my resources were devoted to you, despite the physical and emotional anguish that were the results of his butchery. Only in the few moments before I fell into an exhausted and restless sleep did I have time to wonder whether the uprooting of the core of our love might now render that love impossible.

Initially I was incapacitated, aware neither of what had happened nor where I was. In fact I was locked again into my own room at the top of the house, comatose from the large and frequent doses of morphine administered by my brother. He used drugs to subdue me, regarding the injections as acts of mercy to keep me from my pain and to ensure I caused him no trouble. Only once when he was late in visiting me did I hear your screams and wails. They seemed to go on for ever then abruptly stopped. Shortly thereafter I was once more submerged in a world of abstract imagery, free of human feeling. I confess I welcomed this return to the state of a dreaming vegetable.

You asked me in Toulouse why I hadn't come to your rescue, or at least your assistance, during the days following the surgery. I explained about the morphine, the locked door, the incapacitating visions. It was then you told me what you had endured at Jonas's hands. Not satisfied with maiming, he went on to subject you to further torture. While I had been swamped with drugs, he had denied you painkillers of any sort. He kept you tied to his operating table and, when you began to scream, he simply gagged you, tightened the straps and left you, immobilized, to suffer. He made you pay for your betrayals. And he felt justified in his actions because you were now a mere woman, a defunct whore of no further value to his experiment.

When I learned the truth, I swore I would go back to Paris immediately and kill him. But what would happen to you if I did? I could hardly leave you alone in the hotel. Caring for you was more important than revenge and must, for the present, remain my priority.

Justice would have to wait. I even suspected that it might be out of my hands altogether, and that one day another would assume responsibility for its enactment.

Several weeks after Jonas had finished his work with us and I was allowed out to wander the house like a revenant while you lay silent and sullen in your bed, he summoned us both and announced that we were no longer welcome in his home and were to quit the premises as soon as possible.

Banishment both relieved and frightened me. We had been virtual prisoners since April, with a new housekeeper to maintain internal discipline and a man, perhaps a detective, positioned by the front door. Before I could ask how we were expected to survive, he handed me two envelopes, one with my name on it, one with yours. Inside were a letter and five thousand francs, dividends, I assumed, from the new financial policies he lauded. Or had the Germans rewarded him with a bonus? This seemed unlikely. He told me I might have the cash, provided I swore to keep silent about your history, his part in it and what he had lately done to us. I hesitated, but in the end I accepted his money and his terms for what would be a difficult freedom. I would have to support you, and I had no idea how much money that would require or how I might earn a living. Because we had seldom seen each other since the night of your abduction, nothing had been discussed aside from your physical symptoms. Perhaps I should have acted differently, but I was in a state of shock far worse than anything I had experienced in my life, even during the past five years. I was at a loss as to how I might manage this malign granting of my wish.

Jonas then addressed you. 'Adèle.' He was very formal. 'Your government has requested that everyone who is able to leave Paris do so immediately. I trust you'll hasten to fulfil your patriotic duty.' He smiled as he walked out, leaving me to explain our predicament. I had been so sequestered that I didn't realize war had been declared. It was 4 September 1939, and we were to be evicted at the moment of maximum chaos and danger. I had read no newspapers and had not been allowed a wireless, either of which might have 'distressed' me and impeded my 'recovery'. I had seen none of the official posters, 'Appel Immédiat', pasted on the walls of every city and town, nor passed in the street the ubiquitous warnings about gas attacks. My brother never mentioned these things. But why had I not heard the air-raid sirens tested every Thursday at noon? The housekeeper had said something about her eldest boy boarding a train, along with hundreds of others, at the Gare de l'Est, but I'd failed to grasp the significance of her remark. Otherwise she complained only that the shops were selling candles singly and not by the box.

That night, against orders, I opened the curtains and looked out over a barely illuminated Paris. The blackout was in force. I wondered how my brother must feel. Jonas was opposed to the war. He claimed to be a pacifist, but I knew better. He sided with Germany. Suddenly my terror overcame me so that my hands shook as I closed the curtains.

Four nights later we were ordered, for the last time, to Jonas's study. Our bags had been packed for two days as we awaited his sadistic pleasure like criminals before an execution, unsure of their hour.

'Everyone appears to be travelling south,' he informed us. 'I should leave Paris now, if I were you. Before the roads become impassable and the trains fully booked. Of course the decision is yours.'

You stared at him, uncomprehending.

Jonas did not see us to the door nor send for the housekeeper to help us with our bags. We'd wanted freedom, well, here it was. When we stepped hand in hand on to the Rue Beaurepaire I knew he had deliberately chosen that night for our release. I could not see to the corner of the street. Paris was in complete darkness.

For the first time in my life I had money. You imp, you had stolen your jewellery back from my brother. When I opened your suitcase the next night on the train to Toulouse, I found, instead of clothes, a spangly clutter six inches deep. There was the ivory bracelet given to you by the Descoignes, the diamond earrings from Madame Bianchon, a lapis lazuli necklace from the retired colonel in the Parti Social, and, most precious of all, an emerald ring, which you'd never worn, from the perfumier. I could hardly believe it, and you refused me an account of when and how you'd managed the theft. When I asked if you'd found or felt the combination to the safe, you just smiled. It was a wonderful smile, your old one, not the pale reflection I'd lately been given. Oh, you were better already now that we were far away from Paris and my brother and the war. But how soon before Jonas discovered the empty safe? My only hope was that the war would quickly close all routes behind us, making us unreachable for the duration.

I have worked diligently to train my memory, and I have succeeded, I think. Even at eighty-nine I can still see the great streams of evacuees moving in thousands along the roads of France. I watched them from the window of our first-class compartment costing a fortune, but imperative if we were not to waste another week in Paris. They looked harassed, desperate, bewildered, not knowing what would happen to them next. Among these caravans some walked, carrying children and meagre belongings. Others rode in cars piled high with babies' cots, luggage, pets, bedding and food. Teapots and wine bottles dangled from the doors, filled with petrol in anticipation of getting as far as Tours or Bordeaux. A cross between refugees and pilgrims, they moved slowly under the weight of a national despair. And their despair was my own. I looked at your pale skin, the purple rings under your eyes. I considered the months ahead, uncertain despite our portable treasure. All of us were fleeing south and west in a vain effort to escape the great black wings which spread themselves across Europe and under whose vast shadow we too must inevitably fall.

The landscape through which this sad troupe processed was the golden French countryside whose beauty I had never witnessed: the grapes ripe for the *vendange*, the apple and quince orchards, the paddocks with their goats, sheep, bantams and geese. Ignorant of impending catastrophe, Nature lay ready for the harvest, powdered with silky dust and smiling to please, so like the Adèle that used to be. I longed to stop a while and rest with you and sample the ordinary pleasures that others take for granted.

As it turned out, we stopped in Toulouse, and our rest was an enforced one. Your illness had returned and with it the multiplicity of symptoms with which I felt increasingly unable to cope. For two weeks you lay in bed with a raging fever. You then lost control of your bladder so that I was forced to reimburse the hotel manager for his ruined mattress. Just when I had resigned myself to the possibility of never reaching Bez, you rallied and we went on. The journey grew increasingly difficult until again we were compelled to stop, this time in Lourdes where for three days your temperature soared to one hundred and two. Once more you recovered and once more we set off into less populous country that became wilder with every mile. We begged rides from farmers and local merchants, often stranded at night and sleeping in barns or by the roadside as you held my shivering body. Even in your weakened state, you never minded the cold. One morning we woke to a clear blue sky and, in the west, a view of the Pyrenees, magnificent in the October sunshine. When I turned to gauge your reaction, I found you holding your breath.

I had bought you new clothes, very respectable, which I insisted you wear. I'd had your hair cut simply by an ordinary hairdresser. I made you put on proper underwear and shoes. You were to be my niece whom I had brought to the mountains for her health and to escape an imperilled Paris. I'd been successful to a point, but that unnerving languor still seeped from beneath the bourgeois façade, and I worried that one day you would be seen for what you were.

You must have been convincing enough, because no one in Bez ever penetrated your disguise. Not even the one I most feared – your mother. But apparently she had died or fled. This we assumed, since you never saw her in the village. Unless she appeared after you stopped going out and went to bed for the last time. I asked did you come here on purpose to find your *maman*, and you shook your head firmly no.

While in Toulouse I had sold some bangles, intending to use the profits on a house. At first we found nothing to rent or buy and were regarded with some suspicion by the locals, or so I thought. So we took the largest room in the Hotel St Sauveur, the very same that my brother had stayed in when he discovered and stole you. We found your old house on a gloomy back street and for a few days I nourished the dream of buying and renovating the place, but I was told it was beyond repair, having been deserted for the past five years. At last I rented a cottage that seemed structurally sound and adequate to our needs.

How strange it was to walk the streets of Bez and pass people who might have been your relations or among your early tormentors or even party to your attempted murder. But after our first year in the village I stopped being nervous of them, since by then you had become unrecognizable. I risked an occasional visit from the local doctor who proved to be a discreet man and very kind. Often you looked as if you were about to suffocate. Then I would panic, running from our little house, the last on a rocky street at the end of the village, to knock on his door at two in the morning, and he would come without complaint. For a while your suffering would ease. On each occasion I would insist on paying him in excess of his normal fee, assuring him that I owed him far more than he would ever know, and he would give me a curious appraising look, as if sensing what lay hidden beneath the genteel veneer. He did his best, but your afflictions, being inhuman, were beyond human help. You could not, could never be cured. The source of your magical strength had been torn from you.

The memory of what happened next causes me more anguish than any of your former loves and betrayals. You became enormous. Not simply, humanly fat, but obese, viscous, amoeboid, your exquisite definition of form swamped by undifferentiated flesh. Your breasts enlarged then flattened, sucking the nipples back into themselves so that they were submerged like navels. The swirl of down that adorned your back spread gradually over your entire body until you looked like the animal they'd once accused you of being. In contrast, the hair on your head came out in fistfuls. Your eyes sank into their sockets, immersed in folds of flesh so thick you could barely see. Getting out of bed became impossible, so that I was forced to resort to a bedpan and to long and painful scenes involving its use. Despite turning you constantly and the application of Dr Verneuil's herbal plasters, your bedsores refused to heal. Such were the effects of Jonas Sylvester's revenge. As long as you were able to remain alone, I made rapid journeys – as rapid as possible under the circumstances – to Toulouse. Often I waited days for the Bez train to turn up. In the city I would sell a necklace or a ring. Of course I received nothing like their true worth, but I was not prepared to haggle and wait. I thought of you in the house at the end of the village and dashed out with my money, leaving the avaricious dealer to lick his paws and whiskers.

Aside from these trips I remained in the village and only went out to purchase our necessities, which because of a bad harvest and general chaos were becoming dearer and harder to find. Contrary to my policy of isolation, I came to an arrangement with a local farmer who supplied us with the milk that kept you alive and bags of onions and potatoes for me.

Dr Verneuil insisted I go out more often and suggested walks in the mountains, following old trails worn into the earth by humans and animals. I was not looking well, and he was concerned for my health. He told me I was cutting myself off from life and that such exclusivity would do neither me nor my niece any good. I said I would try. And for a while I did, even forgetting in the beauty of my surroundings the adored burden which grew heavier by the day. Then I would be seized by guilt and race back to the house, tripping and falling over roots and stones so that more than once I fell, cutting my hands and knees. For the next few days I wouldn't even open the front door.

Then Dr Verneuil gave me a wireless. I protested, said he was too generous, that I did not need or want it in my hermetically sealed life. He wouldn't listen. It had belonged to an old man, a patient who had recently died and whose heirs were too far away to come and claim his few possessions under present conditions. Conditions about which I had almost forgotten. That was the point, he said. The war affected us all. It was wrong to hide from the war. I must keep up with events, keep myself informed. Everyone's future was at stake.

Not wishing to appear ungrateful, I accepted the wireless. I did not intend to listen to it. I don't understand serious music and am irritated by the other sort. The sound of a human voice squeezed through electrical components had always strained my nerves to breaking. Finding no appreciable difference between one speaker and another, I preferred silence. So I don't know why I switched it on. Perhaps, because you were sleeping most of the time, I was more aware of my isolation and felt what I almost never feel: boredom.

It must have been mid–May in 1940 that, through the crackle and static, a repeated item of news caught my wandering attention and I actually sat down to listen to the hourly broadcast from Paris. I learned that the French front had been broken at the Meuse. I panicked. Where and what was the Meuse? Then I remembered that it was a river far to the north. I sighed and switched off the machine. But the next morning I was at it again, and at four o'clock was actually making a tiny coffee (rationing myself, there was so little left) and sitting down to the latest bulletins.

Every day I listened. Through squalls of static I followed the evacuation of Dunkirk, then, over the next month, the quick succession of events that brought an end to the French Republic. The Germans had entered Paris. In spite of myself I immediately thought of Jonas. The devoted sister hadn't yet died, which alarmed me. Surely, I rationalized, the highly placed associates to which he so often referred and of whom he was so proud would save his skin. I thought too of all the night people I had encountered in those bars and clubs, the working people guarding their factories when hopes were high. I thought of Moulay. What would become of them all? Suddenly they seemed my friends and I shuddered to think what fates awaited them.

I listened to Pétain's broadcast in which he spoke of an end to hostilities and how the 'decrepit French nation' must now seek an honourable peace with Germany. 'I offer France the gift of my person to assuage her ills,' he said. Dr Verneuil told me that most French citizens (though technically they were no longer citizens) regarded him as a saviour. Was he also, I wondered, to be the father/mother of a New Era?

Life was very difficult and the world was bad. My fears for your health and the physical transformations I daily witnessed were compounded by our potentially dangerous position. Anti-British feeling ran high throughout the country, though I'd experienced nothing of it here. Did the villagers really think we were Parisians? I knew they assumed we lived on a private income from some modest and respectable source, never suspecting how ill-gotten our gains really were. This was one of the points of keeping to ourselves: no noting of accent slips or syntactical mistakes. But officials, to whom such things were important, might trace my whereabouts through my passport records or my brother's report of the theft. I would be evicted, exiled, and what would happen to you? Each morning I woke when the church bell rang five and lay in a rictus of anxiety. I began to wish I had never accepted the wireless. Knowledge is too great a burden. It makes conditions worse. And yet I listened.

October brought the proclamation that henceforward Jews were to be excluded from government, the professions, newspapers, theatre, publishing and cinema. I was used to discrimination in England. My own parents were privately anti-Semitic. But for such prejudice to be legally encoded and enforced – it didn't seem possible. I was nervous that all foreigners might soon be treated similarly. When I asked Dr Verneuil about this new law he tried to reassure me. 'Remember, this is unoccupied France. Thank God we have nothing they want.' He hesitated. 'Except one thing. You probably have no idea.' He leaned closer. 'But all through this area there are houses where Jews are hidden. The ones smart or lucky enough to have got out of Paris early. If you must worry,' he added, 'worry about the winter.'

It came quickly, the terrible winter of 1940–41. A bad harvest made worse by the events of the summer. No men to work the fields. Petrol short and transport often non-existent. The whole country was soon reduced to near-starvation. Perhaps we were better off in the mountains, I don't know. Reports from other departments were dire. I was paying more and more for less and less of your milk. Only sheep's or goat's was now available and had to be strictly rationed. There was no meat. But there was nothing I would not do to feed you. (The dreadful irony was that food had become the centre of your existence, your only remaining pleasure. Yet with every meal, no matter how small, you would swell the more, so that I thought your skin must split from the internal pressure.) I learned to trap and kill poor wild creatures and to cut out their hearts and livers to feed your insatiable appetite for offal. By November I had picked the last of the berries and mushrooms in the fields and woods.

With the arrival of snow, journeys to Lourdes or Toulouse were out of the question, and so I was unable to supply the fruit that you cried for, tears oozing from between the twin lumps of flesh where your eyes lay buried. Then I would sit by your bed and hold your hand, press cold flannels to your forehead, even read to you, unable to compensate for the acid–sweet enzymes so cruelly denied you. Again and again I explained, uselessly, why they were not procurable.

By the summer your physical condition had become so appalling that I asked Dr Verneuil to stop calling, though I'm certain he guessed that what was happening to you bordered on the uncanny. Clearly there was nothing more his limited skills could do for you apart from the continual attentions to your comfort which I could perform myself. I saw no need to risk his learning more. If, in spite of his kindness and discretion, he were to speak a careless word . . . Even when some of our neighbours brought food from their own stripped larders for Madame Jessel's ailing niece, I would say you were not permitted visitors. They would solemnly nod and go away, and I would think how ironic their charity was. I hid you because it seemed criminal to allow others to be repelled by a creature once so beautiful. You had been gaped at long enough. I concealed you like the *mutilés* I later nursed were concealed, except that when we made our last journey together there was no protecting tunnel.

*　　*　　*

Adèle

Your message came one October morning before the sun rose or the church bell tolled six. I was awake as usual, rigid as stone. You moaned loudly, not in pain, I could tell, but as an attempt to summon me. (For some time I had been sleeping in the other bedroom, since your constant discomfort made it impossible for us to share a bed.) These were not your usual noises of distress or memories or dreams. They turned to groans, deep and prolonged, like a man's. I went to your bedside. You were struggling to sit up and pointing towards the east window where the sky was lightening. I assumed you were indicating the place where the sun should have been, but I was wrong. It took me several minutes to understand that you were pointing at the wooded hillside to the left of the house. You grew increasingly agitated until I asked if you wished me to take you there. Immediately your moaning ceased, and something like a smile distorted your flattened face. I returned to my room and lay down, my hands on my pounding heart. My cheeks, arms and chest were on fire. I knew what it was you wanted.

I assumed we'd go that night, but you said nothing; you even slept. The following week was the same. I dared to hope you had altered your decision, such was my selfishness in wanting to keep you with me, whatever the circumstances. Each day I confronted the abyss that lay before me. I worried about the necessity of making our journey before the hunting season or the first snows. But as always, you were sure of yourself. When the time came, you knew.

Getting you into the wheelbarrow took nearly an hour. Not only did you weigh thirteen stone, but you were unable to assist me by the slightest exertion. You seemed without muscle or bone. When we were ready

I extinguished the kitchen lamp before opening the door. It was two in the morning, and the village was asleep. But there were excitable dogs as well as the moans that issued from the pile of blankets in which I'd wrapped you. I prayed no one would wake and see us. We set out, lit occasionally by the moon moving among thin clouds. The wind was cold, but I was sweating profusely. I'll never know how I found the strength required to push you over the rock-strewn road behind the house, then along the trail that skirted the pasture and led to the upland forest of beech, fir and ash where you yearned to be and where there was no more danger of anyone seeing us. For a moment the ruined château stood drenched in moonlight then became a grey shadow as darkness returned.

Your moaning stopped as soon as we entered the cover of the trees, and you began to utter little cries of joy. We pushed deeper into the forest, bumping over roots and crashing into tree trunks. My clothes, despite the temperature, were completely soaked. At last we entered a small clearing, and here the noises you made grew more piercing, reaching an almost ecstatic pitch, and I knew this was where we must stop. I stood panting, trying to gather strength for what lay before me. The last leaves were falling from the beech trees, and in the weak light I could just see one land on you, russet and gold. You must have watched it fall or felt its delicate impact on your cheek, because you brushed your face with your hand and suddenly spoke.

'Qui a tiré sur les oiseaux?' you asked in your own true voice, the voice of Jeanne.

They were the last words you uttered, at least to me.

As gently as I could I removed your blankets and spread them on the forest floor. For what I did next

Adèle

I will never forgive myself. Having reached, then exceeded, my physical limitations, I had no choice but to tip you from the wheelbarrow straight on to the ground. You shrieked, and I rushed to cover you with the blankets, but at the touch of the wool you screamed even louder. I did all I could to calm you as I struggled to contain my own emotions. You began pulling wildly at your cotton shift. Realizing it would be impossible to undress you, I summoned the last of my resources, ripped the garment from the neckline to the hem and peeled it back like the skin of a fruit. It was what you wanted. You lay naked among the dead leaves and pine cones, the cold wind caressing your body that in the moonlight looked like a gigantic mushroom.

Suddenly I became aware of the underground stream that feeds the sulphur baths. It was rushing directly beneath us, and I was certain you had chosen the spot by instinct, dowsing it with your huge and hypersensitive body. I knelt beside you and took your hand, which tried once or twice to press my own, and held it for a long time as your whimpers of pleasure grew fainter. At last you gave me a little push with your knee, then another, more urgent. My signal to go. I kissed you on the forehead, still high and smooth. And there I said goodbye to you and left you alone in the forest.

Immediately I went the wind rose and the moon vanished. Thick clouds roiled down from the mountains skimming the black pines as I stumbled home in the dark. I don't know how many times I fell, but the next day I was covered with cuts and bruises. I spent the remainder of the night at the kitchen table, my hands clasped tight on the blue-and-white cloth. My mind and body ceased to function. I was indeed the petrified woman.

I remember noticing the wind and rain against the window, that is all. When the cockerels crowed and the dogs barked I came to myself in a kitchen full of light. The storm was over. I wanted to rise but I could not, so rigid had I become from remaining static over many cold hours. Feeling as if I should go mad with loneliness, I managed to reach just far enough to switch on the wireless. I listened for a while, not hearing, just needing human voices to assure me that I was not the sole wretched occupant of the universe. Then the news began, luring my attention, recalling me to the world. A by now familiar voice informed me, without emotion, of the assassination of the first high-ranking German officer. In retaliation, the Nazis had executed fifty French hostages. And I thought how there might be no escape for any of us except, thank God, my Adèle.

The next day on my way to the clearing I wondered if you might simply have sunk into the earth and disappeared for ever, at one with the leaf mould and the pine needles, the feathers and fur and toadstools and animal droppings. I half hoped this would be the case, otherwise how could I save you from the scrutiny of unsympathetic, indeed horrified eyes? And how would I explain? I found instead something more miraculous. I stood and looked at you, my arms wrapped round myself, forgetting to breathe. I could only conclude that during the night you had burst, for you lay surrounded by a dark damp stain. All the poisonous liquid your suffering body had retained had seeped away, exuded in an afterbirth of death, and you were restored, very nearly, to yourself. I leaned closer to inspect you. You looked exhausted but very lovely, certainly to me; decidedly older, you nevertheless had regained your former beauty. You were now light enough for me to lift you in my arms, and, after the sun had set and the night had come on, to carry you down the mountain and back to our house at the end of the village. I laid you on the bed, and, leaving you without adornment, washed you for the last time and covered you with fresh linen. Then I went to fetch Dr Verneuil.

Whatever astonishment he must have experienced at the sight of you he sensitively repressed. He just nodded, as if he understood everything, though he could not possibly (nor could anyone), took my hand and told me he would see to the plot and the priest. I thanked him. The only enquiry he made was about your age. I realized that by my brother's calculations you would be twenty-two years old.

When he had finished his mercifully quick examination of the corpse, he stopped by the door and asked me if I had heard about the executions. I said I had. And did I know that most of the hostages were Jews and communists? I did not. But I thought of them; their pale faces eddied like smoke in my brain as I kept watch over you until morning. And I thought too of all the men who were dying, of the wounded who lay with no help or hope, staring at an empty sky, both they and myself unaware that some of them would one day be my patients and, in a bizarre sense, my lovers as well.

These sad images return me to myself, this room, my chair overlooking the graveyard that I can barely see. I know too well I am alive. I can touch my own skin, stroke it with the claws that were once fine fingers, my only attractive feature. I am layering and splitting like the bark of an old tree. Arbitrary ruts and canals have been dug by the years. My surface is lichen-stained, lenticellate, with spiralling boles that

173

widen and deepen almost as I watch. I can feel their rims toughen by the day. If I could tip myself over the window-ledge, swallow arsenic, slash my wrists, I would. I'd welcome death if only I could be sure that I could go on conjuring you for eternity. But who can tell how far a fantasy extends? You might die with me, and this second death I will not permit. I exist for the sake of your existence. I fight to live. If I do not, who will remember you? Even though no one hears, I will tell your story and go on telling it, and you will remain alive in the telling.

One last miracle was granted to me. The following spring when I climbed the mountain and walked through the forest to visit again the place where you had died, I found it covered with little yellow narcissi. On impulse I dug up a few and planted them on your grave where fifty years later their descendants thrive and multiply.

CHAPTER NINETEEN

Tamara stirred a coffee with three sugars. 'He's the nephew,' she informed them.

'*Jessel's* nephew?' Martin's eyes widened.

'No, dummy, Madame Ruiz's nephew.'

'Who's Madame Ruiz?'

'The matron at the old people's home. Madame Jessel kept insisting she wanted flowers put on her niece's grave. She got quite agitated about it, so Madame Ruiz suggested her nephew might perform the service for a small fee.'

They were sitting in a coffee bar on the main street of Bez, killing time until five when Marcel finished work.

'According to him everyone in Bez is related. Trapped in endogamy.'

'But it can't be Jessel,' Martin resisted. 'Not the original.'

'It could, you know. If she were, say, thirty in 1934, then she'd be about ninety now. Not at all impossible.'

'But we don't really know how old she was in 1934.' He remained sceptical.

'All right,' Tamara countered, 'who else could it be?'

Martin shrugged. 'A relative?'

'Blanche had no children.'

'As far as we know.'

'Oh it has to be her.' Tamara had convinced herself.

175

Meanwhile Celia sensed theories undermined and structures crumbling. Would these new developments change everything? If the woman was indeed Blanche Jessel, and if they could meet and talk to her, and if Marcel turned up at all.

In fact he was on time. He took a chair, accepted an offer of coffee and slouched in his seat, his eyes lowered, cleaning his blackened nails with a knife. He wasn't prepared to smile yet, so Tamara smiled for two. He confirmed that he had spoken to his aunt and that a short visit was permissible provided Madame Jessel agreed to see them. They must be prepared for odd behaviour. The old woman had had a stroke four years ago and had lost the use of the left side of her body. Though confined to a wheelchair, her mind was relatively clear and her speech, when she chose to speak, was unimpaired though not always logical.

When Marcel had finished his coffee they set out for the home. Simultaneously donning dark glasses to shade their eyes from the glare, they turned into a dirt road at the end of the village. It led almost vertically up the hill, the melting mud making their climb hard-going. They were soon panting, although Martin continued to film their progress towards the hospital with its majestic backdrop. The building itself was large, four storeys high, and Celia could not imagine that all the rooms were occupied. The place had an air of mournful neglect, despite a few efforts at modernization. It did not seem the most cheerful environment in which to spend one's declining years.

They trudged to the porticoed front door, their feet damp and muddy. At the sight of them, Marcel gave a smile, which was both shy and sly. They were greeted by his aunt who escorted them into a draughty, high-ceilinged hall. The floor, like that of the baths, was laid out in the local marble. Once the place was probably impressive. It was also, like the baths, permeated by the smell of sulphur. Not as strong, but certainly detectable. The lady herself was, like her nephew, rather sullen. Either the psychological effects of working here must not be good or melancholia ran in the family.

'I've told her some people want to see her, but she refused to believe me. I hope you won't be disappointed. What is that?' She scowled at the camcorder.

'A movie camera,' Tamara answered brightly. 'Are they permitted? We've just been filming the mountains. They're really magnificent. We're so impressed. And your church is so interesting.'

Madame Ruiz was less than charmed but beckoned them on. 'Her niece is buried there, you know. Madame Jessel was devoted to her. None of her own, you see.' She shook her head at the calamity.

Marcel announced that he would leave them now. He did not enjoy the company of mad old women. He saw quite enough of them each Friday when he came to collect his pay from the one in the wheelchair. Tamara gave him a wave and they followed his aunt to the lift, their footsteps echoing along the empty corridor. However many patients resided here, they were kept well out of sight. The lift stopped at the second floor.

'*Very very short*,' whispered Madame and knocked loudly on the door. The knock was followed by a silence then a barely audible response.

'She's awake.' She opened the door.

The room was practically dark, since the two sets of curtains had been drawn and the only source of light was the window that faced the church. The place was furnished with a single bed, a chair, a chest of drawers, bedside table, small fireplace, long unused, and a vintage radio on the floor in the corner. The radiator must have been on high as the room was hot. With relief Celia noted that there was nothing of the unpleasant smell she associated with old sick people and which tainted the rest of the building. In fact the room had a light pleasant fragrance. There were no religious pictures.

They waited in the doorway.

'Entrez,' croaked the person in the wheelchair. Her back was to them and she faced the east window. Gnarled fingers gripped the arms of the chair. Next to her was the bedside table with two drawers. It was painted a delicate grey-green and decorated with floral motifs in teal blue. Though hardly expensive and looking a bit fragile, it was charming, the only personal object in the room.

'S'il vous plaît,' came the rasping voice. 'Qui est là?'

Celia and Tamara looked at each other, waiting to see who would take the initiative.

'We're English, Mrs Jessel,' Celia stammered, very nervous. 'We heard you were here. May we talk to you?'

'Talk? To me?'

'Yes.'

'What will we talk about?' Her speech was painfully slow. She might not have spoken English for over fifty years.

'Adèle Louisante.'

Silence.

'I thought you knew Adèle.'

No reply.

'Did you know her? We've been led to believe you did.'

'Who has led you?'

Celia hesitated.

'Was it my brother?' There was agitation in the voice, then resignation. 'No, no. My brother is dead. Adèle, too, is dead.'

'I know,' said Celia softly.

'We visited her grave.' Tamara spoke up.

They heard the buzz of an electric button as the chair swung slowly round. Then they saw the face. At first glance it looked broken and fierce with networks of deep lines. Celia saw Martin take a step backwards. He was afraid of the face. They were all briefly afraid of it, unused as they were to confronting such monuments to great age. In shape it was rectangular, with a long almost elegant nose above puffy lips. The teeth were large and alarmingly healthy, and thin sideboards ran from the ear to the jawbone. The eyes, however, were anxious but interested, suspicious yet surprisingly tender; looking out from a mind still very much alive.

'I don't know you,' said the old woman. 'Why are you here?'

'To pay our respects to Adèle. We're very interested in her – story.'

There was a long pause.

'I don't understand.' Blanche's eyes watered and she dabbed at them with a handkerchief concealed in the sleeve of her inert left arm.

In what she knew to be a crude and halting speech, Celia explained who they were and why they had come, how it all began with the photograph from the Acropolis, how she and Tamara had assembled clues from various sources and pooled their knowledge, about the memoirs of Professor Cone and Jonas's letters, about Paris, their journey south, their accidental discovery of her whereabouts and how pleased they were to find her and how they hoped she might tell them about

179

Adèle and what became of her. Did she feel able to do that? Would she like time to consider it? Or would she prefer that they simply go away? She did not refer to the museum theft or their plans for the Helsinki conference.

Tamara suddenly came forward and knelt beside the wheelchair, her hand on Blanche's living arm. 'Was it you who brought Adèle back to Bez?'

No, thought Celia. Too fast, too soon.

Blanche looked confused. Then she said, 'She was my niece. She asked me to bring her. She was very ill, you see. Very ill. She was my niece.' She stared above their heads at the opposite wall.

'Was she ill because of the operation?' Tamara asked gently.

She fixed ferocious eyes on Tamara who held her ground. Celia slipped past Martin and knelt on the other side of the wheelchair, unconsciously placing herself so that the three of them looked like an icon painting.

'Who told you that?' Blanche hissed. Celia sent Tamara a look that said No, this is too much for her. What if she were to have another stroke?

'I found some letters, remember? Your brother's letters to Professor Cone.'

Blanche raised a trembling hand to her eyes, pressed her forehead against her fingers, returned the hand to its customary position on the arm of the wheelchair. Her neat blue overall was buttoned up to her scrawny neck. Her arms were covered by the sleeves of an immaculate white cotton blouse, well tailored and ironed, but looking almost empty, there was so little flesh beneath it.

'Martin,' whispered Celia, meaning be ready to run for the nurse, and he nodded.

180

Adèle

Then Blanche surprised them completely. 'Pardon my confusion. I'm an old woman and was never very quick. You're talking, I think, about a colleague of my brother, Oscar Cone.'

'Yes,' said Tamara eagerly. 'Like Celia said, he published his memoirs about twenty years ago and they include references to Jonas Sylvester and a girl named Adèle. And also to you.'

'I know him. He visited us twice in Paris, wanting to inspect Adèle. To examine her. It was he who told my brother where to look for Adèle. That was not her name. She was my niece.'

'Please go on,' urged Tamara.

'If you feel able,' Celia added.

'He sent my brother here. Is that correct? Let me think, let me think. We are in Bez . . .'

She was quite excited. They hadn't much longer, Celia felt sure.

Blanche strained to order her thoughts, enunciating carefully. 'He told my brother about these mountains and about the creature, never thinking what would happen. And Jonas came here and he searched for the marvellous child, and after a long time he found her in Bez. And it was true what he had heard, unimaginable but true. And so he bought her and took her away, took her to Paris. Then it was not enough to find her, but he must keep her too, study her like a dissected animal, to increase his knowledge. He must write about her, tell of his discoveries, share them with his dear friend Cone, and the two of them make theories about her. New races and better breeds, all managed and arranged by them. Poor Adèle.' There were tears in her eyes.

'Mrs Jessel,' Celia began, intending to call a halt.

But Tamara could restrain herself no longer.

'Blanche,' she took the liberty, 'that missing part of Adèle – it still exists.'

'Tamara!' Celia tried to prevent her reaching for the bag, but she wasn't quick enough.

'And we have it. Here,' Tamara said triumphantly and handed Blanche the box. 'Look at it!'

Blanche stared at the box. Then she began to shake until the wheelchair, the room, the building itself seemed to vibrate in response.

'My brother sent you,' she accused, clutching the box. 'You've come to punish me.' She raised the box in her fist. 'Leave me alone!' She tried to shout but her voice broke. 'Don't come back.'

Tamara would not be deterred. 'Blanche, we didn't come from Jonas. Jonas is dead. It's 1994 and that box has been in the British Museum for the past thirty years.'

Blanche bowed her head and pressed the box to her chest. Her tears were sparse, their reserves lowered by the drought of old age.

'No, no,' Tamara reassured her. 'We want to – '

Furious, Celia grabbed Tamara's arm. 'That's enough. Mrs Jessel, I'm very sorry. Please forgive us this intrusion. I'll send for the nurse now and we'll go.'

Martin opened the door. His face was white and wore a shocked expression.

Tamara turned to the other two as if she'd forgotten their presence. 'Yes,' she said, rising unsteadily. 'I'm coming.'

'It was a gamble, see?' Tamara lay stretched out in the marble bath, her body beautiful when horizontal and submerged. Celia hadn't spoken to her for the past hour. Immersed in sulphury steam, they were soaking

182

away their troubles, intending to drown them later when they met Martin at Genevieve's bar.

'We could have gone on for ever, tippy-toeing round her, and never found out anything.' No reply. She looked at Celia's tight little mouth. 'Sometimes rough tactics are necessary. You'll see. Something will happen now, I guarantee. I've interviewed a lot of people.'

'And did they have strokes afterwards? How many heart attacks? Any nervous breakdowns?'

'Knock it off, Celia.' Tamara crossed her large legs at the knee and waved one foot up and down. 'I took you for a serious person.'

'Serious. Not ruthless.'

'Oh, I see. And what were *your* alternative proposals? It was be direct or dump the whole operation.' She sat up abruptly, not noticing the tidal waves she sent up over the side of the bath and on to the floor. 'Look, do you really want to go through with this?'

Then she gave a teasing smile. 'I mean I thought you were Our Leader.'

Celia sighed and rested her head against the tiled wall.

'OK, maybe it was a mistake and I went too far. So sue me. But that's all the more reason to keep on pushing.'

Celia looked at her hard. 'You have a peculiar idea of reason.'

Tamara ignored her. 'Besides, mistakes are inevitable. Think of it as two wrongs making a right.'

'For heaven's sake, Tamara!' She was very cross.

'Happens every day, you know.'

The buzzer sounded the end of their twenty minutes.

'Hear that? That is time passing.' Tamara rose, water

cascading over the folds and ripples of her body, and reached for the warm towel handed her by the prompt bath attendant. '*Time*.' She wrapped the towel round her. 'Of which we have very little left.'

CHAPTER TWENTY

Celia dragged herself up out of the chaotic dream that held her and into the terrible bright morning. What was that noise? It was part of her dream, a huge pounding heart, a gigantic pair of lungs expelling gusts of soiled air. 'Don't, don't,' she heard someone plead, then realized that the voice was her own. Next to her Martin lay comatose. The beating continued. She sat up then fell back, her head aching. They'd tied one on, as that very bad influence Tamara Sass had put it. Why had she surrendered once more to her seductions? Was she becoming a spineless sybarite in the early stages of alcoholism? Had there been dipsomania among ancestral Pippets? This must stop, it really must. And now someone was knocking at the door. She recognized the sound at last.

'J'arrive,' she called weakly. She slipped into the flannel dressing gown and opened the door.

Before her stood the bullied receptionist. 'Il y a quelqu'un au téléphone.'

'OK, j'arrive.'

She followed the receptionist downstairs, trying simultaneously to straighten her hair and keep her balance.

'Mademoiselle Pippet?'

'Oui.'

'It's Madame Ruiz. Bonjour.'

'Bonjour, Madame.' Aha. She was beginning to sober up.

'Madame Jessel has asked to see you.'

'Of course. What time?'

'This afternoon. Two o'clock. But alone, Mademoiselle.'

'Yes. I understand.'

'Good. Until then, Mademoiselle Pippet.'

'Goodbye, Madame.'

She replaced the receiver, smiling despite the condition of her head and stomach. Now wouldn't that slag Sass just say I told you so.

As before, Blanche Jessel sat facing the east window. She looked round when Celia opened the door. At this earlier hour the room was brighter, allowing Celia to observe the face more closely. Today it was far from frightening.

'Please come in.' The tone was almost friendly. 'Bring the chair and sit beside me.'

Celia did as she was told.

'You're interested in Adèle Louisante.'

'Very.' Celia took out a pen, opened her notebook and settled herself.

'You and many others.' Blanche studied her through watery eyes. 'I've asked you to come back because I could not say certain things in front of the man and the woman. Excuse me, but you are an Englishwoman of my own class and background, I think, and I − '

I'm not, Celia wanted to shout. I'm nothing like you. Couldn't Madame Jessel tell that she was, or would one day be, the sort of person Tom Cleary might share a joke with?

'I wanted you to understand that, despite his illusions, my brother was right about Adèle. I first realized it when we were travelling south, and her final illness confirmed everything my brother had implied. We had to stop in Toulouse, we thought only for a few days. But she was so ill we were forced to remain in the hotel. The Riart, it was called. You see, even now I remember. It was in that room – it too looked out at a church tower, how odd – that I understood how nothing human could help her once she'd been robbed of her magic. I remembered what Jonas had said about the philosopher's stone: that it is the rarest and also the most common thing. "Found in the rubbish heap, hidden from the wise." Then I knew that she was more than a beautiful freak, more than a priapic woman. She was a third thing. Not one, but two in one, a miracle. About all this he had been correct. She could not live except as a third thing.' Celia gaped. The woman's combination of madness and formality was very unnerving.

'You have come so far. It was only fair that I tell you.'

'Mrs Jessel, what are you saying?'

'And now you will kindly open that drawer.'

Celia reached for the little painted table she had admired the day before. Inside were several envelopes of various sizes and colours. Blanche withdrew them with a palsied hand. Celia noticed the black hairs growing from her knuckles and could not help recoiling a little.

Blanche pushed the stack forward on to her knees. 'The top one,' she murmured.

Celia withdrew a yellow envelope and awaited instructions while Blanche tried to catch her breath.

'You may open it,' she finally said.

It contained two letters dated 4 September 1939. She looked up at the old woman who nodded consent. Celia opened the first letter which was addressed to someone named Jeanne:

I who made you now unmake you. I take back the treasure I discovered. I have earned it and it is mine for good. Without it you are just a woman, with all a woman's afflictions. A pitiful thing.

I believed you were a saviour, the progenitor of a happier species. But you have only spread corruption. Even I was corrupted by you. You betrayed not only me and my sister but your destiny, your true self. Your neighbours were right and I was wrong. I should have let them kill you. They were fulfilling their moral obligation and I mistakenly intervened.

This is my sad conclusion. Leave me alone now. Go somewhere far from Paris. But I will tell you one thing: I do not look forward to being free of you.

Your foster father,
Jonas Sylvester.

The other letter was addressed to Blanche:

My dear Blanche,

I know you resent me for what I have done. Hate me, even. I ask you to understand that, however painful it might be for us both, I was compelled to return you to your original state, which was that of a good and trustworthy woman. The state in which you existed before you fell under the creature's spell.

Sex is too dangerous for you. And so I have made this small necessary sacrifice to restore you to moral health. It is my duty, after all, to guard my sister's welfare. In the future, perhaps the distant future, you will be glad and, I hope, at peace. (You see how I love you and what grief all this has caused me.)

Take the creature and go, if that is what you want, though she'll be of little use to you. At least she is no longer a menace. I have saved you and countless others, including myself, from her pernicious influence. No

one will thank me. That is the fate of the strong.
So be it.

> Your affectionate brother,
> Jonas Sylvester.

'Mrs Jessel.' Celia looked up. 'I'm afraid I don't – '
The letters seemed written by a megalomaniac.

'Do you see? He turned what had been Adèle into
a kind of magic wand. He stole her power and kept
it for himself. It did him no good, though it did us
much harm.'

Celia felt as if she were listening to a person out of
an earlier century. She was amazed by the old woman's
stamina and articulacy.

'Look again in the drawer,' Blanche ordered,
not unkindly. 'You'll find a piece of jewellery.
Take it out.'

Celia groped for it, unable to rise from her chair.
Finding it, she held the bracelet up to the light. 'It's
beautiful.'

'Try it on.'

But no matter which way she twisted her hand, the
bangle would not slide over her second set of knuckles.
She was a girl in a fairy-tale, failing the magic test.

'I can't.' She gave up. 'It's too small.'

Blanche nodded. 'Too small. Even for you.' She
reached forward and Celia passed her the bracelet. She
turned it round and round in her fingers. 'Such a tiny
wrist,' she whispered. 'Such delicate bones . . .'

The piece was made of ebony and silver, simple in
design, yet obviously precious. The fine cartouches
with their rounded extrusions were made of that soft
Saharan silver that wears smooth with time, so that
their scratched glyphs were barely visible and quite
mysterious.

'It was Adèle's,' said Celia.

'Put it back now, please.'

Celia obeyed, moving in a trance.

'Take out the bottle. Open it carefully.'

The perfume bottle was made of golden glass, its surface covered with a pattern of roses and briars. It contained what could not have been more than ten drops of dark-green oil. Celia removed the stopper, and out like a genie floated a scent at once spicy and damp; ferns, chilli and cloves, but with an undertone of something more sensual like tuberose. Within seconds the substance had filled the room. Celia recognized it as the smell she'd noticed yesterday, and felt dizzy from such a delicious concentrated dose of it. Its effects were like eating when hungry, drinking when thirsty, sex after a long time alone.

'This was her scent?'

'All that's left. After Toulouse she stopped using it. By then she'd lost her smell and there was no longer anything to hide. Now the large envelope. The blue one.' She was impatient to get on, concerned, no doubt, for her limited supply of energy.

The envelope contained a blue-silk packet tied with gold string in a complicated knot which Celia carefully undid. She parted the fabric to find a lock of hair, satiny black. She stroked it with her index finger. It smelled faintly of what was in the perfume bottle and was fine yet springy, as though blood still beat beneath the scalp it had adorned. She could not stop touching it.

'Put it back now,' Blanche ordered. 'Take the largest envelope, the white one, and open it. Handle the contents very carefully.'

Inside the white envelope were four photographs, the first being the famous original of Adèle and friends at the Acropolis. Her face peered out through gauzes and silks amongst the other ordinarily pretty girls. The second was of Adèle seated in a chair and wearing a high-waisted pencil skirt with braces and a short-sleeved satin blouse. A kiss-curl swept across the left side of her forehead like a Hokusai wave upside-down. Her beautiful legs were crossed, her feet in high-heels with intertwining straps, the fashion of the day. Her black curls ended at the neck, and there were deep shadows under her eyes which were large and shiny black but without expression. A smile played at the corners of her mouth, lending a sweetness to the long lips. What struck one above all was her perfect ease, a physical grace which could not have been acquired through mere practice. The complete absence of strain implied that everything came naturally to her. Celia started to say as much, but Blanche motioned her to go on.

Next came a close-up of an adolescent of indeterminate sex, tousle-haired, dark-complexioned and looking straight at the photographer. A wistful smile revealed one large front tooth instead of the ordinary two.

The last photo made Celia abruptly sit up. She stared at a breathtaking portrait of Adèle. She looked from the picture to the person in the wheelchair. It was unimaginable, shocking, that someone so old, so English and correct should cherish such an image. How often must she look at it, and how did she bear it? Celia's eyes returned to the photo, unable to believe what they saw, which was Adèle, naked except for a pair of white silk stockings rolled down to the middle of her thighs. She knelt on a tangled bed, her legs spread wide apart, her hands on her hips, regarding the viewer with a challenging gaze. Her arms were adorned with bracelets, and she wore a large amber necklace. Above neat testicles she sported an enormous erection.

All the photos were inscribed to Adèle from Gervais.

Celia opened her mouth to speak, but nothing came out. Blanche snatched back the photograph. Frowning and intense, she stared at it, attempting to rock back and forth in the wheelchair. She had completely forgotten the presence of Celia who turned away in embarrassment. Celia was aware of a freezing sensation in her frontal lobes, as though she had just downed a double Martini or taken a powerful hallucinogen. Then she thought: I am hysterical. It had to be a joke, because it could not possibly be real. Yet here was Blanche Jessel, eighty-nine, anguished and seemingly aroused. She was no trick; she was no hallucination. And maybe, if Celia was patient, she would shortly explain everything. Or not. Her silence indicated that she had finished or given up.

'You saw that all the photos were taken by Gervais. There are many more, I don't know where. When my brother fired him he took all the negatives with him, so I'm sure they – Adèle and he were friends, you understand. Secret friends. So she let him do all these. Put them away now, please.'

Celia replaced the photos with trembling hands, managing a quick final glance at that most spectacular image. She summoned all her scepticism, but it made no impact on her emotional state. She knew that even if she never saw the photograph again she would not forget it. It would remain alive in her brain, and it would change her, like a disease whose symptoms disappear while the microbes live on in one's blood. She was different already, because she proceeded to behave like someone else.

'First I'm going to show you something.' It was the right time, there might not be another. And anyway, she couldn't help herself. She reached for her bag, removed the parcel she'd guarded so fiercely, unwrapped it and handed to Blanche what she'd somehow always known belonged to Adèle Louisante.

'Do you recognize this?'

Blanche took the object then dropped it in her lap as if it had burnt her. She stared at it then lifted to Celia eyes that pleaded to know Where and How and Why. She lowered them again to the mummified phallus. Does she know what it is? Celia wondered. Does she recognize what was once so dear to her?

Suddenly Blanche seized the thing and kissed it, pressed it to her cheek, then kissed it again, passionately, over and over again, while Celia stared out of the window towards the church whose bell was tolling three. She could hear the old woman's rapid breathing and turned to her. Alarmed, she saw that her face was wet with tears. Celia had never intended this. It was mad to do what she had just done. Mad and wrong. Something was robbing her of her will, compelling her to act without reflection. It was not her way. She had a flash of Blanche and Adèle in bed together. It was the one thing, in all her speculations over the past two years, that she had not considered, and it made her feel queasy.

Blanche had stopped caressing the penis. There was joy as well as appalling grief in her contorted face. And they had once imagined her as a hard and devious woman.

'I'm sorry,' Celia stammered. 'I didn't mean to — '

'What is your name?' Blanche whispered, clutching the object.

'Celia Pippet.'

'Miss Pippet, how did you come across this?'

193

'I – I – took it from the British Museum. From the same drawer as – '

'I don't understand.'

'When I took the clitoris that my friend gave you, I found this in the same place. I think it was Adèle's. Is it?'

'Yes.'

'And the clitoris in the box?'

'It is mine.'

'I see.' Celia raised her hand to her face. 'Excuse me. I feel a bit dizzy.' She leaned her head on her fingers and pressed them into her forehead until she felt the nails bite.

'Put your head between your knees,' said Blanche automatically, once more the efficient nurse.

'I'm all right, thank you.' Celia looked up and tried to smile. She shook her head and gave a short laugh. 'Please tell me,' she begged, 'Madame Jessel, is all this true?'

'I have no reason to lie.'

'Then it would be correct to say that Adèle was a woman and also a man.'

'I've already told you what she was.'

'I know, but I need more.'

'This interests you?' She was almost teasing. She turned and looked out the window for a very long time. 'Come here,' she said more kindly. 'Sit down beside me while I recover myself. And then, for as long as I am able, I will tell you everything you want to know.'

CHAPTER TWENTY-ONE

'It's like this: Aphrodite fucked Hermes and gave birth to a double-sexed child called – no surprise – Hermaphroditus. He symbolized the unification of opposites, an important concept in early religions and alchemy as well as psychotherapy. He was quite a number, with breasts and long hair, and everybody ran after him. Later on in Hellenistic times, his divine aspects deteriorated into a popular erotic image, a sort of pin-up like that statue of the sleeping hermaphrodite in the Louvre. Do you know the one? There's also the bearded goddess, the male aspect of Venus, who was worshipped on Cyprus. But lots of gods have female attributes, Dionysus, for instance. Graves says that double-sexed gods tend to appear during transitional social phases, especially during the change from matriarchy to patriarchy.'

'Blanche said Adèle was a saviour. Or that she would have been if she'd lived.'

'Hermaphrodites are also healers.'

'Maybe.' Martin interrupted Tamara's lecture. 'But has anybody ever seen one?'

'I have,' Celia reminded him.

'You saw a photo. And photos can be faked.'

'We realize you're not at ease with ambiguities.' The doctor smiled indulgently. 'A lot of men aren't. Unlike the Dyaks. Their male shamans were bisexual and impotent because their function was to act as intermediaries between earth and sky. (Earth feminine, sky masculine. The usual.) The female shamans were prostitutes as well as priestesses and both practised thievery. Sort of holy burglars.'

'Please be quiet,' said Celia, 'I'm trying to think.' Her short hair was standing up in punkish peaks because she'd been running her hands through it for the past hour. Martin observed that she looked like a stressed pixie. (He was pressing her to have it cut even shorter like Jean Seberg's in *Breathless*.)

'But this bisexuality,' Martin went on, ignoring her, 'it's just symbolic.'

'It isn't, you know. Parthenogenesis is not uncommon in the lower vertebrates. Plants and worms are true hermaphrodites and there's a species of Russian lizard – '

'But not mammals.'

'You think so? Well, just look at all the humans walking around with the wrong secondary sex characteristics. Not to mention transsexuals, who don't really figure in this argument since the operation wasn't available in the thirties.'

'So what about Adèle then? Her sexual apparatus, I mean.'

'From Celia's description she sounds to me like the Greek hermaphrodite. Female body, very graceful; male genitals, very able. More boy/girl than man/woman.'

'And that's all. No vagina, no clitoris. Just tits and hips.'

'And a pretty face. Celia? Am I right?'

'Probably. I don't know any more. I can't relate to your terms; this isn't a treatise, Tamara. It's real.'

Tamara sighed. 'Darling, I am simply in the habit of placing things in context.'

'Well, my mind doesn't work like yours.'

'Tell me about it.'

'Hang on,' Martin intervened. 'Aren't you getting carried away? OK, and me too,' he added before they could attack him. 'I got carried away. I admit it. But now I'm thinking: Yeah, this is all very interesting, very exciting, but is it really that important? Consider it: how is a mummified clitoris going to help women's advancement? Maybe instead of playing detectives you should be fighting for equal pay and free nursery care and more women in Parliament.'

That was Frances speaking, and Frances was right.

'You think we're *not?*' Tamara's head shot forward.

'Well, you might be, but you're also having too good a time.'

'Don't jive-ass me, Cleary. I can mop the floor with you.'

'Don't I know it. But with respect, Professor, you two seem to have completely forgotten that Adèle wasn't only a woman. She was also a guy, and she was exploited as a guy. The SHE was purely for convenience.'

Tamara smoked fiercely. 'I assume you've finished.'

'Yes, ma'am.'

Celia stared into space. 'When I was listening to Blanche I felt as if I were under a spell. I believed her completely.'

'Obviously,' snapped Tamara. 'You left our most precious possessions behind.'

'*Her* most precious possessions. They belong to *her.*'

'OK, OK. Technically they're hers. But we're the only ones who can do anything with them. I mean what if she goes bananas and destroys them, or the nurses throw them out by mistake? Anything can happen in a loony bin. What about the conference, our evidence, our TV programme?'

'That's why I should film her before any terminal freakiness. You can arrange it, Celia. She obviously likes you.'

Celia covered her ears. 'Please, Martin, I haven't recovered. It was a bizarre afternoon and I'm trying to sort it all out.' She wanted to tell him that something – Some *Thing* – had happened to her that might have changed her for good. But she was without the right words.

'She hasn't recovered,' Tamara teased, addressing Martin in a stage whisper. 'She's sorting it out. Quiet on the set.'

Celia glared at her.

'Listen, sweet sisters,' Martin intervened, 'it's no wonder everyone's rattled after the day's events. Why don't we all go downstairs and interview a bottle of local plonk?'

'Good idea. Let's do it,' said Tamara, changing tack. 'And stop moping, Celia. What happened to the spirit of the BM?' She put her arm around her and hugged her in a friendly way.

The moper managed a smile. 'All right.'

Back in the café two girls at the window table stared at their empty coffee cups, looking up whenever a pedestrian passed, which wasn't often. The three friends took a table in the furthest corner. Celia ordered *thé citron*, Martin a *pression* and Tamara a pastis.

She inhaled deep breaths of the yellow liquid. 'Clears the tubes.'

'Well, Celia?' Martin asked. 'Anything else we should know?'

Celia scanned the nearly illegible notes she had taken. 'Apparently there's a journal. Jonas kept an account of

Adèle's progress and what he called his experiments.
Five years' worth, Blanche said.'
'They'd make interesting reading.' Tamara's eyes
sparkled. 'Where are they?'
'She's not sure. She'd have stolen them if she'd
been able to find them, if only for the incriminating
descriptions of the operations. He may have destroyed
them because of that very evidence.'
'Or given them to his good friend Cone.'
'In which case they're also in the museum.'
'But what exactly did he mean by experiment?'
'I think he was attempting some primitive form of
genetic engineering. He wanted to find out if Adèle
could reproduce, either by herself or with a woman.
He was preoccupied with race and believed it was
possible to create a new one of which Adèle would be
both mother and father with he himself as midwife and
commandant, arranging and controlling it all. He made
contact with some German doctors, through Cone, I
think, and convinced them he was on to something.
They were fascinated and offered to subsidise him
in exchange for sharing his discoveries. They had
reservations about skin colour, though, and Jonas had
to promise that if Adèle proved capable of reproducing
he'd mate her exclusively with Anglo-Saxons. He even
hoped to make brown eyes a recessive trait.'
'Jesus, there wasn't anything those bastards wouldn't
try,' Tamara muttered. 'No stone unturned, fingers in
every goddamn pie. The energy is terrifying.'
'Finally Jonas decided that Adèle was no moth-
er/father but an eternal child and a very naughty one,
unworthy to manifest his mad ideas. He was also in
love with her.'
'Blimey.' Martin swallowed the last of his beer.
'And therefore jealous,' Celia concluded.

'So he went for the ultimate prophylactic. Ye gods and little fishes, what a yarn.'

'If you can believe it.' Martin remained unconvinced. 'Now could we please get back to the present? Like filming Mrs J., for instance. Isn't that what we're here for?'

Celia frowned. 'But is it fair to make her expose herself to a lot of strangers? It must seem as though we're punishing her. Hasn't she suffered enough?'

Tamara grew impatient. 'Oh come on. You just said she wants to out her brother. No more sturdy British secrecy. Let's have the truth. Is there any other way?'

'You're right, of course.' Celia gave in. Tamara had a genius for annihilating alternatives.

'When she died I purchased her plot in the churchyard and one next to it for myself. I assumed I'd shortly join her.' Blanche sighed. 'I didn't know I'd have to wait so long.'

'Mrs Jessel?' Martin tried to attract her attention.

'I sold her amber necklace to pay for them. It hurt me, but I went to Toulouse and I sold it. She had such wonderful taste in jewellery and clothes. Where could it have come from?'

Madame Ruiz said Blanche had been quite deranged after her interview with Celia. Her temperature rose and she'd been unable to sit up or lie down or keep still. So she'd had twenty-four hours' rest and her three interviewers had taken a day off. Even when she had rallied, the nurses considered forbidding another visit, but she'd been wily enough to lie, telling them that Celia was a distant relation. Since Madame Jessel never had a visitor after the death of Dr Verneuil (other than Marcel when he came for his wages) Madame Ruiz could hardly refuse her. There was, Blanche pleaded, so little time.

'Yes?' She turned to Martin.

He moved her wheelchair to align with the shaft of light from the window. 'Look at the grave, please, Mrs Jessel.'

'I'm always looking at it.'

'Head to the left, please. Tamara, could you . . .?'

Gently Tamara adjusted the head that once had frightened her. It flopped to one side, and she tried again, smiling at Blanche who was long-sighted and could barely see her.

'Right, Mrs Jessel. We'll start now if that's OK.'

'OK.' Blanche spoke the word as though she had never heard it, pronouncing it slowly to see how it felt.

The camcorder started. She sat perfectly still.

'Great.' The whirring stopped.

'Great,' Blanche repeated.

'Do you feel ready to talk now?' Celia knelt beside her.

Blanche was suddenly alarmed. 'What do you want me to say?'

Celia placed the two organs in the old woman's lap. 'Talk about these.'

'Why?'

'So that others will know about the terrible thing your brother did to you and Adèle.'

'But *you* know. Isn't that enough?'

Blanche scanned the room like a frightened child, sensing some terrible trick about to be played on her. 'Will other people want to know?'

'Yes. They will.' Celia did not hesitate. 'Why don't you start with Bez? You could say how Adèle was born here and how your brother found her.'

201

'Must I tell it all again?' Her lower lip trembled.

'If you could, if you feel able, it would be a very good thing.' Celia cursed herself for being a brute. 'You needn't hurry,' she added, though hurrying was essential.

Tamara rose from the bed and, at a signal from Martin, turned the wheelchair to face him. She put her hands on Blanche's shoulders which were sharp and surprisingly strong under the black fabric of her dress. Slowly Martin brought the camera closer to Blanche's face and switched it on. She stared fixedly into the lens and, opening her mouth, began to speak.

She spoke quietly, without emotion, her voice harsh but clear. Occasionally she wobbled, and they stopped for her to catch her breath. Once, in mid-sentence, she asked if anyone else would arrive and force her to perform all over again. They swore this wouldn't happen, that they would safeguard her privacy, and she seemed to believe them, though, if they were honest, they had not given the matter of her future protection much thought. How could they when there was so little time?

When she had told her story to the end, they congratulated her on her performance. Then Martin paused to change the cassette. He'd like one more take, he said. But when they were set to shoot again, they found Blanche asleep in her chair.

Celia placed a hand on her arm. 'May we take them now, Mrs Jessel?'

Blanche's head shot up. 'What?' she gasped.

'You agreed that we would bury them for you. With Adèle. That's what we're going to do now. Is it still what you want?'

Blanche's head fell forward like a baby's and she

moaned. When she lifted it tears were running down her cheeks. 'Did I say that?'

Celia froze.

'Yes, I did say that, didn't I?' She sighed. 'Take them, my dear.' She surrendered her treasures to the girl she believed at that moment to be her distant relation.

Celia kissed the top of her head with its hair like an antique doll's. It occurred to her that it was unlikely anyone since Adèle had done the same, and her flesh stood up in goose bumps.

'We'll come tomorrow to say goodbye,' she said. 'We're going to the churchyard now, and after that perhaps you'll feel more peaceful.'

Blanche leaned as far towards Celia as she was able. She suddenly wore a sly expression and spoke in an eager whisper. 'But I can watch, can't I? You promised I could watch.'

Down in the valley the weather was fine with no clouds or mist to blur the mountains. Circumstances could hardly be better.

The yellow narcissi bent to the breeze that carried their sweet scent. Martin, Celia and Tamara stood by Adèle's grave. On the ground beside them was a black leather satchel and a trowel.

'Just start talking,' Martin said. 'Talk now.' He'd had this idea that they should convert their narratives into dialogue instead of merely reciting their pieces like smarty-pants schoolgirls. It was working well, a big improvement.

The two women looked confident, pleased with themselves and all they'd achieved, animated by indignation and clothed in a beautiful righteousness that was in tune with the clean blue of the sky and the bright snow. Clearly they were good women who had tried hard, done their best, risked themselves for the sake of justice. They exposed Professor Cone and his crimes. Courageously they incriminated themselves. They closed with a mention of Dr Sylvester's note-books, a reference to the current campaign against clitoridectomy and a last reminder to their prospective audience that much remained to be discovered in this strange case.

When they had finished, with more footage than they could possibly use, they commenced the business of the burial rite. Sharing the honours, Celia and Tamara lifted the slice of pre-cut turf then took turns with the trowel. They dug in silence while Martin kept an eye out for the verger. When they had gone almost deep enough, he put the camera to his eye and shot the finale to their odd performance.

First Celia then Tamara placed an organ, each wrapped in a piece of the green silk, in Adèle's grave. Then with their four bare hands they refilled the hole, placing the square of turf on top and pressing its edges smooth and tight. They looked at each other and smiled, almost shyly, suddenly self-conscious now that the job was done.

They remained on the cold grass as Martin filmed them from various angles. At the rattle of an approaching blue Renault, they rose and hurried to the wall that overlooked the chasm below, arranging themselves like normal tourists admiring a Pyrenean sunset.

'That was close,' whispered Martin, pretending to film the glistening range of mountains to the south.

Celia was experiencing a great satisfaction, greater even than founding *Dia* and watching it modestly prosper. She was alive with an unprecedented sense of completeness. As if the burial had been hers alone.

'Isn't it strange,' she mused. 'Blanche isn't at all what

we supposed. She did truly love Adèle. She sacrificed her life for her.'

'I think Blanche Jessel was just masochistic. She enjoyed being abused and humiliated.'

'Martin,' fumed Celia, angry at his wrecking of their mood. 'That is crude and reductive.'

Why did he insist on playing the subversive? Perhaps he was simply nervous, out of his depth. Anyway, the pose didn't suit him.

Tamara was equally offended. 'Her devotion was saintly. Surely even you can see that.'

'OK. Canonize her if you like.' He slipped his arms around both their shoulders and looked from one to the other. 'Know what?' He smiled. 'You're both obsessed.'

'You've noticed,' drawled Tamara. 'Of course we're obsessed. Who wouldn't be? I've never heard anything like this in my life, and I admit it's blown me away. In fact, it makes me want a pastis. And do not look askance at me, Celia Pippet.'

No one spoke.

Then Celia groaned. 'Who on earth is going to believe us?'

Simultaneously Tamara said 'Everyone' and Martin said 'No one.' At which they all three burst out laughing.

CHAPTER TWENTY-TWO

Celia and Martin lay in their separate beds thinking their separate thoughts. He was soon asleep, but she did not close her eyes. She stared at the ceiling watching a band of afternoon light travel slowly across its cracked surface and trying not to imagine what it would be like to go to prison. She recalled gruesome accounts of Holloway. And she would not be treated as a political prisoner. Perhaps she'd be declared legally mad instead and spend a year or two in the bin before finding herself at the mercy of Care in the Community. Or would she be utterly discredited and pronounced unfit to edit *Dia*, having dragged it into the tabloid realms of freaks and sexploitation, not to mention larceny.

'Martin,' she whispered, but he did not wake up. All day, since she'd opened the curtains at seven-thirty, she'd been wanting to tell him but hadn't found an opportunity to mention the tall man on the bridge. It was his reappearance that had triggered this imagined incarceration and disgrace. When a chance to talk did present itself, after they'd returned to their room, she'd hesitated, wary of being scolded or laughed at. Then she remembered Tamara's remark at the baths. Well, she thought, I am the leader, aren't I?

'Martin,' she tried again, but there was no response. Whatever happened, she would protect him. Neither torture nor pain of death could make her reveal the name of the film-maker.

An hour passed. There were footsteps in the

Adèle

street below, a few cars. She should get up and turn on the heater – the room was cold. But she continued to lie still, trying to assimilate all the unexpected developments and what appeared to be the complete success of their project. Then she heard Tamara next door. She stumbled against something and swore. The doors of the armoire squeaked as they were opened and closed. Water beat against the plastic walls of the shower. After that, Celia remembered nothing until she woke to the sound of a bed creaking.

By the light of the bedside lamp she could see the muscles on Martin's shoulders and under his arms move and swell as he pulled on a fresh T-shirt and tucked it into his jeans. Until this moment she'd hardly noticed how smooth and white the skin on his back was. Hardly noticed the Milky Way of freckles. Studying them, she forgot the man on the bridge.

Next door Tamara was speaking in French, laughing her horse laugh. Then came a male voice – Marcel's. Had they invited him round? She didn't think so. Perhaps Tamara had off her own bat, and quite right too. Without Marcel they'd never have found the truth. Celia smiled. Tamara's laugh really was infectious.

'You were dreaming,' Martin said without turning round. He didn't need to look at her to know she was awake.

'Was I?' She stretched.

'Yeah. Woke me up.'

'Sorry.'

He was wearing the black wool jumper with the unravelled sleeve Frances insisted he must mend himself. It wasn't fit even for Oxfam, but he couldn't part with it. He'd worn it five years ago in Scotland during a shoot. His single credit in a major film. It was his lucky jumper.

'Was I saying things?'

'One or two things.'

'Like what?'

'Like "Ahhh, ohhh, ahhh, mmmm – *uh!*" Followed by genteel thrashing and some sweet little snores. Why, are you trying to find out what you've been thinking?'

'Yes, actually.'

'Aren't you just glad?'

'Of course. What's going on next door?'

'The nutty professor seems to be entertaining a gentleman friend.'

'Marcel, isn't it?'

'Yup.'

'Did you invite him?'

'Nope.' He hitched up his belt and pushed the prong through the hole. 'Look at that,' he crowed. 'The fourth notch – easy-peasy!' He thrust out his chest and stomped around the room so that the furniture shook. Then he rushed at Celia, shooting her close-up through an imaginary lens. 'Are we pleased with ourselves now, eh, what? Good girl, clever girl, let's hear it for Celia Pippet.'

She laughed and covered the finger-made aperture with her hand. 'Please, no pictures. Flash-bulbs give me migraines.'

'Oh let me, let me. You look just like Isabelle Huppert in *Lacombe, Lucien.*'

There was a loud thump from next door followed by more laughter.

'What are they *doing?*' Celia stopped play.

'Opened a bottle, sounds like. Shall we investigate?'

'In a minute.'

'OK, but you know how the Yank knocks it

back. If you want even a whiff you'd better mosey.'

It occurred to Celia that the pair might not want company, and the thought made her uneasy. But they were due a celebration, after all. So she combed her hair and slid her feet into her flat shoes and put on her blue trousers with cotton tights underneath and a dark-green jumper on top and – on second thoughts – her Indian earrings, and went to Tamara's room.

Dr Sass was sitting on the bed in her stockinged feet with her hair hanging loose, still damp after a shampoo, filling a tumbler to the brim with red wine. She gave Celia an enormous smile.

'Ennntrrrez!' she called, very merry. 'Care to join us?'

'I'll fetch some more glasses,' Martin offered. 'Let's have the key, Celia.' She tossed it to him and off he went.

She was startled to see Marcel not only smiling but missing his two front teeth.

'Look at Bugs, will you.' Giggling, Tamara pointed at him with the tumbler as wine sloshed unnoticed over her skirt. 'Show Ceely-weely,' she commanded. 'Do it again for Mommy.'

Quick as a flash he put his hand to his mouth, removed it and grimaced, displaying this time a complete set.

Tamara shrieked. 'I knew those chompers were too damned good to be true. When it comes to dentistry, you can't fool an American.'

Martin returned with the glasses and Marcel again removed the false teeth. At Martin's astonished expression they all burst out laughing.

'It's a birth defect,' explained Tamara, filling Martin's glass. 'He was born with one massive front tooth instead of the usual two. His family considered it disgraceful –

bad luck or bad karma, something – and had it removed. Pas at all amusant for our little Bugs. They took him to Toulouse and the new porcelain was duly installed.' She scrutinized Marcel's mouth. 'Not a bad job either.'

His lips closed and he assumed a no-nonsense attitude.

'Apparently it happens sometimes around here. A local genetic deviation. You'd think they'd be proud of it.'

Celia, however, knew why they weren't proud, and the realization made her catch her breath. She studied Marcel's face, searching for more of Adèle. He felt the gaze and turned to her, and she quickly looked away, lest he think she was admiring him. She must tell the others about the significance of this family trait, but of course it couldn't be now.

'My great aunt had a complete set behind her upper gums. She was a celebrity in Cork.' Martin eyed the three other bottles in the corner, and Tamara caught his look.

'I was going to take them to Helsinki, but what the hell. We'll drink 'em now.' She turned to Celia. 'Assieds-toi, chérie.' She patted the chenille counter-pane and bounced herself up and down as the springs creaked and groaned. 'This is a marvellous occasion. We're marvellous people. Here's to the marvellous!'

They clinked glasses.

Two hours later they were surprised to find the bottles empty. Marcel went downstairs and across the street to his cousin's. He returned with two more bottles of wine and a smaller frosted bottle whose pretty label was adorned with raspberries and green leaves. Celia realized, much later, that it was this particular bottle that had caused all the trouble.

210

She could not remember quite when the trouble started.

But the contents of the frosted bottle proved delicious. Drink me, it sweetly charged, and she was Alice. And then Tamara was singing and suddenly she wanted to sing too, very much, and so she did, and that too was marvellous. All of them were slumped on the bed singing and passing the bottles around. The glasses had been abandoned, and besides, gripping the same green-glass neck between their lips and fingers seemed appropriately intimate. And now Marcel was one of them and they were intimate with him too. Marcel, who had squared their triangle. Without him there would have been no discoveries, no magic. He wasn't even aware of the discoveries or the magic or their victory for justice. Yet he had made them all possible.

But with the square comes conflict, conflict and excitement. Celia had never associated conflict with excitement. Only fear and boredom. She didn't think Martin had either. Tamara clearly did. She was arguing with Marcel in French, her cheeks burning, her eyes big and sparky. She sat on her heels, legs apart, hands on her thighs. It was then Celia noticed that Tamara had removed her tights. Her thighs were dimpled in the pink light. The sight of them silenced Martin.

Celia sensed that Marcel might not really be angry with Tamara, and that his grabbing the hair-dryer where she'd abandoned it on the carpet – still connected – and turning it full force on her was only a make-believe punishment. Her hair blew wildly around her head, like a spectre in a symbolist painting. It was all over her face and arms, in her eyes. She tried to wrench the dryer from Marcel's hand, but he was too quick for her. Laughing, they moved this way and that in an absurd ballet to the accompaniment of an electric wind. She reached for the dryer again and again until she lost her balance and fell back on to the pillows.

Marcel jumped back on to the bed, nearly tipping Celia off, and got to his knees, still wielding the hair-dryer. What happened next made Celia stop singing. Facing the supine Tamara, now helpless with giggling, he placed her legs on either side of his own and thrust the whirring dryer under her skirt. She screamed and called him names. And though he held her down by one arm and the dryer must by now be hot, it struck Celia that she was not struggling especially hard to get away. Not even when he lifted her full red skirt and began to slide it upwards did she throw him off her. He pushed the skirt past the top of her thighs so that it lay bunched on her belly, exposing to the other three and to the hair-dryer's teasing ministrations the red-brown fur between her legs.

Celia scrambled off the bed. Hands twisted on her flat stomach, she stood watching. Tamara was still faking struggle, though her noises and her movements had changed. Marcel exercised his machine along the inside of each thigh, while with hurrying fingers she undid her blouse. When the last button refused to loosen, Martin came to her assistance, drawing the blouse aside from the breasts spilling from a coral-coloured bra. She undid the centre fastening and out rolled the fabulous contents the bra had constrained. Martin took a big brown nipple between his fingers and began gently to squeeze it. Tamara stroked and pressed his hand until Marcel prised it away.

Irritated, he turned to Martin. 'In a minute,' he said in harsh English, and Martin withdrew.

He had by no means finished his games with the hair-dryer. Tamara yelped and squirmed. Celia couldn't

212

tell whether the noises she made were expressions of pleasure or pain.

'Stop!' she wanted to cry, but she could only stare, unable to tear her eyes from the scene. She remembered a similar experience at a demo when fighting broke out between protesters and police. Everyone kept saying Let's leave, run, get away, but nobody moved. It was just too fascinating. They were compelled to watch.

Martin sat mesmerized, waiting his turn.

Now Tamara was on her back, smiling at Marcel as he masturbated.

'Go in,' she whispered.

'In a minute.' The phrase seemed to be the only English he knew.

Why wasn't Martin saving her, Celia wondered. She herself was powerless to intervene. She could only observe the conflict, feel the excitement.

With a reluctant sigh, Marcel accepted the condom Tamara produced from out of nowhere and pushed himself inside her. Celia marvelled at the speed with which his small bottom rose and fell. Then, with a short moan, he came. Tamara stroked his back until his shudders subsided. Still unsatisfied, she began to clutch his shoulders and rotate her pelvis beneath his. He kissed her on the mouth, raised his torso with his hands and glanced mischieviously at Martin.

'You do it,' he said. Marcel extricated himself, pulled up his jeans and threw him a condom. Then he sat on the floor with his back to the wall, wiped the sweat off his face with his arm, lit a cigarette and smoked it while, with an impassive face, he watched Martin gratify the American woman. When they had finished and Martin had rolled off her, there was a moment of silence before all three of them collapsed in laughter. Marcel stood up, brought her a cigarette and lit it for her.

Tamara leaned back and blew a lungful of smoke at the ceiling. 'Pass me that bathrobe, will you, darling.' She pointed to a chair. Marcel obliged. She spread it over her body like a satin blanket and stroked it tenderly.

'Cost a bomb,' she said to no one in particular.

Celia remained in the middle of the room, wrapped in her crossed arms. The others had forgotten her presence, and she wondered if she'd become invisible until she felt Marcel looking at her. She didn't want to look at him. She was frightened of Marcel. She was frightened of Tamara too, and of Martin. Marcel studied her calmly, his face expressionless. Only his eyes showed anything like interest. She imagined herself a slave before the appraising gaze of a potential buyer. She prayed to go free, yet she wanted to be bought.

Martin had got under the bed covers with Tamara, her white satin dressing gown covering them both. They whispered together like children, his head on her shoulder, her hair spread behind them. They *had* forgotten her. Who were these people, who *were* they? She was horrified by her inability to resist them, to run from the room, to scream for help, flee into the night or at least next door where she could lock herself away from their malign intentions.

Marcel cocked his head. His eyes questioned her: What's wrong with you, English girl? Why do you stand like that, all timid and trembling like a bird? Why not enjoy yourself like a real woman? Why not enjoy yourself with me? Or if not me with one of them? They're your friends, aren't they? And that's what friends are for. Why make everything so serious? Just have fun and forget. Celia summoned the energy to turn her back on him. She was shaking with cold while they were all warm and perspiring. Marcel shrugged and took another swallow, then raised the bottle to the couple in bed.

'You want?' he enquired of Tamara. Oh Tamara was no problem; she knew how to handle him and how to let him handle her. She held out her glass and regarded him in a manner suggesting she might like to be handled again.

Celia had never made love more than twice in twenty-four hours. And Tamara once had a lover who could do it six times a night. And here she was having two in one evening. So why not Celia Pippet? Oh she must go. Just go to bed and leave the others to it and never mention the incident again. But it was too late for that because Marcel's hands were already on her shoulders, kneading at the tense muscles. She tried to move away but he wouldn't let her and went on kneading and putting his soft lips on the back of her neck and kissing her there, then sliding his tongue down to her throat, lapping and kissing, then into her ear, exploring its ridges as his breath roared through her brain. His hands slid from her shoulders to her waist as he grabbed her to him and rubbed himself against her. Then up they went, under her jumper, and grasped the bare flesh of her hips. If he did not stop now, she was in serious danger of never making it to the door.

Martin, she called, though no sound came out, put a stop to this. Tamara, rescue me.

The two of them were sitting up in bed, all attention, the audience for whom she was about to be the entertainment. They settled down to watch the film, all comfy and warm and excited. The projector was loaded, a beam of light pierced the darkness, and there on the screen was her own face. She saw her parted lips, the little teeth, the large eyes spilling tears. She watched Marcel caress her breasts from behind. How insignificant they must seem after Tamara's. His practised fingers undid her trousers, removed her jumper, slid beneath the elastic waistband of her ugly tights, clutched her bottom and steered her towards the bed.

She saw herself naked, stretched across the bed, as Marcel ran his hands over her body. The other two bent over her, watching the spectacle like owls with gleaming eyes. And it was all because of that Adèle. The three of them had fallen under her spell. It was only a matter of time until the others discovered what she already knew: that Adèle had come back, through Marcel, to lure them towards this lewd adventure, to twist their sensations and feelings into weird confusion, so that the barriers that normally defined and separated them could no longer be relied upon as a defence and they could never be the same towards each other.

When he entered her Marcel's face was terrible. Yet she watched herself respond, move with him, clutch and desire him; not him personally, just what he could do. Then Martin was on top of her, barely recognizable with an expression she'd never seen. She closed her eyes to shut out the face and simply feel him inside her and that was good and she also wanted what he could do. She wanted him, herself, all of them to be anonymous.

Unsure of how it had happened, she had become both victim and leader, the focus of all their attentions. At her unspoken commands they assaulted each other, played and wrestled like children, until there was no difference, no separation between them. They did as they liked to her, yet she controlled them rigorously, demanding her rights and fulfilment. Alternate tongues flicked between her legs, nibbling sweetly away at her and igniting a brief panic that what could never last long enough might shortly end. And when a talented mouth drew back, planning, no doubt, some new treat for itself, she grabbed it hard with both hands and held it where it was.

Later she woke up in Martin's arms. They'd got into bed, and she was returning his kisses. She felt rather than saw that Marcel was gone.

CHAPTER TWENTY-THREE

Something tickled Celia's face – spider webs, ragged ribbons, seaweed. She brushed them away but they came straight back. She opened her eyes and saw that they were strands of Tamara's hair. Dr Sass was asleep beside her, breathing heavily, her mascara smeared, her skin blotchy. Martin, also asleep, held fast to Celia's midsection. If only she could crawl over him without waking him. She tried to rise but was prevented by a sharp pain in her head. Martin tightened his grip as she struggled to free herself. She was nauseous. She must get to the loo. Fighting her way out of bed, she put on Tamara's dressing gown and went as fast as she was able down the corridor to the WC.

Vomiting eased her stomach, but the headache went on pounding. Where should she go? Back to her own room, she decided, for another hour's sleep. Tamara came staggering towards her, wrapped in the counterpane.

'So *you've* got it.' She tugged at the dressing gown and disappeared into the loo. 'Wait for me,' she called as Celia hastened to her room and bolted the door, leaving the dressing gown neatly folded on the floor outside.

She did not wish to see Tamara. She did not wish to see Martin either. Shivering, she pulled on her pyjamas, took four paracetamol, got into bed and curled up in a foetal position. She clutched her body to assure herself that Celia Pippet was still present and accounted for after recent events. Something awful had happened in the night. A dark shadow had passed over the village, leaving destruction in its path, and she was both shattered and elated by the visitation. She wondered what would come next and how she would ever face those two next door (who might at this very moment be up to new mischief). She could hardly complain of their behaviour when she had so obviously enjoyed herself. Not that she wanted a repeat performance. She most certainly did not. God, what a tragedy, what a farce.

She slept until ten-thirty when the banging roused her. It was Martin wanting to come in. Why didn't he just use his key? He was an irritating boy. Then she remembered the last twelve hours. She also remembered that the door to their room had been open. He must have forgotten to lock it last night when he returned for the glasses. Somewhere inside her an alarm went off, raising her headache to an intolerable pitch. She stumbled to the door.

'Martin, don't you have – '

'God, I'm ill.' He clutched his head. 'You look pretty good, all things considered.' He tried to kiss her cheek, but she pulled away. 'Hey,' he exclaimed, 'what the fuck!' and made a dash for his open rucksack.

Celia already knew that the camcorder would be empty. She also knew that the second cassette would be missing. She'd known when she'd entered the room but had been too devastated to acknowledge it.

'Shit, where are they?'

'Better search before we panic,' she advised, calm out of habit.

'Yeah, yeah.' He was opening drawers and pushing furniture around. Ten minutes later they conceded that the cassettes were gone.

'If they'd been ordinary thieves they'd have taken the camcorder as well. Any money missing?'

'No, but my wad's pretty resistible.'

'Well, then.' Celia rested her throbbing head in her hands as the room surged and swam around her. 'It's Mole, isn't it?'

'Mole.' Martin stared at her stupidly then with reluctant comprehension.

'Think about it. I have to go to the loo.' She ran out of the room.

As she made her way unsteadily back from the WC, Tamara appeared in her doorway.

'You too?' she sighed.

'Come quickly.' Celia beckoned her. 'Something's happened.'

They were so crapulous that at first the magnitude of their loss registered only a distant distress. They knew they should care more but they couldn't.

'Ring up the museum,' Celia ordered miserably. 'It might clarify a few things.'

'Like what?'

'Like whether Mole's been fired.'

'Or taken a vacation.' Tamara lit a cigarette, retched, stubbed it out.

'Mole? On holiday? He despises pleasure.' The calamity had righted Martin's brain and stomach and he was quite well again with plenty of energy for guilt and regret.

'Perhaps he has a lot of sick leave?'

'You mean he used it to take off and follow us?'

Tamara and Martin seemed to have forgotten the night's activities. Celia was almost grateful that the new developments had superseded a post-mortem and its emotional consequences. Perhaps the others were as well. She was on the verge of tears and couldn't help repeating her refrain.

'I *told* you I saw him.'

'You did, babes, and I wouldn't believe you, and now I'm sorry.' He looked down at his feet.

'So much for computer games.' Tamara made another attempt to smoke a cigarette.

'Tamara, stop it,' snapped Celia. 'It's making us all worse.'

'OK, OK.' Again she extinguished the Gitane. 'Obviously the BM is on to us.'

'So they dispatched Mole to retrieve the artefacts?'

'Or he took off on his own before his bosses found out they were missing.'

'You mean he intends to replace them on the sly and hope for the best?' Martin slid off the bed and on to the floor next to the two women. A low centre of gravity seemed more inviting.

'Why not? There's a perfectly good chance the curators will never notice. You said even the mavens have no idea what's really stashed in that pile. If he's quick enough —'

'This is our punishment for tricking him,' pronounced fatalistic Celia. 'For being so ruthless.'

'Oh stop bragging. What do you know from ruthless?'

'Yeah, when it comes to ruthlessness, Mole takes the biscuit.'

'He's also smart. You never told us that,' Tamara accused.

'Brainbox actually, Oh shit.'

'Mole, Mole,' Celia sighed. 'Where is he now?'

'Wherever he is, he's smiling,' Tamara said bitterly.

'Maybe he's planning to blackmail the museum.'

'And jeopardize his job for life?' Martin shook his head. 'Not the Mole. He's deeply conservative, even if he did belong to the SWP for eighteen months.'

Martin snapped his fingers. 'I know! It was agents!'

Tamara groaned. 'Agents! Agents of what, agents of whom? Dear God, agents . . .'

Things were sliding towards the preposterous. They all fell silent and sat in dull confusion until she spoke again.

'Well, troops, where do we go from here?'

Martin gave a wry smile. 'Can't exactly ring the plods, can we?'

'I don't see why not.' Tamara brightened, a fresh flicker of life in her eyes. 'Go downstairs immediately and report the theft to the gendarmerie. Give them an exact description of Mole. Be bold.'

'But I can't speak French.'

'Well, why the hell not, you lazy xenophobic Brit?'

'Steady on, girl. I got an A-level in Spanish. And by the way, I'm an Irishman.'

'And when you've done that,' ordered Celia, 'telephone the British Museum, as I told you, and ask to speak to Mole or whatever his name is. By the way, what *is* his name? Here, here's some money.' Her mind was beginning to function. 'We might get the cassettes back,' she mused. 'It's not impossible. He accepted a bribe before. In a pinch we could – Oh God, oh God!' Her hands flew to her face.

'What, what?' cried Tamara.

'What?' echoed Martin.

Celia looked from one to another, her eyes huge with dismay. 'The grave,' she whispered.

★   ★   ★

222

They walked in silence, partly out of tension and partly to conserve their minimal energies. Tamara wore her coat over her white satin dressing gown and Caterpillar boots. Dark glasses concealed her smeared mascara and her uncombed hair was loose. People stared at her in the street. It was another beautiful day. On their left the river crashed and glittered in the sun. Simultaneously all three looked back towards the garage.

'What if Marcel . . .'

'Don't be crazy, Celia. He doesn't know anything. He thinks Adèle is Madame Jessel's niece.'

'But if he led us to Blanche, wouldn't he lead someone else?'

'That's a nasty thought.'

The churchyard was quiet. No one was about. From the bend in the road they could see the yellow narcissi. How profuse they were. They thrived on Adèle's remains. Walking faster now, they crossed the cemetery and made their way to the grave. It appeared undisturbed. They knelt beside the place where, the day before, they had buried the organs. Celia felt for indentations in the grass then removed the trowel from her bag and lifted the turf they had so carefully replaced. The hole was empty.

Digging frenziedly, she plunged the trowel into one spot after another, tipping over several narcissi without noticing. She would have destroyed the lot if Tamara had not grabbed her arm.

'Don't, sweetie.' She took away the trowel.

Celia sat back on her haunches then tipped slowly towards the ground as her eyes rolled back in their sockets.

She came to lying on the grass with Martin and Tamara leaning over her, their faces expressing concern and affection, not the lechery of the night before. Martin shook her gently.

'I'm all right, thank you,' she said as they helped her to sit up. Her glasses had come off and the snow was blinding. Her friends held her steady as she took deep breaths of reviving air. How embarrassing this was. Then she remembered why it had happened. She turned towards the home. Its windows were lit up by the sun's reflection, as if a fire were burning behind them. She imagined she could see Blanche in the second-floor window, her visage transformed by concentration and fierce love. She could feel the pale-blue eyes watching, puzzled, sensing defeat. What would she say to the old woman now?

CHAPTER TWENTY-FOUR

The police had not been encouraging. Why all the fuss over a couple of cassettes? He still had the camcorder, didn't he? In execrable French Martin had explained that he was a film-maker and that this was irreplaceable footage. They shrugged and said they would make enquiries. On the way back from the gendarmerie he'd spotted Marcel who'd given him a non-committal wave. He went over to the garage, wondering why he was so reluctant to speak to the Frenchman.

Marcel had left the St Sauveur at six in the morning. He'd seen no one, not even the cat. He was *désolé*. On his return, Martin rang the museum. Then he rang his wife.

'Guess what. Mole's on holiday. Not expected back for another week.'

Celia gave a sigh of morbid satisfaction.

'But how on earth did he know where we were going?' Tamara was reaching a pitch of frustration. 'How could he have found out about Paris and Toulouse and Lourdes?'

'I was just coming to that,' Martin replied sheepishly. 'In fact, it's been on my mind for a bit, despite making fun of Celia's hallucinations. And now my dad's confirmed it.'

'Your dad?'

''Fraid so. See, I also spoke to Frannie just now, and she mentioned someone had called my parents asking for me.'

'But why would Mole – '

'Because he's like a childhood mate, right? Knows my folks for donkey's years. Says he wants to look me up – "Auld Lang Syne" and all that. Well, the old man bought it and tells him I've gone to Paris with a lady friend. Mole insists it's urgent, so the world's very good friend Tom Cleary gives him Tamara's Paris number and an entire itinerary.'

'How the hell did he know that?'

'I gave it to him.'

'What?' shrieked the women.

'OK, OK, I didn't tell you. But they're parents and they're old, right? They want to know where I am. They think one of them will die and they won't be able to find me. Or that I'll have a fatal accident.'

'Their worst fears may shortly be realized,' Tamara muttered.

It was now four-thirty in the afternoon and they had adjourned to the café. None of them had eaten and none of them was hungry. Tamara tapped her cigarette on a tin ashtray.

'We can't do it,' she said. 'I mean no organs, no point. We can't re-shoot without exhibits A and B, and Blanche could be any old dame with a weird story. The film would be perceived as interesting speculation, if that.' She swept her hair back from her face. 'Meanwhile, what am I supposed to say to all those women in Helsinki? Hi, folks, we had these amazing treasures, but gee whizz, we sort of lost them? Face facts, my dears. The party's over.'

'Not for me.' Celia finally spoke.

Tamara patted her hand. 'It's not like we didn't make a damned good try. We even got lucky – for a while. We just can't deliver our Big News Item the

226

way we planned. Best to accept it,' she advised when Celia didn't answer.

How healthy she was, this Dr Sass, thought Celia bitterly. How philosophically and sensually sound. She looked out of the café window to hide her tears. There was a bluish light in the street.

She had rung to enquire after Madame Jessel's health, to send her greetings and find out if she had received any other visitors in the past twenty-four hours. Madame Ruiz was not available, so she spoke to a nurse who informed her that Madame Jessel was sleeping, that she was as well as could be expected and that she had seen no one.

'So, Professor,' asked Martin, 'what will you tell all those women eager for your words of wisdom?'

'Plenty. I'll tell them plenty. They won't be disappointed, believe me. I've got lots of ideas — like take some of our material and put a new spin on it; use the hermaphrodite as a focus to discuss sexual ambiguity and the breakdown in the gender contract. Should be able to do it. Let's see. I'll have from 8 a.m. tomorrow to get my act together. I just love working on trains. And I'll be home about two. Plus there's all of Sunday.' She stopped, realizing what she'd just said. The others didn't know about the booking she'd made for the next morning's first train to Paris, nor the taxi she'd already hired to drive her to Lourdes.

'Sorry, Celia. I only thought — well, things being what they are, we'd better cut our losses and now you wouldn't want to — oh hell, why don't you come with me? Come anyway. Just come.'

Celia looked down at the table and shook her head.

'OK, I won't press you. But you've got the plane ticket to Helsinki. I mean it's expensive and not transferable. I'm not sure you could get your money back. You could say you lost your ticket, I suppose. I got away with it once. But be prepared. The Air France bureaucracy is a nightmare.'

'We still have an extra day.' Celia's argument sounded feeble, even to herself. 'There's tomorrow. We could – '

'Frankly, darling, I can't hang around on the off-chance.'

Martin agreed. 'And if I don't put in an appearance on Monday I'm dog food.'

He was right, of course, so right. She watched the bubbles in her mineral water rise lackadaisically to the surface, their thrust and purpose nearly spent.

'Besides,' he confided, 'I miss Tom.'

'Bet you do.' Tamara smiled. 'You're so lucky.'

He nodded. 'I know.'

Lucky? Celia had always thought of Martin as talented but singularly unlucky. She tended to overlook Frances and Tom. But then what if these very compensations were preventing his advancement? It was probably true, but not worth thinking about. Nothing seemed worth thinking about, and so she lapsed into a condition of simple pain like a little girl moaning over and over again, Why couldn't it have all worked out? Why didn't I get what I wanted when I wanted it so badly? Why, why, why? And the answer came that perhaps more was required than wanting. She began to feel a stirring of inner resiliency, and it occurred to her that not quite everything had been denied her. She need only abandon these old moans, open her large eyes and look objectively at what remained.

'There's Blanche still,' she said.

'You mean we should tell her.' Tamara took a quick swallow of pastis. 'Well, of course. We're obliged.'

228

She hesitated. 'Hang on, though. I'm not sure. Mmm. Maybe not. Not now, anyway. Is it really such a good idea?' She folded her hands on the table, assuming, like a schoolmistress, an air of defensive calm. 'Now I know you don't like the thought of her staring at that grave every day and assuming all's right with the world, and I'm not too happy about it either. But be realistic; she hasn't much longer to live, especially now that she believes we've shouldered responsibility for Adèle's eternal memory.'

'Well,' asked Celia. 'Haven't we?'

'I guess we have.'

'Then we can't lie to her.'

'We won't lie. We just won't say anything.'

Celia looked at them both in dismay. 'That's appalling.'

'Celia.' Tamara leaned towards her and looked at her gravely. 'I admire your integrity and all, but you're a dangerous moralist. You'd do what you believed was Right with a capital R, even at the risk of chaos and pain and death. It's irresponsible. You're compelled to tell Blanche the truth because you can't bear to tarnish your precious image. Little Celia Does Not Lie. I call *that* appalling. I'm the one who's concerned for Blanche, not you.'

'You're also the one who's leaving.'

'OK, but I'm also the one who's doing the conference, and that's no laughing matter. *Ergo*, you do Blanche. Division of labour. See?' Then she softened. 'Sure you won't come with me?'

Celia shook her head.

'Well, then.' She was all efficiency, as if in her mind, at least, everything was settled. 'What are your plans?'

'I don't have any.'

'Oh Celia . . .' Tamara sighed and squeezed her

other hand. 'Don't be blue. I'll be with you in spirit, whatever happens, as I trust you'll be with me.'

'Of course.' She forced a smile as Tamara raised her glass, encouraging the others with her eyes to do likewise.

'I was hoping to end on a high. One always should, you know. Anyone care to end on a high?' She looked from one to the other. 'Come on, help me, guys.'

The harsh overhead light exposed the creases and pits on her skin, the lack of sleep and food, the consumption of too much alcohol. And yet, thought Celia, she was beautiful. Beautiful and strong and unstoppable.

Her face went suddenly mischievous. She *would* get the response she required. 'And then there's last night as well. I assume you two reticent Brits enjoyed yourselves.'

Martin and Celia looked at each other. A new kind of look. With wan smiles they touched their glasses to hers.

CHAPTER TWENTY-FIVE

He knew by her devastated expression that the photos were gone.

'And the two letters,' she added, almost with satisfaction that the disaster should be so complete.

He'd been very kind, waiting in the hospital corridor, keeping invisible while she paid her last visit to Blanche Jessel, sick at the thought of what she had to tell her. He put his arm around her shoulders and steered her towards the lift.

Celia didn't speak until, for the last time, they closed the front door and started down the hill towards the village.

'I found out something.' She stared straight ahead. 'Blanche *did* have a visitor. Marcel came for his pay on Friday afternoon. No one thought to tell me when I phoned because they don't consider him a visitor.'

'But why would Blanche give him – '

'She didn't, of course. He must have waited until she fell asleep. Or hidden somewhere in the building. She's easily tired lately. Since *we* arrived, I suppose.'

'So he took the cassettes and the organs as well. I guess no one would be surprised to see *him* digging up Adèle's grave. Think Mole paid him to do it?'

'Looks that way.'

And now Mole had everything he must have wanted: their treasures, Blanche's treasures and, God knew, even a few of his own.

'But what the hell will he do with them all? Stage an exhibition?'

'Maybe he wants what we wanted. What did Tamara say? "It'd make great television".'

He smiled at her imitation of a Brooklyn accent. Then he shook his head. 'Nope. Not his style.'

'Well, in any case, I'm going to find out.'

He stopped in front of the hotel entrance. 'So you do have intentions.'

In fact she did, but suddenly Martin was the last person in the world to whom she'd reveal them. She asked for the tenth time when his bus was leaving, and he accused her of wanting to be rid of him. Quite the reverse, she nearly said, but thought better of it.

They drank a coffee and he grilled her anxiously, trying to make her confess her plans. She'd only reiterate her unwillingness to abandon what they'd originally called the Project.

'But what will you do? Where are you going?' He was clearly distressed, sensing what was coming.

'I'm going to recover our losses.'

'By any means necessary?'

'Probably.'

'And that entails?'

'Oh blackmail, bribery, spying, intimidation, you know.'

'Bribe the Mole? You're nuts.'

'Not at all. He's ripe for it.' She considered the matter. 'You still haven't told me his real name.'

'Can't remember. He was always just Mole. Let's see.' He scratched his head in mock perplexity. 'Something like Clive Bamber. Or maybe it was Rumpelstiltskin. Anyway, you'd have to make the offer very much worth his while this time round.'

'I would do.'

232

'Oh yeah? With what?'

'I'd sell *Dia*. It wouldn't be a fortune, but it's a tidy sum. It's a start.'

'Celia, you don't – '

'Mean that? No, of course I don't.'

As usual when Martin sighed, his drooping eyelid slid further down his face. 'Good. In that case we won't have to have you committed.' Relieved, he returned to their earlier conversation. 'What still bothers me is how Marcel knew about Blanche's photos and letters.'

'Someone told him, didn't they?'

'Who?'

Who indeed. Perhaps the someone who had left for Lourdes that morning.

(Celia had not gone downstairs for a last hug. Shivering in pyjamas and bare feet she'd watched her departure from the window feeling bitter and lonely and ill. It was 6.30 a.m. when Tamara flung her suitcase into the taxi's boot, slid into the front seat and sped away, already in lively conversation with the driver. Forward, Dr Sass. Hail and Farewell.)

'Three guesses.'

'Not Sass.'

'She did mention seeing Marcel on Wednesday.'

'But why blab to him?'

'Over-excitement? I don't really know. Possibly she only implied there was something worth finding. More to Madame Jessel than meets the eye.'

'Yeah. I can sort of imagine it.'

Martin tried to brighten a bad moment. 'Know what this reminds me of? The end of *The Maltese Falcon*.'

She raised her eyebrows. For a moment she looked almost coy.

'Lorre and Greenstreet scampering off to Constantinople in pursuit of that mad-arse bird. Excited like kids because the game's not over after all. And suddenly you see that it's the chase they love, even more than the money.'

They rose to leave and Martin collected his bags.

'Yes, but doesn't Mary Astor – I mean Miss Wonderly – doesn't she go to prison? Doesn't Sam Spade "send her over"?'

He kissed the tip of her nose. 'Not in my re-make, precious.'

They should never, she thought, have made love last night.

'This is it,' she said as they entered the car-park. 'This is your bus, Martin Cleary.' Through squinted eyes she scanned the river, the bridge, the snow, the mountains, the sun.

'I don't want to leave you like this.'

'Like what?'

'Alone. In a predicament. All these mysteries to solve and people to see who might not be very nice.'

'Stop feeling guilty. It's not your fault. You have to leave. This is the only bus. You'd better get on it.'

He hugged her. 'God, you smell wonderful. What is that stuff – shampoo français?'

'Scent. A very old brand.' She embraced him then pushed him gently away. 'I'm not sure when I'll be back in London.' She folded her arms both as a gesture of protection and to keep herself from touching him. 'I won't call you and I won't write. Please don't try to contact me. I hope you'll do well. I really do. Goodbye.'

She left the car-park as the bus backed slowly on to the road. She hadn't intended to turn round for a parting glance, but something made her act against her will. When she looked she saw Martin with the camcorder to his eye. He filmed her standing there in front of the Hotel St Sauveur until the last moment as the bus lumbered up the hill, rounded the bend and was gone.

She set off immediately for the garage.

Marcel was standing outside, a greasy rag in his hand, as if he'd been expecting her, waiting for her alone. His eyes smiled, or she thought they did. He did not display his nice teeth until he said, 'Ça va, toi?'

'Très bien,' she replied, thinking this was the last chance to abandon her plan and run.

He asked about Martin and 'Madame le Professeur'. Both gone, she informed him, and he gave her a puzzled look.

'Mais pourquoi n'es-tu pas partie aussi?' Not very flattering.

'Parce que je voudrais parler avec toi.' She winced at her awkward French.

He did not respond other than to say that the garage closed at noon, and if she waited ten minutes they could have a coffee together.

'OK,' she agreed. Marcel disappeared inside and she rested against the smashed fender of a Citroën, positioning herself so that she could see him in case he slipped out the back. He was now all that was left to her of Adèle. He would not elude her like his ancestor.

A single striplight illuminated the work room. No one was about, either inside or on the street. Lunchtime. Then Marcel reappeared. He had tidied himself and was wiping his hands on a communal towel. She watched him dry each digit. He leaned against a Peugeot with two flat tyres and asked what she wanted.

Celia cleared her throat. 'I wondered why you came to our hotel on Thursday evening.' There was no way she could make her voice sound casual, but Marcel was unperturbed.

'L'Américaine m'a invité.'

'When?'

His smile faded and there was a flicker of annoyance around his mouth. 'Mercredi, je crois,' he answered in a tone that implied it was none of her business.

'I see. And when you saw her on Wednesday did she tell you there was something interesting in Madame Jessel's room, or did you already know?' She made herself look him in the eye. 'Where are the contents of Madame Jessel's drawer and where are Martin's cassettes?'

He didn't answer.

'I won't do anything. I'd just like them returned along with Madame Jessel's photos and letters and, above all, what you dug up from her niece's grave.'

His innocent surprise was quite convincing. She pressed on.

'And the man who paid you to do this. Is he still in Bez or somewhere nearby?'

Again no response.

'I do *know* what happened.'

'Moi non.'

Celia marvelled at the accomplished acting. Just his stance, the way he placed himself against the car, seemed to make him invulnerable. They stared at each other then in opposite directions. Two wary cats.

He rose and stood apart from the Peugeot. 'I must close the garage,' he said in English.

Celia didn't move. He motioned her to come with him.

'Will we talk?'

'Si t'insistes.'

She followed him then hesitated. The overhead light

had been switched off, but a small room at the back was lit by a battered desk lamp. She could see a table covered with several coffee cups and an old armchair where someone had tossed the morning paper.

'It's the weekend.' She spoke with surprising confidence. 'We could go somewhere. Toulouse . . .'

Marcel turned and gave her an enquiring look. Then he smiled, extended his hand and beckoned with the fingers. She approached and took the hand he offered and let him guide her past the hydraulic lift, greasy jacks and rusted body parts into the darkness of the garage.

CHAPTER TWENTY-SIX

Who was she, that girl who left in tears? We've met before, I'm certain. In Montparnasse, at the Select or the Dôme. Perhaps one evening we conversed, though it seems unlikely. I remember now. She was a nurse. She worked with me at the veterans' hospital. She's rather pretty, though she's a pale thing. White skin has never appealed to me. At least she has kept her youth, whereas I —

I should have helped her in her distress. Shameful, for I am still a nurse, after all. But what could I do, being also an invalid and a cripple? And I was never good at consoling words.

She seems a kind person, but her persistence upset me. Asking questions to which it was plain I did not have the answers. Begging to search my little cabinet. Really it was quite intrusive, quite alarming. Yet she was so agitated that I could not refuse her, and so I let her look. Clearly it did not contain what she wanted because she immediately opened the other two drawers as well, this time without asking permission. Finding them empty only increased her vexation. One would have thought she had failed in some life-or-death mission. Then she proceeded to ask impertinent questions about you and Jonas. What could I say? My brother has been dead for many years. Liver cancer. A terrible end. But she must be aware of that, having had medical training.

She behaved as if I were some sort of expert who held the key to a great secret. I assured her she was

mistaken. I tried to explain that I have lost all talent for
the present; I am not in control of it. It slips in and out
of consciousness like other people's pasts. Often I am
unaware of its existence. She claimed she understood
this. So why besiege us this way? Why do they all come
with their enquiries that leave me in such confusion?
Don't they realize it does them no good; that they
only make matters worse for themselves? Why even
the boy who, like me, is normally so reticent, even
he has begun to pester me.

Then she told me a story. Such a dreadful story,
about you and me. How could she have known so
much about us? Since when have we become a matter
for investigation and research? We live quietly and
harm no one, a poor widow and her niece.

I have even, I trust, done a little good, while you
are a victim angel.

No, I don't believe her story, though at first I think I
might have. There were reasons to believe it at the time,
coming, as it did, from a relative, albeit a distant one.
I suppose the family connection explains her intense
curiosity. Yes, she seemed kind. But persistent; much
too persistent. I trust she will not come again.

Daylight. Morning. I must have slept. What grinding
of gears the simple raising of my eyelids involves. How
sickening to experience again the sensation of being
trapped in the coffin of my body. Buried alive, for I
am alive. Of that I'm certain, at least this morning. It
is not a certainty I enjoy. Indeed I never enjoyed it
except with you. Until you I was always buried alive,
a walking corpse, a zombie.

Something is different. The room has changed since
yesterday. People have come and gone. I remember,
but can I trust the recollection? I must hold it hard

or it will shortly vanish, and what was substantial will dissolve before me. What is the meaning of this change and what brought it about? Why even try to understand? I am tired of trying. I'd give up if only my old vice, curiosity, did not keep gnawing at me like a rat.

Those visitors, when was it they came? They mentioned justice, didn't they, several times. Now, it appears, justice has been thwarted. That was her news, the reason for her despair and my agitation. Such presents and promises they bestowed on me. Here are your lost treasures, Madame Jessel, the missing pieces of your holy puzzle. They are for you and for your niece who died. Now we remove your treasures. We take them in order that you may keep them. We hide them in the earth so that you may see them. And now suddenly they have gone where they can neither be seen nor found. And there are so many reasons why.

Never mind, poor girl, you did your best. Please don't cry, it's only failure. As if I require anything but what I already possess.

Daylight. Afternoon. I can tell by the shadows. Yesterday, when I was young, I used to go at this time to the window. For hours I would gaze at the church and the graveyard. But not now. Not any more.

Instead, to their amazement, I asked to listen to my wireless. I was told that it no longer worked properly and that it would cost a great deal of money to repair. It took all my energy to order them to switch it on. I know that they did because I could see its tiny light in the shadows. A green dot of light out of which your voice would shortly issue, announcing my death to the darkness. Then one afternoon the light went out. I pointed to the wireless. They told me it was broken for good. Send for Dr Verneuil, I said, but no one heard me.

The nurses bring me treats: white crustless bread with margarine, stewed apple, a little baked fish smelling far from fresh and, lately, a television. But my interest is not aroused, and the food is removed untouched, the television switched off. My eyes follow the nurses' activities, my ears attend their voices, but I say nothing. I watch. I am she who watches. None of me moves, no part of me. Whatever persuasions are worked on me I will never move again. They tend me like a plant or a machine, and I submit to their ministrations. I allow them to perform their jobs, earn their living, practise their art. I don't make a fuss. I just lie here. And I can endure this stasis because my patience is enormous, as you know, dearest Jeanne, and as I have proved.

I have something to tell you. I have given our story away. That someone else now shares it and assumes responsibility for its care and protection is to me a hateful relief. Both my goal and my extermination. But I hope to tell it once more, if only to myself. To make a final journey round the stations of my own private cross. There may be time or there may not.

So I won't listen for your voice on the wireless. I won't look at the church, the cemetery, your grave. They may open or close the curtains. It is the same to me. All that I need is within me, just like – strangely enough – the Kingdom of God.

CHAPTER TWENTY-SEVEN

The clock on the bright-yellow wall said 4.45 p.m. Celia synchronized her watch. He was such a prompt person; it was essential she catch him at 5.10 precisely or she would miss him for the third time. And she had lots to tell him, lots. And offers in the way of wicked bribes and financial improvements. She sipped a mint tea. (They presented it to you loose here in a tiny white pot.) At home she drank it in the mornings if she was sick, which was often.

She was re-reading a letter from the Gervais Estate. They were sorry, they said in reply to her request. They were unaware of any early photos such as she described, though they might certainly exist. Perhaps in a private collection or in museum or gallery archives. They suggested she contact the Triangle Gallery in Montreal. Celia copied the address into the small notebook she always carried. Since her sabbatical from *Dia*, she had more time to pursue what had become her second most compelling interest.

The waitress asked if she'd like a *mille-feuille* and she accepted. Clotilde's served wonderful pastries to which she was rapidly becoming addicted. And now, after so many visits, Edith knew her preferences. Celia attacked the *mille-feuille* with a small fork, keeping an eye on her watch. Ten minutes to go.

Martin had rung that morning to tell her about the job he'd been offered on a crew going to the Northern Sahara to film the festival at Ton-Ton. She'd stood beside the answering machine, hands folded on her tight already swollen stomach.

'Pick up the phone, Celia. I know you're there . . . OK, don't talk to me. It's just to tell you I'm leaving for Morocco in two days. We'll be shooting for a couple of weeks, so don't be stubborn and give me a call. You haven't sworn a solemn oath, you know. You think you have, but you haven't. Anyway, I suppose I'll call you. Like I always do. Bye.'

She missed him badly. She hadn't spoken to him since that morning in the Bez car-park. So he couldn't know that she was more than two months gone.

Five minutes left. She began to bolt the remains of the pastry, stopped, signalled Edith and resumed cramming it into her mouth, capturing stray crumbs and blobs of *crème anglaise* on the tip of her finger.

5.06 p.m. Celia waited outside the Museum pub, refusing friendly offers of seats. The rain had stopped and a weak sun stained the roadside puddles blue and gold and made even the museum seem less intimidating. Everywhere the petals of flowering trees were carried on a damp wind. Millions of them fell like pink snow on to the pavements where they turned brown, rotted and eventually fused in slimy clusters that were kicked or swept into the gutters. Celia studied some that had landed on the sleeve of her jacket. She thought of Adèle's grave and of Martin's footage of the two women standing beside it. Where was that footage now? And where was Tamara Sass? With her 'in spirit', she supposed.

Looking up she saw Mole descend the steps and cross the courtyard to the huge iron gates. In her haste to catch him she was nearly knocked down by a van. The driver shouted at her, but she paid no attention, and, risking her life a second time, accosted

Mole next to the hot-dog stand. He was taller than she remembered, though the spectacles were the same — large and black-rimmed, magnifying the eel-coloured eyes behind them. She noted his large misshapen ears, the disagreeably soft lips. For a moment she was afraid she might strike him.

He must have sensed aggression because immediately he saw her he made an abrupt left-turn and strode rapidly towards the corner. She took off after him, breaking into a run. Hearing her footsteps, he glanced back through the iron railings then started to jog, clearly something he seldom did. Frightened she'd lose him, Celia sprinted after him, faster than she'd ever run.

'Clive,' she shrieked, prompting stares from passers-by. 'Clive Bamber!'

He ran straight into a flock of schoolchildren. Her heart leapt as she felt a surge of second wind. He had collided with three six year olds who were giggling madly and pointing at the odd frustrated person with his flapping coat. He stumbled through the unruly mob and had almost manoeuvred past them when she caught him up and grabbed the sleeve of his worn mac. He yanked and yanked, muttering curses, his teeth bared, but she would not release him and now clutched at the coat with both hands. The children broke ranks and, surrounding them, laughed, pointed and cheered, thrilled by the antics of these badly behaved grown-ups. Their teacher tried, without success, to restore order as pedestrians stopped to gape at the bizarre social ballet.

Then there was a great lunge and a tearing sound as the sleeve gave way at the armpit.

'You're crazy, Pippet,' he yelled. He faced her, furious, as she stood panting, his sleeve in her hand. 'You ought to be locked up!'

She tended to agree with him. She was so breathless and, to her immense chagrin, tearful, that she could barely speak. 'We could make a – We could make – ' she gasped, unable to complete her sentence.

He snatched back the dangling sleeve. 'Piss off!' he hissed and turned on his heel. But he was also too tired to run, and so was compelled to walk as fast as he was able, the ruined mac flying open in the breeze, his exposed arm swinging by his side.

Celia's ankle hurt. She must have stumbled on a paving stone but could not remember doing so. What a spectacle they'd made of themselves. Oh so bloody what, she thought, and limped after her prey who was walking determinedly past the Mesopotamian Galleries and might soon be able to run again. Dragging her aching foot at first, then half-running despite the pain, she trailed him down Montague Place shouting at the top of her voice, 'Clive Bamber! Let's make a deal!'

A NOTE ON THE AUTHOR

Mary Flanagan is the author of two novels,
Trust and *Rose Reason*, and two volumes of
short stories, *Bad Girls* and *The Blue Woman*.
She lives in London.